I0612258

STILLMAN'S WRATH

Ben Stillman 14

PETER BRANDVOLD

WOLFPACK
PUBLISHING
— EST 2013 —

Paperback Edition
Copyright © 2019 (as revised) Peter Brandvold

All rights reserved. No part of this book may be reproduced by any means without the prior written consent of the publisher, other than brief quotes for reviews.

This book is a work of fiction. Any references to historical events, real people or real places are used fictitiously. Other names, characters, places and events are products of the author's imagination, and any resemblance to actual events, places or persons, living or dead, is entirely coincidental.

Cover photography by Rick Evans Photography

Published in the United States by Wolfpack Publishing, Las Vegas

Wolfpack Publishing
6032 Wheat Penny Avenue
Las Vegas, NV 89122

wolfpackpublishing.com

Paperback ISBN 978-1-64119-728-1
eBook ISBN 978-1-64119-727-4

Library of Congress Control Number: 2019946659

STILLMAN'S WRATH

Chapter 1

"Hello, there, pretty lady. You mind if I sit down beside you?"

"In fact, I do."

The man frowned. "How come so sour, my pretty?"

"I'm not one bit sour. In fact, I'm feeling quite happy to be heading home after a week away. You asked me a question, and I answered it. I am disinclined to welcome the attentions of an unwashed scalawag such as yourself, much less a drunk one, to boot. Please make yourself scarce, sir."

Fay Stillman gazed up at the man hovering over her in the depot station of the Musselshell River Stagecoach Company in Rocky Ford, Montana Territory. The man scowled down at her. He was a little younger than she, probably in his late twenties, and he looked like a thirty-amonth-and-found cowpuncher.

"Say, now, that's no way to talk to a stranger who's just tryin' to be friendly!"

Slurring his words, he smelled like a distillery. His breath reeked like a saloon on the wrong side of the tracks, which was the sort of place the man likely patronized.

He dropped heavily onto the bench beside Fay, near the station's front door that opened out onto the main street of Rocky Ford. "I thought you looked lonely, sittin' over here all by yourself, is all. I come over to be polite an' keep you company."

He glanced across the nearly empty waiting room at two other men, dressed similarly in worn trail garb, sitting on a bench against the far wall, beneath a monotonously ticking round-faced clock. They had saddles, saddlebags, bedrolls, and Winchester carbines piled to each side of them.

They grinned, glassy-eyed, at their friend and Fay. Just a moment ago their friend had been sitting there with the others, passing a bottle, eyeing Fay lewdly, muttering. They'd snickered like schoolboys gathered behind the girls' privy.

"I don't need company, thank you. I have my knitting." Fay looked down at the socks she'd been knitting for her son, whom she and her husband, Sheriff Ben Stillman, called "little Ben," while waiting for the stage to roll through town and to carry her back to her hometown, Clantick, seventy-five miles north in the far northern reaches of Montana Territory.

The man ignored the knitting. He kept his gaze on her. He leaned closer to her, bringing his face to within inches of hers, and swept a sausage curl of dark-brown hair back from her pale left cheek. His voice cloyingly intimate, he said, "Say, now, you're even purtier close up. An' you smell fine." He glanced at the other two snickering, red-faced men on the other side of the room. "Real fine!"

"Say, boys," he said, raising his voice. "She smells as good as she looks!"

The others howled.

"Give her a kiss, Utah!" said one of his friends—a stocky man with a broad, deep-lined face trimmed with a bulbous red nose and flat, close-set eyes. He leaned forward, playing with the hondo loop at the end of the lariat in his hands. "Give her a big old wet kiss right on the mouth. I'll give you a dollar!"

Utah turned back to Fay. He gave her an oily, heavy-lidded smile.

"What do you say, sweetheart? You wanna make me a dollar?"

He leaned farther into her, turning his mouth toward hers. He stopped suddenly. He frowned as he stared into her eyes.

There came the menacing click of a gun hammer being rocked back.

"Go ahead, Utah!" encouraged the big-nosed man on the other side of the room. "Give her a big, wet kiss. What're you waitin' for? She wants you to—I can tell!"

He and the other man, a little taller and a few years younger than the big-nosed man, loudly guffawed.

Utah, his face still only inches from Fay's, sat as still as a rabbit being mesmerized by a snake. His face now wore a nervous expression, his eyes dilating.

Moving only his eyes, he glanced down to where Fay held an over-and-under, pearl-gripped Derringer between his thighs, the .44-caliber maws pressed taut to the bulge at the saddle tramp's crotch.

"Go ahead," Fay said very softly, giving a devilish half-smile. "But it's going to cost you."

"What the hell you waitin' for, Utah?" said the younger man on the other side of the room. He and the older, stockier gent frowned now, impatient, incredulous. "Go ahead an' kiss her!"

Keeping his eyes on Fay, Utah smiled, his mouth corners twitching nervously. "Nah," he said, pulling his head away from the woman's. "I, uh... I reckon that wasn't such a good idea, after all."

Fay pulled the Lady Derringer from between the man's thighs. She kept it cocked and aimed at him, however, from just above the knitting on her lap. She held the gun low enough that the two men on the other side of the room couldn't see it, but only their partner's decidedly abrupt change in demeanor.

"I think you're making a wise choice, Utah," Fay said softly.

"Easy, now," Utah said tightly, rising stiffly from the bench. "Easy, easy..."

Looking as if he'd just swallowed a whole pitcher of sour milk, he walked slowly back to his partners, who scowled at him doubtfully.

"Ah—you chicken-livered cur!" the younger man said, and whacked Utah on the leg with his hat as Utah sank down on the seat beside him. "Can't even depend on you for a little entertainment...somethin' to fill the time before the stage pulls in."

Faith returned the Derringer to her fawn-skin reticule then took up her knitting needles once more. She was glad Ben had reminded her to take the Derringer on her stagecoach trek down here to Rocky Ford. Montana Territory was growing more and more civilized by the day. Two separate railroads crossed the territory, connecting even the little backwater of Clantick with both coasts.

Still, pockets of depravity remained. She'd had a first-hand look at it right here while she'd been doing nothing more daring than waiting for the stage that would take her back to her husband and little boy. She was glad that Ben had reminded her of the gun, and that he'd taught her to be accurate and confident with it, as well.

She smiled fondly. A good husband she had. She couldn't wait to see him again.

"Why don't you give it a try?" the big-nosed older man cajoled the younger one, then took a hard pull from the bottle they'd been passing. "Go on over there an' get a kiss off that purty li'l thing. Don't be a chicken-livered coward like Utah here."

"Nah," Utah said, wagging his head resolutely from side to side. "You don't wanna do that, Clem!"

Utah cast Fay a quick, dubious look then looked down at the floor, color rising in his cheeks carpeted with several days' worth of sandy beard stubble. Fay smiled with satisfaction and clicked her needles together as she continued to work on little Ben's socks. A few minutes later, she lowered the work to her lap and glanced up, frowning.

She'd heard the clatter of a wagon or a buggy pulling up before the depot. Along with the clatter and the thumping of a horse's hooves, she'd heard a familiar male voice. The male voice was accompanied by that of a woman—a woman whose voice was filled with laughter.

Still frowning curiously, Fay set aside her knitting and rose from the bench. She turned to the window in the depot's front wall, and stared through the dirty glass. A smile brightened her pretty, brown-eyed features, for the man just then climbing down from the single-seater, red-wheeled carriage pulled by a stout cream gelding was none other than the doctor from Clantick—Clyde Evans.

Chuckling, Evans stepped to the ground then accepted the white-gloved hand of the pretty young blond woman still seated in the carriage. He helped the girl to the ground.

Yes, judging by the smoothness of her skin, the subtle curves of her figure clad in a cream-colored, form-fitting day dress with ruffled sleeves and fine embroidery accentuating the bodice, she was still a girl, not quite a woman.

She and the doctor stood laughing together over some private joke. The girl gazed admiringly up into Evans's bespectacled face, and placed her hand to her mouth as a sheepish flush rose in her pale cheeks.

Evans placed his hands on the girl's shoulders

then leaned forward to whisper into her ear, causing her cheeks to grow positively crimson. Laughing bawdily, he kissed her cheek.

"Doctor!" the girl said, tittering behind her hand.

Evans laughed then straightened the brown bowler on his head. "Let me get my bags, and I'll be on my way, my dear," he told the girl, walking behind the carriage where a leather grip, a black medical kit, and a single large leather traveling bag sat side by side on the carriage's small bed.

"I hate to see you go, Doc," the girl said, stomping up beside him in a mock pout. "I feel like we were just starting to have fun!"

Fay snorted a laugh to herself.

She turned and made her way over to the depot's front door. She pushed through the door and stepped out onto the boardwalk fronting the building. She crossed her arms and manufactured a severe expression as the stocky Evans, clad in a somewhat bedraggled but freshly brushed three-piece suit, strode toward her.

He carried the two larger bags while his young companion carried his medical kit, chattering away like a schoolgirl, hurrying to match his quick stride.

"Well, well, well," Fay said in a castigating tone. "I can't let you out of my sight at all—can I, Clyde Evans?"

The doctor stopped in his tracks. "Fay!"

The girl stopped beside him, gazing curiously at the pretty dark-haired woman before her clad in a brown traveling dress with white polka dots, and a round-brimmed brown felt hat standing.

"Who's this, Clyde?" she asked.

"Who am I?" Fay said, coolly. "Who're you?"

The girl's cornflower blue eyes widened. She gulped. "I...I, uh..."

Fay slid her recriminating gaze to the doctor. "I came down here to make sure you've been behaving yourself, Clyde. I see I have my answer, don't I!"

To the girl, whose face had gone nearly as white as a sheet, she said, "I am Missuzz Evans. I'll ask you one more time, young lady--who are you and why do you insist on addressing my husband by his first name?"

"Hu...hu...husband?" the girl croaked, sliding her terrified gaze to the doctor once more, her cheeks again turning as red as a blood-red, midsummer rose.

"Come along, Clyde," Fay ordered haughtily, tossing a lock of her long, chocolate-colored hair behind her shoulder. "I see you have some explaining to do. You'd better get started!"

"Oh, gosh, Clyde!" the girl said. "I mean... Doctor Evans! I didn't..." She looked at Fay. "I swear, ma'am—I didn't know he was married. With kids, to boot! Why didn't you tell me, Cly—I mean, Doctor Evans! Why, you said you were a bachelor!"

"Bachelor, hah!" Fay intoned, tilting her nose in the air.

The girl hurried forward, set the medical kit down on the boardwalk. "Here's your kit, Cly—er, I mean Doctor Evans! It was a great pleasure to, uh…to, uh…to work with you, Doctor. I mean, to assist you and Doc Barney with the surgery on Mr. Haney!"

Evans gave Fay the wooly eyeball, pinching the left side of his mustached mouth together broodingly, despite the amused twinkle in his eyes behind his glasses.

Fay raised a hand to her mouth, ready to stifle the laughter she felt building inside her even thought she knew the joke she was pulling on the girl to be a tad cruel.

The girl backed up, breathless, red-faced. She waved quickly, gave a stiff smile. "Bye, now!"

She wheeled, scrambled back into the carriage, swung the cream gelding out into the street, and slapped the reins against its back, putting it into a ground-eating gallop. She tossed an anxious, pink-cheeked glance over her shoulder, then turned her head forward again and clattered off around a dogleg bend in Rocky Ford's main street.

Evans furled his brows at Fay. "Awful woman! Who sent you here to spoil my fun?"

"You're lucky I showed up when I did," Fay scolded him. "Do you know who that girl is?"

"I...well, I, uh..." Evans furrowed his thick, auburn brows, which matched the color of his hair, now mostly hidden by his frayed-brimmed bowler hat. "Well, I think...if I remember right... her name is Deirdre..."

"You think?"

Evans tugged at his lower lip with an index finger, sheepishly pondering. "Wasn't that her name, or was that the name of the girl in Madam Marmaduke's place...?"

"It's Dixie Conway," Fay said. "Her father is the town marshal here in Rocky Ford. Burt Conway is no man to trifle with. I met him once when he came to Clantick to pick up some prisoners Ben had arrested. I saw Dixie with him at my former tutor's funeral the other day. He is a very uncompromising man, and his daughter—who is young enough to be your young daughter, I might add— is his pride and joy. If he were to find you working with her...and I don't mean assisting with some surgery on Mr. Haney...he'd likely toss you in his jail at the very least, shoot you down like a dog in the street at the very most!"

Evans was still pondering, gaze on the ground, frowning, mashing at his lip with his finger. "Are you sure her name was Dixie? That doesn't ring a bell."

"Get up here, Doc, before an angry father or a jealous boyfriend runs you down in the street."

Fay wrapped both of her arms around his left one and, with a mother's stern but loving affection, led him up onto the boardwalk. "Though it would be no less than what you deserve."

"Ah, heck, I was just having a little fun," Evans said, setting his bag on the boardwalk with his medical kit. "She truly was assisting Gerard Barney and me on a surgery. Talented little urchin, I will say."

"Oh, I bet she's talented in many ways, Doc." Fay snorted a mocking laugh.

Evans blushed, which surprised Fay. She didn't think the lusty sawbones was capable of feeling embarrassed about his infamous and notorious hound-dog ways. "She's the one who insisted on the picnic...after the surgery. You know—as a way to wind down..."

"Oh, yes, I'm sure it was a wonderful way to wind down."

"What're you doing down here?" Evans was scowling at her now, curious as well as indignant. "Did Katherine send you down here to spoil my fun? I wouldn't put it past her!"

Chapter 2

Katherine Kemmett was the woman in Clantick—a minister's widow, no less—whom Evans had almost married before Katherine caught him in a less than gallant situation with the young lady, Evelyn Vincent, who worked as a waitress at Sam Wa's Café. Evelyn might have been a few years older than Dixie Conway, but not by much.

Most of the town, Fay included, were still fuming at the shabby way the doctor had treated the good widow, who'd fallen in love with him in spite of his penchant for drink and women—mostly women of the fallen variety, as well as a young waitress now and then, to keep his life interesting.

Despite all that, and despite the town's anger, there was not a single Clantick citizen—at least among those who knew the doctor—who didn't harbor a soft spot for the loveable fool. Everyone seemed to believe, whether they pontificated aloud on the subject or not, that Evans was as much a victim of his own devilish weaknesses as was Katherine Kemmett or anyone else.

Fay truly did love the man, in a familial sort of way. He was a good friend to her and Ben. That didn't mean she didn't feel like throwing him off a cliff from time to time, and this was one of those times.

"Katherine had nothing to do with my being here, Doc," Fay said, chuckling at the man's unfounded wrath at the woman whom he himself had cheated on. "I don't think she cares one whit about what you do with your life anymore, and why should she, after what you did to her?"

"Please—let's not go into that again!"

"You're never going to stop hearing about that from me, Doc. But I did not come down here to devil you. I came down here because the private tutor I had as a child growing up on my father's Powder River Ranch, Miss Magdalena Merchant, who has lived here for years running a boarding house and school for orphan girls, died the other day from a cancer.

"I was sent word she was taking her last breaths, so, daring to leave little Ben alone with big Ben, I hurried down via stagecoach. Fortunately I arrived in time to sit with Maggie for a while before she passed. I helped her daughter plan her funeral. That was yesterday. I'm heading home today to see what a shambles my husband and son have left my house in."

"Well, I reckon we'll be riding together, then," Evans said, sounding none too excited about the prospect. "If you're fixing to lecture me about Miss Conway and Katherine all the way home, it's shaping up to be a long ride, indeed."

Evans reached into his broadcloth coat and pulled out a leather-cased traveling flask. "I'd best fortify myself. Might even ask the driver if I can ride up on the roof with him and the shotgun messenger."

"Chicken-liver!" Fay teased him.

Evans chuffed and held out the flask to her. "Snort?"

Fay rolled her eyes. "At eleven o'clock in the morning, Doc? Really?"

"It's eleven o'clock already?" Evans said. "In that case, I have some catching up to do. Excuse me."

He tipped the flask back once, twice, lowered it and smacked his lips as he returned the tangle-leg to his pocket.

"Yes," Fay said, only half joking. "It is shaping up to be a long ride back to Clantick." She glanced through the open door behind her, at the three drunks inside the depot building. "It will be nice to have company--besides those three, I mean."

Evans glanced through the door, squinting against the shadows inside the building. "They've given you trouble, have they?"

"Nothing I haven't been able to handle." She swung the fawn-skin reticule hanging from her wrist.

"Yeah," Evans said, smiling ironically. "They look like no match for you. No match at all. I pity them, in fact."

Fay snickered.

Hearing the rumble of galloping horses, she turned to gaze south along Rocky Ford's broad, dusty main street that was only four blocks long. A humble-looking four blocks, at that. Rocky Ford had never grown into much beyond the small ranch supply town of its origins.

Down here, thirty miles south of the Missouri River, was prime ranching country. There were several large spreads, mostly foreign-owned, sprawled throughout the broad, bowl-shaped valleys stretching between several relatively small, isolated mountain ranges from the Two Bears in the north to the Little Belts in the south. The town itself wasn't much except for two large mercantile stores, two churches, Magdalena Merchant's Boarding House and School for Orphan Girls, one hotel, a bank, a couple of saloons, and the stagecoach station flanked by a stock barn and corrals.

There were a few other sundry shops as well as the town marshal's office, but the town was almost deathly quiet most days of the week until times like now, when the stage hurtled in from the south. Fay shaded her eyes with her hand, watching the dusty Concord rush toward her from the town's far edge.

The driver was bellowing at his six-horse hitch and cracking his blacksnake over the horses' backs as though he were trying to outrun a wildfire. Fay knew the jehu was only showing off for the town, knowing his appearance was one of the rare, highly anticipated occurrences that relieved, however fleetingly, Rocky Ford's general malaise.

"Stage!" a man bellowed south along the street, on the street's left side. Cupping his hand to his mouth, he shouted, "Stage is here! Stage from White Sulphur is here!"

As if the driver's bellowing and the team's thundering hadn't announced it loudly enough...

Several men and one woman hurried off the street to keep from being bulled over and torn asunder by the hard-charging team and rocketing carriage. In the high driver's boot sat the jehu, the shotgun messenger beside him holding a double-barreled, sawed-off coach gun across his thighs. Both men wore bandannas pulled up over their noses against the powdery dust.

When the driver got the coach stopped in front of where Fay and Clyde Evans stood on the boardwalk fronting the stage station, he jerked his red neckerchief down off his nose to reveal his long, craggy face.

Tying his reins around the brake handle, he peered down at Evans and Fay blinking up at him against the billowing, clay-colored dust, and said in a thick Irish brogue, "Well, I'll be hanged if it ain't the Mrs. Ben Stillman her ownself! Twice in one week, Morley." He elbowed the shotgun messenger sitting to his left and winked at Fay. "Now, ain't we the lucky ones?"

"Hello, Rocky!" Fay greeted the man—Rocky O'Sullivan, another old friend of her husband. "Rather daring, aren't I?"

"Why--whadoya mean, pray tell?"

"It's a known fact that when a person takes a ride on one of your coaches, Rocky, they rarely make the same mistake again."

"Yeah, a two-way ticket usually becomes a one-way," Evans put in, crouching to scoop his bags off the boardwalk, chuckling, "even if the poor traveling soul has to take up residence where you let him off rather than risk life and limb on the return journey!"

"Insults, Morley," O'Sullivan said to the shot-gunner batting his hat against his knee beside him. "We come all this way to be met with insults! From such a pretty lady, no less. Makes a grown man cry to be insulted by such a beauty. The doc I can understand—why, he's ugly as sin, an' he cheats at cards—but you, Mrs. Stillman. You break my heart, ya purely do!"

He'd recited this soliloquy with his high-crowned, dusty brown Stetson held over his heart and a deep, mock sadness in his light tan eyes circled with red from the irritation of the dust swathing him. The shotgun messenger, Dave Morley, chuckled.

Only half-listening to the comical Irish jehu, Fay began dragging her luggage out of the depot building and grunting with the effort.

"No, no—stop there, ma'am." Rocky O'Sullivan scrambled down the side of the Concord, dropping to the street and lifting more dust around his high-topped boots. "If you was to hurt yourself movin' your luggage around, Ben Stillman would hunt me down an' shoot me like the lowliest of lowly cattle rustlers! Both me an' Morley, an' roll us into the same shallow grave!"

"Thank you, Rocky," Fay said, straightening.

"There's one more in the station. I do apologize about all the luggage. I guess I got carried away."

"Never knew a woman not to, ma'am," O'Sullivan grumbled as he hefted Fay's large carpetbag and tossed it into the coach's rear luggage boot.

"I got the rest!" Dave Morley said, hurrying up onto the boardwalk ahead of the driver.

O'Sullivan stopped and shook his fist at the stocky man roughly the same age as the Irish jehu—mid-sixties. "Ah, stop showin' off, Dave. We both know who she'd set her hat for—if she wasn't already married to that scoundrel, Stillman."

He glanced at Fay and said with a cordial dip of his chin and an affable glint in his eye. "And that wee little insult, you can relay to the sheriff himself, my sweet."

"I will do just that," Fay said, laughing as she stepped up to the near-side open coach door. "Just as soon as I see him again."

"I see you're a mite eager," the driver said, offering Fay his hand while holding the door open for her.

Fay slid onto the forward-facing seat nearest the door, and smoothed her brown print frock flat against her thighs. She set her Derringer-packing reticule on her lap and gave a lonesome sigh. "I don't know which Ben I'm, more anxious to see—the little one or the big one. It's six of one, half-dozen of the other, I guess."

The driver leaned against the door casing. "That handsome devil has you wrapped right around his middle finger, don't he?"

"He does, indeed, Rocky," Fay said. "He does, indeed. In fact, they both do."

"Ah," Rocky said with his own sigh of dreamy longing, smiling at the beautiful woman seated inside his carriage. "To be such a lucky man. To be such a lucky, lucky man..."

He wagged his head wretchedly and turned away as Doc Evans entered the coach from the side opposite Fay.

"Say, Rocky?" Fay called.

The driver headed up to supervise the changing of the teams, which was well underway, three hostlers having led the fresh team up from the corrals flanking the station while two others unhitched the weary, dusty six that had pulled the coach into town.

The jehu stopped and arched a brow over his shoulder at her.

"Please greet Mrs. O'Sullivan for me, will you?" Fay winked.

The Irishman flinched at the mention of his wife's name. Flushing with chagrin, he smiled sheepishly and said, "Aye. I will surely do that for ya, Mrs. Stillman. I surely will."

He set his hat back on his head and slogged away as though under a heavy burden.

***

The stage lurched away from the depot station not ten minutes later. Rocky O'Sullivan took pride in the tight timetable he was known to keep.

Unfortunately, Fay found herself seated facing the three drunk saddle tramps she'd had to contend with in the station.

However, the three had passed their bottle around so many times earlier, that by the time the stage hit the open country, rocking gently, almost soothingly on the leather thorough braces running beneath it, they were all soon fast asleep.

Chins on their chests, they snored loudly, fluttering their lips. One was so deep asleep that he slumped down against one corner of the carriage, mashing his face against the wall, which somewhat muffled his raucous snores.

"Now, isn't that a sweet sight?" Evans said, sitting to Fay's left. "As sound asleep as baby lambs."

"Yes," Fay said. "Let's just hope they remain that way until we pull into Clantick."

"I wouldn't count on it. We have two team changes and then noon lunch at the Election Creek Station. They won't sleep through a meal.

Not these fellas."

"No, I suppose not," Fay said, wincing regretfully.

"Mind if I smoke?"

She glanced at the doctor, who held a fat stogie in one hand, a lucifer match in the other. Fay scowled at him. "They smell bad enough!" She glanced at the three saddle tramps likely heading to the Hi-Line country for summer ranching jobs.

Evans drew his mouth corners down and stuck the stogie and the match back into a pocket of his waistcoat. "You're not still miffed about little Miss Conway, are you?"

"Little Miss Conway did remind me of Evelyn." Fay turned her reproving frown on the doctor. "What you did to both of those poor women was unconscionable, Clyde."

His eyes widened in disbelief behind his dusty spectacles. "I didn't do anything to poor Evelyn that she hadn't been fishing for for a good long time!"

"Oh, Doc! Do you really believe that?"

"Yes!"

Fay turned her head forward and groaned in frustration. The stubborn man would never accept responsibility for his actions. He was like a child that way. A child who would never learn from his mistakes because, to his mind, he never made any mistakes!

Fay was about to give Clyde a harsh rebuke, but stopped when a rifle crack sounded from somewhere outside. At least, Fay thought it was a rifle. She glanced at Evans, who must have heard it, too, for he stared back at her, frowning curiously.

"Ah, hell!" came Rocky O'Sullivan's agonized voice from atop the stage. "Dave! Oh, Dave!"

Fay turned her head toward the window on her right in time to see the bulky figure of Dave Morley drop from the top of the Concord. The man was a blur as he fell past the window and onto the trail below with a loud thud and a wail of pain.

"Dave!" O'Sullivan cried again.

Fay gasped and turned her attention to the coach's ceiling.

She gasped again when she saw the three saddle tramps holding cocked pistols on her and Evans. The oldest of the three grinned crookedly, the tip of his nose as red as a railroad lantern.

"Just sit still, pretty lady," said the one who'd accosted her in the depot station.

Utah winked lasciviously.

Chapter 3

More guns popped around the stage. The shooting grew louder as the shooters drew closer.

Fay flinched at every shot, expecting one of those bullets to tear into the carriage's thin walls. Meanwhile, the three saddle tramps aimed their pistols at her and the doctor.

Her blood ran cold as she gazed back at those round, black maws and the grim faces of the men staring at her, eyes dark and vaguely sneering beneath their hat brims. The cocked revolvers bounced around with the sway of the coach.

It wouldn't take much of a nudge to trip one of those triggers.

The thunder of galloping hooves rose from behind, mixing with the dwindling gunfire, which became more sporadic and half-hearted as the coach slowed, Rocky O'Sullivan bellowing to the team, his voice pitched with anguish at the loss of the shotgun messenger, Dave Morley. Fay glanced out the windows on each side of her. Dusty horseback riders were converging on the coach, swarming like vultures.

The riders of the horses, hard-eyed men in dusty trail garb, aimed revolvers or rifles at the driver's boot. The stage began slowing more abruptly now as, up top, Rocky O'Sullivan bellowed, "Whoaaaahhhhh! Whoaaaaahhhh, now, team!"

Sitting across from Fay, the man called Utah angled his cocked Colt at Evans. "Keep still, Doc. And keep your hands where we can see 'em."

Evans glared at him, said flatly, "I'm a doctor, not a regulator. I'm not armed."

Utah angled the Colt back at Fay then leaned forward and grabbed the fawn-skin reticule from her lap. He opened it up and shook her Lady Derringer onto his lap. As the stage ground to a halt, he tossed the little popper out the window on his left.

"Won't be needin' that, pretty lady."

"What's happening?" Fay said, her chest tight with fear.

"What do you think is happening, pretty lady?"

She knew what was happening. Hold-up. The word was a sharp bone in her throat. She'd lived most of her life on the frontier west and knew well that holdups were dreaded by even the bravest and most adventurous of travelers. She was neither. She was just suddenly deathly afraid she would never see her husband and little boy again.

As the coach rocked to a shuddering halt, Rocky O'Sullivan bellowed, "What in the holy hell is going on here? You men just murdered Dave Morley! Dutch Wayne—is that you?"

"It's me," returned a raspy, older-man's voice outside the coach. "I shot ole Dave because he's just too damn good with that Richards of his. Sorry, Rocky, but I got my boy here, and I wouldn't want to risk his getting a bad case of double-aught buck!"

"Hey, Rocky!" said a younger man, his voice pitched with condescending mockery. "How you been, you raggedy-heeled old mossyhorn? Ugly as ever, I see!"

O'Sullivan cursed the younger man as Utah wagged his pistol at Fay and Evans, directing them to the door on the doctor's side of the coach. "Out. Hurry it up, now. We ain't got all day!"

Fay and the doctor shared a dark glance.

"Out, Doc!" yelled the younger man sitting across from him. Fay remembered his name was Clem. "Get out now an' keep showin' your hands. I don't believe you about not goin' heeled. Not even a sawbones is that stupid in this country!"

"Easy," Evans said, opening the door and stepping out. When he had his feet on the ground, he reached back in to take Fay's hand in his own, and he helped her down out of the coach.

As the three outlaws stepped from the coach behind her, Fay looked around, blinking against the dust kicked up by the coach and its team, as well as the horses milling around them, lifting even more dust. More dust than was swirled by the hot mid-summer breeze.

She saw at least a half-dozen men, maybe more, on horseback. There was one mule and three horses without saddles being led by the others. The human vultures swarmed around the stage, all holding their guns on Fay, Evans and Rocky O'Sullivan, who still sat in the driver's boot.

O'Sullivan glared at one of the men sitting a big zebra dun off the coach's left rear wheel, grinning up at the driver. This man appeared the oldest of the bunch—a short, pot-bellied, gray-bearded man in a red-and-black checked shirt beneath a ragged buckskin vest.

His eyes were bright with a hard, angry kind of humor. He held two pistols in his hands, both aimed at the driver. On his head sat a low-crowned, gray felt sombrero with a braided rawhide band.

A younger man sat close beside him, holding

a Winchester rifle on his shoulder. His round face was plump with baby fat he hadn't quite grown out of, and he had one lazy eye. He didn't look much over twenty, if that. His eyes were on Fay—at least his good one was--making her feel suddenly even more vulnerable than she had felt before.

Glancing around at the others, she saw the eyes of all the men on her now, and that the contentious conversation O'Sullivan had been having with the oldest of the outlaws had broken off abruptly. The older man gazed down in apparent surprise at Fay, his shaggy gray brows arched above his eyes.

The young man sitting beside the older man smiled a dimple-cheeked smile at Fay. He whistled and said, "Well, I'll be damned, Daddy. Get a load o' that!"

O'Sullivan cursed and reached for a rifle on the seat beside him. Quickly levering a round into the chamber, he swung the rifle down toward the older man on the zebra dun. The older man had seen the move, and jerked both his pistols at the driver.

Fay was only dimly aware of herself leaping forward and crying, "No!"

The old man's big pistols leaped and barked, flames lapping from the barrels.

O'Sullivan grunted as he triggered the carbine wide, the bullet punching dirt several feet behind its intended target. He jerked back in his seat, then collapsed forward over his knees, rolling awkwardly out of his seat and tumbling from the coach. He struck the ground hard, with a grunt and a heavy thud.

"Rocky!" Fay screamed and ran to the crumpled man, dropping to a knee beside him.

"That was your fault, Missy!" barked the gang's older leader. "We was all distracted. If I'd kept my guns on Rocky, he wouldn't have tried nothin', but we was all distracted on account o' you bein' such a purty li'l thing."

Fay wasn't listening to the old fool. Rocky writhed on the ground before her. The Irishman glanced up at her from pain-racked eyes as blood oozed from two holes in his checked shirt, between the flaps of his dust-caked, black broadcloth jacket from the torn breast pocket of which two long-nine cigars poked up.

"I'm sorry, Missus." He choked, shoulders jerking. "I'm so sorry, Mis--"

His voice cut off as he jerked once more then dropped his head to the dirt. His body relaxed all at once, the air leaving his lungs in a long, ragged exhalation.

Fay stared at him in shock. She hadn't realized

until then that Clyde Evans was kneeling beside her.

He placed his hand on her shoulder, gave it a firm squeeze, and said, "He's gone, Fay."

"Damn dirty shame," said the gang leader. "But I had to do it. It was on account of you, Missy. We was all distracted, lookin' at you!"

Fuming, Fay rose slowly. Clenching her fists at her sides, she glared up at the man. "You cow-stupid old fool!"

"Say, now!" the man said, jerking back on his dun's reins. The horse lifted its head sharply and sidestepped. "I don't take no sass off no--"

"She's Ben Stillman's wife."

Fay glanced at the man who'd accosted her in Rocky Ford. He still stood near the coach's open door, grinning coldly at her, his dark eyes amused as well as new-penny bright with lust.

"What's that, Utah?" the old gang leader asked.

"Sure enough, Dutch—I heard her an' the man there talkin'. She's Stillman's wife. You know—the county sheriff up in Clantick? Used to be a deputy U.S. marshal…?"

"Yeah, I knew who he is," said the gang leader, regarding Fay thoughtfully. "Had us a coupla run-ins over the years, Stillman an' me. He's married, eh? To you?" His eyes shone with disbelief, deep lines of consternation cut across his forehead, beneath the bullet-crowned felt sombrero.

The man's lazy-eyed son studied Fay, as well. "He done well for himself—didn't he, Daddy? She's right purty, ain't she?" Obviously soft in the head, he turned to his father as though he'd asked a serious question to which he awaited a reply.

"She's trouble—that's what she is. Look what happened here."

The older man peered at O'Sullivan, who lay slumped on his side in death. He clucked re-provingly and said, "Well, we don't got all day palaverin'. One of you boys climb up on the stage and grab the box. Hurry up now—we don't got all day. Rocky was known to keep his schedule come hell or high water!"

The old man turned his angry gaze on Utah and the other two who'd ridden the stage, all standing side by side near the coach's open door. "You three are drunk!"

Utah opened his mouth to respond, but closed it again when the older man said, "Don't lie to me, Utah. You an' Clem an' old Fritz been drinkin' when I told you not to. I told you what happens if you don't follow orders."

"I'll fetch the lockbox, Daddy!" the gang leader's son said, apparently oblivious to the verbal dustup.

He scrambled off his horse, dropped the reins,

and hurried over to Rocky O'Sullivan, saying politely, "Pardon me, Miss," as he brushed past Fay. As he crouched to go through the dead jehu's pockets, his father continued to dress down the three drunkards with:

"I told you when you joined my bunch, Fritz— you take orders from me. You don't follow my orders, you get a bullet in your consarned guts!"

Fritz's large red nose grew redder and his eyes blazed as he lurched forward, gritting his teeth and thrusting an angry finger at the older man on the dun. "You got no right to talk to me like that, Dutch! We was kids together! We come from the same damn place! Just because you had a ranch—a ranch which you lost!—you think you're so damn high an' mighty!"

Fritz thrust his hands high in the air and waved them as he did a bizarre little dance there on the trail between Fay and Evans and the old gang leader called Dutch. Suddenly, he thrust an accusing finger at Dutch again, and said, "I'll take a drink any damn time I wanna take a drink, you old devil!"

Fay had seen it coming. She didn't know why Fritz hadn't. She'd seen it coming, all right, and now she braced herself as Dutch angled both his revolvers down at Fritz, and smiled cagily. He blinked and then he triggered first the right-hand

Colt and then the left-hand one.

The staccato blasts slammed against Fay's ears one at a time, spaced about a second apart.

Fritz shuddered as though deeply chilled.

He screamed and stumbled backward into Fay, who reflexively threw her arms out to catch him. Unable to hold him, they both dropped to the ground together, the howling Fritz on top of Fay. Fay was so preoccupied with the wailing Fritz writhing on top of her, she was only vaguely aware of several horses comprising the stage's six-horse hitch giving a shrill whinny, and of the stage jerking forward.

She was a little more aware of another high-pitched scream—a man's scream.

A half-second later, just as Fritz rolled off of Fay, clutching his bloody belly, Dutch's son flew off the coach's roof to smash against the iron-banded lockbox that had fallen down ahead of him, six feet to Fay's left.

The boy yipped and yowled like a coyote that had suddenly found its foot in a trap. He flopped onto his back, wailing, his left arm hanging an odd angle.

"Ahhhhhh...ohhhhhhhh!" came a fresh set of wails behind her.

It took Fay a few seconds to realize the new batch of vocalized sorrow came from Dutch himself, staring down in horror, and pointing his finger at his son, who writhed on the ground beside Fritz, whose own body merely shuddered now as he gave up the ghost.

"Oh, god!" Dutch said, scrambling awkwardly from the dun's back. "Oh, god...someone help him...oh, please help my boy!"

But as others dropped quickly from their own saddles and ran over to the young man, Dutch pushed them aside, barking, "Outta the way! Outta the damn way!" He dropped to both knees beside his son and started to place his hands on the agonized boy's shoulders but stopped, keeping them in the air before him, fearing he might make matters worse.

The young man's left arm hung at an odd angle.

"Help me, Daddy! I'm hurt bad, Daddy!"

Dutch stared at his son in shock, yelling, "Where does it hurt, Waylon? Tell Daddy where it hurts! Oh, no, no—how did this happen? How bad you hurt, son?" He was sobbing now himself, moaning.

Still sitting on the ground near Fritz, Fay looked up to see Doc Evans standing beside her, just off her right shoulder. Evans stared at something on the ground in front of her.

She followed his gaze to one of Fritz's two holstered pistols. The revolver's handle jutted toward her and the doctor, taunting them both with its closeness.

Evans glanced at Fay. His eyes were glazed with anxiousness, with the prospective weight and implication of the revolver in his hand.

He stepped forward and, taking advantage of the outlaw's attention on the injured young Waylon, crouched low and extended his right hand to Fritz's gun.

Chapter 4

Sheriff Ben Stillman cracked the dark-brown egg on the edge of the beer schooner.

The shell opened cleanly.

The yoke inside its colorless jelly-like cocoon rolled out from the shell. It burst through the beer's two-inch froth to tumble like a miniature sun through white clouds in a saffron sky, shedding the flames of golden air bubbles every which way as it tumbled down…down…down at a slight slant through the glass.

It struck the bottom of the mug and bounced once before rolling to one side, wobbling slightly in its weightless new world. More, weaker flares of the miniature sun's demise continued firing from the dying star, rising toward the foam above, glinting like dust motes illuminated by several shafts of light angling through a window beyond this self-contained, honey-and-cream, liquid world.

"Ahh," Stillman said to the little, blond-headed boy he'd set on the edge of the bar in the Drovers Saloon on First Street in Clantick, Montana Territory. "Ain't that a sight to behold, little Ben? Two of our favorite foods together in one glass!"

The boy thrust his soft, pale little hand toward the glass, tapped his pudgy index finger on the rim. "Baza!"

"Beer," his father corrected the child.

"Baza!" little Ben said, slapping his finger against the glass, sometimes missing the rim, sometimes not.

"Beer," Stillman said, raising the glass as though in salute to the boy. "Can you say beer?"

The blue-eyed boy, pudgy-faced and curly-haired, waved at the glass, index finger extended, and said more loudly, "Baza! Baza!"

"Imagine that," remarked Stillman's black deputy, Leon McMannigle, standing to Stillman's left at the bar. "A child of yours unable to say 'beer'."

The slender man a few inches shorter than Stillman's six-two, and a former Buffalo Soldier during the ongoing Apache Wars, McMannigle shook his head with mock sadness then sipped his own mid-day ale.

He'd been nibbling at the ham sandwich he'd built from the free-lunch platter on the bar beyond him and which three businessmen in three-piece suits and cravats were plundering while arguing quietly over some proposed business venture.

"Maybe he's an idiot," McMannigle opined.

"Damn," Stillman said. "I never thought of that." He crouched down to look closely into the boy's large, frosty blue eyes—the same blue as his father's eyes. "Are you an idiot, little Ben? If so, your mother'll kill me. She'll assume you got it from my side."

"And rightly so, I would add," said his deputy before snorting a chuckle and taking another sip of his ale. "He certainly wouldn't have gotten it from the Beaumonts."

"Oh, there has to be an idiot or two in the Beaumont woodpile," Stillman disagreed. "Every family has an idiot or two." He was still inspecting his son's eyes, looking for evidence of folly. "I just hope this ain't one here. His mother will purely kill me!"

"What the hell are you two talking about?" said Natalia "Nat" Drucker, who had taken over management of the Drovers just last year. She was a mannish little dark-haired woman in her early sixties, though she looked far older.

She didn't only look like a man and dress like a man, in dungarees and flannel shirt and suspenders; she spoke in the low, froggy tones of a hard-edged old mossyhorn, as well.

The woman seemed perpetually on a royal tear, madder than the proverbial old wet hen. She hadn't been in Clantick more than a year—nobody seemed to know where she'd come from--but even in that relatively short space of time, Stillman couldn't remember ever having seen her crack a smile.

"What's this blather about little Ben bein' an idjit?" she demanded, slapping the bar with her crab-like, nearly black little hand. The noise startled little Ben, but he just whipped his head around to gaze at her in bright-eyed fascination, wet red lips parted. He'd seen her before when Stillman had secretly—against Fay's wishes—slipped him into the saloon to show him off to Nat and the parlor girls, but the toddler still seemed to find Nat eminently interesting.

"Baza!" little Ben said as though to reinforce his father's concern, slapping the rim of the beer glass while keeping his gaze on Nat. "Baza! Baza! Baza!"

"So what's wrong with 'baza'?" Nat inquired.

"He doesn't seem able to say beer yet," Stillman said.

"How old is he?"

"Three."

"How long's he been three?"

Stillman winced, dreading her response to his own. "Three months and pocket jingle."

"Oh, hell," Nat said, whipping her hand off the bar in disgust, as though she were casting to the floor a fly she'd just killed. "That's early yet." She leaned forward and said right up close to the boy's face: "Baza, little Ben. Baza! Baza! Baza!" She sounded like a crow cawing from a widow's walk.

All excited now, Little Ben kicked his feet, clad in small black boots, down below the edge of the zinc-topped mahogany and waving both hands at his father's beer glass. "Baza! Baza! Baza! Baza!"

"All right, all right—'baza' it is," Stillman relented, stirring the egg around in the glass, whipping up a heavier foam, into which the yoke disappeared. "If he's still calling this stuff 'baza' when he's thirty, I'll know who to blame." He raised the glass, tipped it at the boy's plump, pink lips, and said, "Here you go, little Ben. Beauty before age."

"Sheriff Ben Stillman, what in tarnation do you think you're doing?" came a female screech from somewhere to Stillman's right.

Stillman turned to see one of Nat's parlor girls, Tonya French, hurry at him from the bottom of the stairs rising to the second floor, where the doxies plied their trade. Tonya French was what the girl called herself, though Stillman knew her real name was Clara Hansen, born and raised on Clear Creek in the Two Bear Mountains south of Havre.

A pretty little freckle-faced blonde, she was clad at the moment in only a bustier and pantaloons, with a powder-blue housecoat hanging from her slender shoulders. As she wasn't working at the moment, a cornhusk cigarette drooped from one corner of her mouth, and her eyes were half-closed against the smoke curling into them.

She removed the quirley from her mouth as she drew up before Stillman, McMannigle, and little Ben, whose interest in Nat died immediately. Now he feasted his gaze on the blonde's deep cleavage, swinging his short legs and waving a hand at same.

"What do you mean—what am I doing?" Stillman said, with one hand holding the boy on the bar so he didn't throw himself head first into Tonya French's bosom. "We skipped breakfast up at the house on account of Fay sold all the eggs from the coop the day before she left for Rocky Ford. The hens haven't been laying lately, so…"

"So," Tonya said, gesturing haughtily at the egg-drop beer, "you're going to feed this child a raw egg in beer?"

"Well," Stillman said, glancing at McMannigle,

who had also turned to face the doxie, grinning at little Ben's obvious enjoyment of the man-pleasing wares before him. "Yeah...that's what I was about do, all right."

"Does your wife know you feed little Ben raw eggs in beer?"

"Well, it's not like he's on a steady diet of the stuff. Just a few glasses a week, mostly for breakfast. Gives his cheeks a healthy glow, puts a shine in his eyes."

"Oh, my god!" Tonya exclaimed, blowing out a long smoke plume at the ceiling then turning her castigating gaze back to the sheriff. "I'll ask again--does his mother know about this?"

"Well...no." Stillman chuckled, sliding his amused glance toward his deputy, who gave a sheepish chuckle of his own. "I wouldn't tell her. She doesn't need to know what we men do when she's not around. By god, I know times are a-changin', but--"

Tonya gave a disgusted chuff and then leaned toward the toddler, who was still waving his hands at her corset and chortling loudly. Stillman had to admit he had the impulse to do the same thing when he saw the pretty blonde pleasure girl parading her stuff around the Drovers, as she tended to do, so he didn't see anything overly untoward in the toddler's display.

"Come here, little Ben," Tonya said.

She picked the boy up off the bar. Little Ben went to her immediately, wrapping his arms around her neck and curling his legs over her bosom. He whooped and slapped the air with both hands.

"Wait," Stillman said. "Where are you taking my son?"

"I'm taking him into the kitchen for a proper meal." Tonya turned away with the boy in her arms and said over her shoulder, "The cook got a fresh batch of eggs in yesterday, and I have a few oats left from breakfast. Fried eggs, oats and milk. That is a proper breakfast for a growing little child. Not raw eggs and beer."

She gave a groaning wail of raw disdain punctuated with: "Men!" then disappeared through the curtained doorway at the back of the room, gone.

Stillman still heard little Ben whooping and hollering like a soldier on furlough. He could also hear the German cook, Nils Schumacher, greet the boy in his jovial way, as he always did when big Ben brought little Ben around.

Leon took another drink of his beer. "Well, it looks like your son's just been kidnapped, Ben. Want me to form a posse?"

Stillman winked. "I was counting on that."

McMannigle frowned. "Huh?"

Stillman turned to the bar and took a couple of big sips of his beer. Setting the mug back down and smacking his lips, he chuckled and said, "The neighbor lady, Mrs. Finnegan, who usually looks after the boy for Fay, took ill suddenly. Something she ate, she said. She couldn't take little Ben today. I didn't have anywhere else to go, so I came here." He broadened his grin at the deputy.

"Why, you devil!"

"There's nobody in town better with babies than whores! Besides, it's only for a few hours, till Fay's stage pulls in this evening."

"Hmmm...I wonder what Fay would think about that," McMannigle said, frowning off across the room in grim speculation. "If she knew..."

Commandingly, and with no little threat in his voice, Stillman said, "We'll never know what she thinks about that, Deputy, because she's never gonna find out. Correct?"

"Oh, right, Ben. Right! Leastways, she'll never hear it from my lips, because you're the only man fool enough to give me a job. I just hope she doesn't hear it via the moccasin telegraph or any other way, because I got me a feeling that if she did, she'd take you to the wood shed and you'd be spending a good couple of months in the dog house afterwards."

They both had a good laugh at that, though McMannigle's laugh was more unbridled than Stillman's. Both men's mirth had cooled to a few last chuckles and Stillman was moving down the bar toward the lunch platter when a man yelled his name from the front of the room.

Stillman turned to see the Western Union agent, Darl Simmons, standing between the batwings, beckoning. He held what appeared a thin pink telegraph flimsy in his long-fingered right hand trimmed with a gold ring on his pinky.

"Hmm," Stillman said, unhappy about having his lunch interrupted. "Wonder what that's about..."

"Only one way to find out."

"I reckon."

Stillman set his beer down on the bar then strode through the noon crowd of drinkers and diners to the front door. As he did, the telegrapher stepped out onto the stoop fronting the saloon, and Stillman and his deputy walked up beside him, the batwings shuddering into place behind them.

"What do you have, Darl?" Stillman asked.

The tall, gray-haired, long faced man in a blue wool waistcoat and leather-billed Western Union hat waved the flimsy. "Looks like trouble, Ben. The stage up from Rocky Ford is late getting into the Chadwick Relay Station."

Stillman felt cold fingers of apprehension press against the small of his back, near the site of the operation he'd had recently to remove an old bullet from where it had snuggled too close to his spine, threatening to paralyze him. Fay was supposed to be riding that very coach, the next one up from Rocky Ford, where she'd spent the week sitting with and then helping to bury a woman who'd tutored her as a young girl on her family's ranch near Milestown.

Simmons read the trepidation darkening Stillman's frosty blue eyes. "I know that's the stage your wife is on, Ben," the man said grimly. Simmons doubled as the stage agent for the Musselshell Line here in Clantick. "I booked it for her."

"Chadwick Station..." Stillman said, his heartbeat increasing. "That's the next station north from Rocky Ford..."

"Yes, I know."

"Ben, the doc's on that stage, too," McMannigle put in.

"Evans?"

"Yeah—I thought you knew. The doctor down in Rocky Ford asked him for help with some operation he was performing on a fella's ticker."

"That's right," said the telegrapher. "Your wife

and the doctor are both on that stage."

"How late is it getting into Chadwick's?" Stillman asked.

"Three hours. At least, it was three hours late when the message was sent. Billy Chadwick sent his son J.J. back to Rocky Ford to notify the marshal down there—Burt Conway. Conway sent this telegram to you." He shook his head. "Apparently, there was no sign of the stage between Chadwick Station and Rocky Ford."

"So," Stillman said, his heart beginning to kick in earnest. "It's missing..."

Softly, the deputy said, "I'll saddle the horses, Ben."

"No." Stillman pushed his fear aside to organize his thoughts, to plan coherently. "You stay here, Leon. Someone needs to keep an eye on things here. I'll check it out."

"Shouldn't we form a posse?"

"Probably, but I'm not going to take the time. Besides, there could be a simple explanation. Rocky might have taken a different route and just lost a wheel or something like that. They might have even rolled into Chadwick Station by now. I'll check it out..."

He stepped down off the boardwalk and looked around, trying to get his bearings. He knew the town like the back of his hand, but everything looked different now in the light of the possibility that…

No. Don't even think it. You won't be able to climb onto your horse, weighed down with a thought like that.

"Sheriff Stillman!"

Stillman turned around to see four men coming out of the Drovers behind his deputy and the telegrapher. All four were dressed in dusty Stetsons, checked shirts, billowy neckerchiefs, and brush-scratched chapparreras. Stillman recognized them as rancher Phil Triber's men, from Triber's Milliron Ranch southwest of Clantick.

The one who'd called Stillman was one of Triber's top hands, Cyrus Green—a lean, thin-lipped redhead in his mid-thirties. Stillman had seen all four hands nursing beers and enjoying the free lunch in the Drovers.

Inwardly, the sheriff cursed. He didn't care for Triber or the man's men. They were a hard, tough bunch led by a hard, tough man. A man known to take the law into his own hands. Stillman had a feeling he wasn't going to like Triber or his men any better after he'd heard what Green had to say.

He tried to forestall the conversation. "Not now, fellas."

"Hold on, Sheriff." Green and the others walked out from behind McMannigle and the telegrapher, lightly nudging both men aside. Green walked up to Stillman. "I overheard. The stage is late getting into Chadwick's?"

"That's right."

"Mr. Triber will be sorry to hear that. He has a good bit of money coming in on that coach, Sheriff."

"He does, Ben," Simmons said.

"Payroll?" Stillman asked, scowling incredulously. Most payrolls were shipped up from Helena or Great Falls by train.

Green shrugged. "I don't know what it is, exactly. He's been pretty tight-lipped about it. Money for some business deal, I think. But it's a good bit of cash, and if the stage is late, he's gonna want us to help you look into it."

At the moment, Stillman didn't give a damn about the rancher's money.

"I'm going to look into it alone," Stillman said, and turned around.

Green and the other men strode forward. "We'll ride with you."

"You'll only slow me down and get in my way." Stillman started to cross the street.

"I'm afraid I'm going to have to insist, Sheriff."

Stillman whipped back around. This time he'd dragged his ivory-gripped Frontier Colt .44 from the holster angled for the cross-draw on his left hip. He cocked the long-barreled revolver, and aimed at Green's freckled forehead. Gritting his teeth, he said, "What don't you understand about no?"

Green stopped abruptly. The others did, as well, gazing at Stillman in shock. Green raised his hands chest-high, palms out. He opened his mouth to speak, but Stillman cut him off with: "If I catch you four on my back trail, I'll blow your damned heads off!"

He glanced at McMannigle. "Little Ben…"

"Don't worry about the boy. I'll keep an eye on him." McMannigle's molasses-black eyes were grave as they stared into Stillman's. "Good luck down there, Ben."

"Right." Stillman gave the Milliron men another threatening look then holstered his Colt, wheeled, and headed for the livery barn.

Chapter 5

Breathless, Fay stared at the hand Evans was sliding toward dead Fritz's holstered revolver.

Crouched over the man's bloody body, Evans nearly had his hand around the gun when one of the outlaws said, "Hey!"

The dark-haired man in a torn canvas coat shouldered Evans aside and pulled the revolver from the dead man's holster.

"Here ya go, mister—this what you're lookin' for?" the dark-haired man said, clicking the gun's hammer back and ramming the barrel against Evans's belly. The man's two front teeth were silver, and he flashed them now as he said, "How 'bout if I give you a belly full of it?"

"Hold on!" Fay took a step forward. "Don't hurt him. He's a doctor. He can help Waylon."

Silver Teeth looked at Dutch, who was administering to his writhing son beside the strongbox while the other gang members stood around looking uneasy, maybe a little impatient with the delay.

"Hear that, Dutch?" Silver Teeth asked, glancing quickly at the outlaw leader down on one knee beside his son. "She says this fella's a sawbones." He raised his voice to the distracted outlaw leader. "Hey, Dutch!"

Dutch snapped a harsh look at the man with the gun. "What the hell you want, Dude? Can't you see my boy is injured here?"

"Yeah, but this fella's a sawbones, Dutch."

Dutch glanced at Evans.

"His shoulder is separated," Evans said, his bespectacled gaze on the boy.

Dutch scowled. "Huh?"

Evans brushed past the silver-toothed Dude, who still held Fritz's revolver on him, and moved to where the boy writhed and thrashed in terrible agony. "Look at his arm. See the bulge? The shoulder's been wrenched out of its socket."

Dutch's brown eyes glinted hopefully. "Can you do somethin' for him, Doc?"

Evans took another step forward, nudging two other outlaws aside. Waylon was moaning and kicking his legs and waving his right arm while the left arm hung down at a strange angle.

Evans grabbed the young man's wrist with his

own right hand, then planted his left knee against Waylon's chest.

"Hey, what're you doin' there?" Dutch yelled, closing his hands around the grips of his own two holstered six-guns.

Evans grunted as he gave Waylon's left arm a hard tug.

A cracking sound rose from the young man's shoulder.

The boy threw his head back. His face turned as white as freshly laundered linen. He howled shrilly and banged his right arm against the ground.

Dutch and the others stood gazing at Evans and the boy in hang-jawed shock, most with their guns drawn.

"Look at that," Dutch said, pointing at his son's injured shoulder. "The bulge is gone."

One of the others gave a raspy whistle of amazement.

Waylon still sobbed but was obviously in less pain than before.

"That should take care of that problem," Evans said. He gently probed the young man's ribs with his fingertips. That sent Waylon into bawling agony again; the young man lifted his chin and hurled several more screams at the blue Montana sky.

Glancing up at the old outlaw leader, the doctor said, "He's got some broken ribs on his left side. By the way he yelled, I'd say he's got some internal bleeding, too. Those broken ribs might be chewing into a lung."

"How bad, how bad?" Dutch asked.

"We need to get him into a bed, so I can examine and treat him. We need to get him to Gerard Barney's office in Rocky Ford. Dr. Barney is well-outfitted to handle such injuries."

Dutch stared at him, thinking it through.

"We can't take him to Rocky Ford, Dutch," Dude said, laughing his disdain for the idea. "Wouldn't Marshal Conway love that? We need to take that strongbox and light a shuck. Besides, we can't trust this fella." He glared at Evans, his silver teeth glinting. "He made a play fer Fritz's six-gun!"

"Wouldn't you in my situation?" Evans glared at the man. "You men are a bunch of lowdown, unwashed, uncouth killers!"

Fay had never seen the doctor so furious. His face was beet-red, and he didn't appear to care that his dusty spectacles were sagging low on his nose. She grabbed his arm to try to calm him down.

Dutch angrily swiped his sombrero off his head and ran a brusque hand through his close-cropped gray hair in frustration. "Ah, hell!"

"This never would have happened if you hadn't killed Rocky," Fay said, her voice quavering with emotion. Her own internal wolf was threatening to break its chain. Now that the initial shock of the situation had worn off, she was both enraged and heartbroken at what these men had done to the driver and shotgun messenger.

Dutch straightened quickly and cast his fiery-eyed gaze at her. "Shoot her! She's nothin' but a distraction. One of you boys shoot her! I can't do it because she's a woman, gallblastit!"

Fay gaped at him, taking one faltering footfall away from him.

Evans moved in front of her, spreading his arms as though shielding her from a bullet. Several of the outlaws had turned toward Fay, bringing their pistols or rifles to bear.

"Shoot her and you'd best shoot me, too, Dutch," Evans said. "You need me to help with your boy. If those ribs aren't set, he'll die." The doctor shook his head stubbornly. "But if you shoot her, that kid will get no more help from me." He touched his voice with a dark chill. "And he'll die."

Dutch glared at him for nearly a minute. He looked at Fay and then returned his gaze to Evans. Gradually, the bright flares of fury in his eyes faded, and he looked down at his sobbing son and said, "Can we move him?"

"Only if I wrap his ribs. If they're cutting into his lung, moving him could kill him. We need to get him back to Rocky Ford."

"No." Dutch studied the ground, wagging his head. "No. We can't go to Rocky Ford. Conway's there. We can't go to no town." He turned, lifted an arm and pointed his index finger at the southwest. "We go there."

All Fay could see in that direction was a jagged, purple line of mountains on the far horizon.

"Where?" Evans asked.

"The Highwoods. That's where we're headed. My boy goes, too." He pointed at the doctor and narrowed his eyes threateningly. "You keep him alive, you understand? If he dies, Doctor—you die. But first you watch her die. Understand?"

Evans glanced at Fay, drew a deep breath, and released it. He turned back to Dutch. "I don't recommend it, but all right."

"Get to work on my boy," Dutch commanded, peering down at his son. "And if either of you tries another dirty stunt like the one you just pulled, it's all over. For both of you."

He gave Fay and the doctor each a hard look in turn.

***

Fay helped the doctor wrap young Waylon's ribs.

They'd sat the boy against a large rock beside the trail, in a patch of shade offered by a small cedar. They used strips Fay had cut from one of her petticoats, which she'd pulled from one of her bags in the coach's rear luggage boot.

While they worked, Fay glanced up at the silver-toothed outlaw, Dude, whom Dutch had ordered to keep watch over her and the doctor.

The man grinned down at her in goatish male fashion.

Fay curled her nose distastefully, and looked at Evans. Quietly, she asked, "Is he gonna make it, Doc?"

At the moment, the young man appeared to be unconscious. That was likely due to the several sips of whiskey the doctor had given him to dull the pain. But his breathing sounded raspy, shallow. He grunted and groaned as his chest rose and fell when he breathed.

"I honestly don't know," Evans said, tying one of the petticoat strips, straining with the effort of drawing the wrap as taut as possible without pinching off Waylon's breathing altogether. "See that pink froth on his lower lip?"

Fay leaned forward to peer at the young man's

mouth, and nodded.

"He's expectorating oxygenated blood," Evans said.

"What does that mean?"

"Lung's likely pierced. Hard to say how badly. If it's bad, he won't make it. Not without getting him to Rocky Ford and cutting him open to repair the torn lung and set the rib."

Fay sighed. She glanced at the man guarding them.

Dude sat on the ground fifteen feet away now, leaning against another small cedar, his knees drawn partway up to his chest. He was smoking a cigarette with a desultory air. His rifle lay across his belly. Four of the other nine men, including Dutch, were leading the stagecoach toward a canyon to the east.

They'd placed the bodies of Fritz, Rocky O'Sullivan, and the shotgun messenger, Dave Morley, inside the coach. Dutch had decided to run both it and the team, as well as the three dead men, into the canyon to prolong the chance of their discovery. Four of the other men had gathered wood and rope and were busy rigging a travois for Waylon.

The strongbox sat near Fay and the doctor and their patient. A stocky mule had been tethered to the cedar. The beast hung its head sleepily, occasionally switching its tail at flies. It had been outfitted with a packsaddle for hauling the loot to the out-laws' lair in the Highwoods.

"Is there any chance at all he can survive the travois ride, Doc?" Fay asked Evans, who was wrapping another strip of cloth around Waylon's chest. She turned toward the jagged purple line of the mountain range. "All the way to those mountains?"

Evans glanced at Dude, then gave his head a subtle shake. Keeping his voice just above a whisper, he said, "Doubt it. Let's just hope we can keep him alive long enough for a posse to find us. Because if he dies…" The doctor let his voice trail off and glanced with foreboding at Fay.

"Yes, I know," she said soberly, holding the cloth firm while the doctor tied it.

When he finished tying the last bandage, Evans looked at her again. He reached over and wrapped his hand around her wrist. "You all right?"

Fay drew another fateful breath, nodded. "I'm all right, Doc. Just scared. How 'bout yourself?"

He shrugged. "What choice do we have, right?"

Fay gave a start when a horrible din rose from behind her in the east. The shrill collective cry of the six-horse hitch, followed by the thunder of the team and stagecoach crashing to the bottom of the canyon a couple of hundred yards to the east surged in the air.

Fay clamped a hand over her mouth as she stared toward the canyon and the four men milling on the lip of it. "Oh, my god!"

Smoke roiled up from the canyon before them. The outlaws had filled the coach with dry brush and set it on fire before running the team into the gorge. Fay had heard Dutch give the order, but she hadn't been able to work her numb mind around the significance of his plan until now, having heard the raucous screaming of the terrified horses and the explosion-like sound of the coach and team landing on the bottom of what was now their burning grave.

Evans sat back on the heels of his half-boots, gazing in shock at the smoke and the four men striding back to him and Fay. The men were little more than black stick figures from this distance.

"Savages," he muttered, and gave a deep chuff of disbelief. "Stupid, soulless savages."

He glanced at Fay and shook his head.

"Shut up, Doc." Dude had walked up to stand over the two of them, holding his rifle on his shoulder and rolling a match stick around between his lips. He looked at Waylon. "He better be able to travel—that's all I got to say about him." He narrowed his cow-stupid gaze on the sawbones. "And for you."

Evans rose to his feet.

"He's as ready as he'll ever be," the doctor bit out, unable to disguise his disdain for the cutthroats.

"Easy, Doc," Fay whispered.

The guard crouched over Waylon. The young man leaned against the rock, chin dipped to his chest. He appeared asleep, but it was a miserably painful sleep. He grunted and fluttered his lips and shook his head slowly from side to side. More pink blood froth stained his lower lip.

The guard peered at Evans and rolled the matchstick from one side of his mouth to the other. "He ain't gonna make it, is he?"

"He will."

"I heard you and the lady talkin'. He ain't gonna make it."

Fay rose, absently brushing at the weeds and dirt clinging to her dress. "Doc Evans can pull him through if anyone can."

"Not sure he's worth the trouble, though... really."

The guard smiled menacingly at Fay and Evans. Dutch and the other three outlaws were walking toward them from the direction of the canyon but had just disappeared behind a hillock. Only the crowns of their hats were visible above a watery heat haze.

The guard lowered his rifle toward the sleeping young outlaw. "Waylon's a damn fool, soft in his thinker box. I never been able to figure why Dutch keeps him around. I ain't sure he's worth slowin' us down, riskin' a posse over-takin' us."

"What are you sayin' over here, Dude?" The four men who'd been putting the travois together walked toward Dude and Fay and Evans. Two of the men carried the hastily constructed travois between them. One of the carriers had asked the question.

Dude glanced at the four newcomers, narrowing one eye against the sunshine. "I'm sayin' why let Waylon here slow us down? A posse's liable to overtake us. Leastways, one'll track us easy if we're draggin' that crazy rig of yours."

"What do you propose we do', Dude?" asked Clem, the other man carrying the travois.

The two others held back a little, as though wary of the implications of the conversation, not sure they wanted to be part of it.

"I'm sayin', Clem," Dude said, "is why don't we just put him out of his misery right here and now?"

Dude grinned as he pressed the barrel of his rifle against Waylon's wrapped, broken ribs. "Shouldn't be too hard..."

Waylon groaned and jerked his head as he

slept, scrunching up his eyes against the pain.

"No!" Fay said.

Evans hurried over and gave Dude a hard shove. "Leave him alone, you damn savage!"

The comment didn't sit well with Dude. The silver-toothed outlaw hardened his jaws. A crimson flush rose in his cheeks behind his thin beard. He whipped up the rear stock of his Winchester and rammed it butt-first into the doctor's gut.

Chapter 6

Evans gave a fierce grunt as the air exploded from his lungs. Clamping his arms across his belly, he dropped to his knees, groaning.

"Doc!"

Fay leaped forward and took a knee beside the doctor, glaring up at Dude. She stretched an arm across the doctor's back. "You all right, Doc?"

Evans groaned. He had his head nearly on the ground, trying desperately to suck wind back into his lungs, making guttural strangling sounds as he did.

"Easy, Doc," Fay said, patting his back. "Try to relax..."

He gave her a dubious look.

She glared up at Dude again. "You son of a bitch!"

Dude walked over to her, scowled down at her. She could see raw fury again darkening his face behind his sandy beard. "You might think you're all high 'n' mighty 'cause you're Stillman's wife, but I don't have to take that from no woman!"

"Go to hell!" Fay screamed at him.

He dropped his rifle. Fay screamed as he pulled her violently up by her hair. He held the back of her head with one hand and wrapped his other hand around her neck, nearly strangling her. He shoved his face up close to hers, pinching his face up with diabolical rage.

His two silver front teeth shone between his stretched-back lips. "I don't care who you are--I'm gonna show you what happens to women who sass me!"

He glanced at the other four men standing around grinning at him. "Fellas, mind the saw-bones. I'm gonna take this purty little sheriff's wife off in the bushes an' show her what happens when she sasses me!"

"All right, Dude," one of them said, chuckling. "You do that, Dude!"

Evans choked out a garbled objection, trying to gain his feet.

"Stay there, Doc!" one of the others ordered, snugging a rifle barrel against his left ear.

Fay tried to fight against her attacker, but he was far stronger than she was.

"Get over there!" the man bellowed, giving her

a hard shove.

She flew into the brush on the trail's west side. She fell and rolled. She came up on her butt, shaking her hair, which had tumbled out of its bun, away from her face. "Get away from me, you son of a bitch!"

Grinning icily, the man sauntered toward her, his eyes raking her body through her thin black cambric jacket and light brown dress.

Fay scrambled to her feet. He grabbed her again, gave her another hard shove. She flew farther from the trail, taking three lunging, off-balance strides before hitting the ground again, and rolling. As she once more tried to scramble to her feet, Dude grabbed her hand and dragged her a dozen yards to the west then threw her to the ground behind three ragged cedars.

He gave a devilish laugh then threw himself on top of her, pressing his body against hers, holding her head as he tried to kiss her. She writhed against him, cursing him, terror gripping her, weakening her. She tried to turn her head away from him, but his grip was too strong.

He laughed mockingly as he ground his body against hers.

He was too strong for her. He was going to take her. The thought enraged her again, tempering her fear.

"No!" she screamed and somehow managed to ram her knee into his groin. As he lifted his head and howled, she raked her fingernails down his right cheek. She dug them deep, tearing his flesh, feeling the wetness of blood under her fingernails.

Dude howled again, louder this time. Shriller.

Cursing, his raised his fist. "Why, you—"

Before he could bring his fist down against her face, Fay saw Dutch step up to them both and plant the barrel of a rifle against the back of Dude's head.

"Get off her, Dude!"

Dude stopped. "Leave me alone, Dutch. Just gonna have me a little fun, is all!"

Dutch loudly cocked the Winchester then set the barrel against Dude's head again. "Get off her now, Dude, or I'll drill one through your head!"

Dude swung around. His voice was low and hard. "Leave me alone, Dutch. You can have a little taste later." He grinned.

"That ain't the way you a treat a lady." Dutch narrowed one eye as he aimed down the barrel at Dude's forehead. "You get off of her now, Dude!" He tightened his grip on the Winchester. "Get off her now, dammit, or so help me…!"

"All right, all right! Stand down, Dutch!" Dude rolled off Fay and climbed to his feet.

The other men had followed Dutch to Dude and Fay. Doc Evans strode to where Fay lay on the ground, her heart still racing, fear sparking in every nerve in her body.

Evans didn't say anything, but he held her gaze with his own. He helped her to her feet, then closed his hand around her arm and said, "You all right?"

Fay drew a breath, shook her loose, tangled hair back from her face. "Yes." She drew another calming breath and turned to him. "How 'bout you, Doc?"

Evans nodded. His clothes and his short, auburn hair, normally parted neatly on one side, were badly disheveled. His cravat was loose, and it hung to one side. His spectacles were so dusty, Fay could barely see his eyes through them.

"I do apologize Mrs. Stillman," Dutch said, genuinely contrite, casting an angry glare at Dude. "That ain't how this group treats a lady. I want you to understand that."

The elderly outlaw leader lowered his rifle and now stood facing her and Evans. Dude brushed dirt and bits of grass from his clothes, chuffing angrily, cursing under his breath. Blood dribbled from the long scratch on his cheek. Dutch was flanked by the other men of his gang, none of whom, it appeared, shared Dutch's sense of honor regarding the fairer sex. They eyed Fay lustily, elbowing each other, snorting ribald laughs.

Dutch turned to them and said, "That ain't gonna happen again, fellas. I will not allow this woman to be mistreated. Now, if she's too damn much of a distraction, I'll just go ahead and shoot her," he added, glancing sharply over his shoulder at Fay, who felt a cold stone drop in her belly.

Turning back to his men, Dutch said, "I will not have her mistreated in any fashion. You boys understand that much? You mind your manners, and you clean up your talk while she's around, an' act like gentlemen from now on or I'll cut ya loose. So help me, I will. I'll cut ya loose!"

Fay stared at the hard cases. It was hard to tell what they were thinking, but they were a rough-looking bunch. The oldest of them appeared a good twenty years younger than Dutch. Dutch was the old wolf with an unruly pack behind him, and Fay didn't think they respected him all that much. Or feared him.

Which, as far as her safety was concerned, was not good.

She glanced at Evans. His own dark expression said he was likely thinking the same thing.

Dutch said, "Now, all we're doin' over here is wastin' time. Let's get that travois rigged to my hoss. I'll pull my boy. He's mine to carry. Dude, you an' Scrim an' H.G. get the loot out of the box and onto the mule. Clem, Mort—you fetch Fritz and Waylon's hosses for the doctor an' the woman."

The old outlaw leader clamped his rifle under one arm and clapped his hands. "Come on, now. Get movin'. Sober up, Utah, gallbastit, anyway! That stage is already late pullin' into the Chadwick station, which means old Billy Chadwick an' that half-breed son of his will be lookin' for it soon. So come on, now—let's fog some sage, boys!"

Dutch glanced at Fay and Evans. He gestured at the trail with his rifle, giving his head a mock-formal dip. "Doctor," he said. "Mrs. Stillman..."

Fay shared another glance with the doctor then started walking back in the direction of the trail. Evans fell into step beside her. "What do you think, Doc?" Fay asked, trying to slow her heavily thudding heart. "Are we going to get out of this alive?"

"I don't know," the doctor said, casting his gaze across the hard-faced men around them. "As a betting man, as a veteran of the green baize and the craps tables, I won't tell you where I'd place my silver."

"Yeah." Fay also looked around. "Please don't."

***

Twenty minutes later, they were all mounted and heading southwest toward the Highwoods.

Fay had torn a long slit in the skirt of her dress, so she could sit a regular stockman's saddle. She was mounted on Waylon's claybank while the doctor rode a mouse-brown dun with a blaze down its snout and white spots splashed across its hindquarters.

Waylon rode behind his father's horse, strapped to the crude travois. He was tucked into his own bedroll. Only semi-conscious, he moaned with nearly every jarring stride of Dutch's horse.

Fay and Evans rode side by side, to Dutch's left. The other men, one leading the mule outfitted with the packsaddle bearing the loot they'd taken from the strongbox, flanked her, Evans, Dutch and Waylon. They didn't appear to be following a trail but were riding through open country. Occasionally, Fay spotted cattle peppering distant hillsides.

It was a vast, gently rolling country punctuated by distant midget buttes and small mesas topped with pines. The colors were all greens and the light summer browns of brome, buffalo, and rye grass with occasional stretches of dusty green or purple sage. Wildflowers added surprising splashes of color as bright as oils on a painter's pallet. The sky arched broadly, a broad cerulean bowl with the only clouds those stacked high against the western horizon.

It was warm, not hot, and a gentle wind blew. It would have been a nice day for a ride.

Fay enjoyed riding on such days, leaving little Ben with her neighbor, Mrs. Finnegan, and taking her sorrel filly, Miss Dorothy, for a long trek into the Two Bear Mountains to visit her and Ben's friends, Jody and Crystal Harmon and their son, Billy, named after Jody's deceased father and Ben's old buffalo hunting partner, Wild Bill Harmon.

This would have been a nice day for such a ride...

Occasionally, as they rode along, Fay's knees and elbows still sore from the battering they'd taken when Dude had shoved her to the ground and she'd fought for her life, she stared off into a ravine. She daydreamed, however briefly, that she was on just such a carefree jaunt right now, jogging along the ravine's bottom and maybe stopping occasionally to pick a berry or a wild plum, to enjoy the explosion of flavor on her tongue.

Every time her mind drifted, it was brought back by Waylon's tormented grunts or sobs until, finally, after a particularly aggrieved cry of pain, Dutch stopped his dun and turned to Evans. "Dammit, Doctor—ain't there anything you can do for my boy? You hear him back there? It sounds like every step this horse takes is killin' him!"

The doctor checked down his own dun, and sighed. "I'll take a look at him."

Evans swung from his saddle and wrapped his reins around the horn. He'd removed his suit coat and tied it behind his saddle. He'd rolled his shirtsleeves up his forearms; his watch chain dangled from a pocket of his brown wool vest. His bowler hat was covered with a thick layer of dust and weed seeds.

Wearily, he walked to where Waylon lay on the travois angling down at a gentle slant from the hind end of his father's horse. Fay swung down from her own saddle and walked to the travois.

Evans knelt beside the semi-conscious young man. He looked into each eye then laid his hand across Waylon's forehead. He glanced fearfully up at Fay and then looked at Dutch, who sat hipped around in his saddle, regarding the doctor anxiously, impatiently.

"Well?" Dutch said.

"Fever," Evans said. "I was afraid he'd get one, and he has." He shook his head. "He really needs proper tending, Dutch. I just can't do for him out here what I and Dr. Barney could do for him in Rocky Ford."

"Well, you'd better!" Dutch cursed and swung down from his own saddle. Doing so, he got one boot partly hung up in his stirrup. He cursed again as he nearly fell, then, recovering his balance and flushing with embarrassment as well as with anger at the doctor, he marched back to Evans and said, "You remember what I told you, Doc. If my boy dies, you die! And she dies, too!"

"That isn't fair, Dutch!"

"I don't care about fair. I just care about you makin' my boy well again, gallblastit!"

"Dutch, for godsakes!" came another voice.

Fay turned to see the other men gathered behind her, all sitting their saddles, leaning forward, elbows crossed on their horns. The man who'd spoken was the one she'd come to hate with a zealot's passion, with a raw ache inside her, so she could hardly stand to look at him.

"Dutch, look," Dude said, swinging down from his saddle and walking over to where Dutch stood with Fay and Evans. He pointed down at Waylon. "You're torturin' the poor kid."

"What're you talkin' about?"

"Look at him, Dutch."

"I am lookin' at him!"

Dude glanced at the other mounted riders

forming a semi-circle behind him. Returning his gaze to Dutch, he said, "Dutch, I know it's a terrible thing to think about, but…"

Dutch's eyes blazed at the taller, sandy-bearded man with the deep scratches on his face. "What's a terrible thing to think about, Dude?"

"I don't think he's gonna make it, Dutch," Dude said, keeping his voice soft and sympathetic, though Fay also heard a sharp, vaguely patronizing edge in it, too. "Don't you think it might be better just to…"

He let his voice trail off meaningfully, holding the older man's gaze with a feigned compassionate one of his own.

Dutch walked around Fay and Evans, around the travois. His eyes blazed as he stared up at Dude. "You'd like that, wouldn't ya?" he said through gritted teeth.

Dude raised his hands in supplication, shaking his head. "Nope, I wouldn't at all, Dutch."

"Sure, you would."

"Dutch, listen to reason," said one of the other mounted riders. He had nearly white, shoulder-length hair, pale blue eyes, and an old scar angling across his nose. "I love the boy, like we all do, but he's slowin' us down, Dutch."

"You, too—eh, Thorn? What? You want me to kill him? That'd be a bigger split for the rest of you, then, wouldn't it?"

"That ain't what I mean," Thorn said. "Look at him. He's dyin', Dutch. Like Dude says, he's miserable."

Dutch shucked one of his big Colts. He cast his angry gaze from Thorn to Dude and then to the other mounted riders. "Waylon's gonna make it. The doc's gonna pull him through. No, I ain't gonna put him out of his misery, 'cause he ain't that miserable. The doc's gonna make him so he's not. Get to it, Doc!" The old man's craggy face was brick-red behind his thin, gray beard.

Returning his gaze to his men, Dutch said, "You seen what I did to Fritz. Fritz was a good friend of mine. Leastways, he had been. But he crossed me, so I shot him. I ain't been with none of you even half as long as me an' Fritz was together. And it was me that got us all a damn good payout there on that mule. You remember that. I see any of you lookin' even crossways at my boy again...or suggestin' anything like Dude suggested...I'll drill a bullet through your guts an' leave you howlin'. Understand?"

That last word had issued like a strangled cry from a dying hawk.

The cutthroats didn't say anything. They just gazed down at the older, feeble-looking man holding the pistol up near his belly bulging behind his red and black checked shirt.

Dutch turned to Evans, who still knelt beside Waylon. "Doc, dammit, can't you make him stop breathin' like that?"

Waylon's breaths were loud rasps ensconced in a deep groan or a choked sob.

Evans looked up at Dutch. "All I can do is give him more whiskey. That's the only thing that will ease his pain."

Evans had given the boy a good amount of whiskey already, before they'd lashed him to the travois. In fact, he'd emptied his traveling flask. Fay could tell the doctor didn't think more liquor was going to make much difference, but Evans was at a loss.

Her heart thudded at the idea the boy would die. When and if Waylon died, her chances of ever seeing her husband and son again would dwindle to nothing.

She and Evans would be dead within a minute of Waylon's final breath.

"All right, all right! Why didn't you say so?" Dutch turned to one of the mounted riders. "Mort, toss down that bottle of yours."

Mort looked back at him, his mouth corners drawn down behind his droopy, red mustache.

"Come on, come on," Dutch said. "There's more tangleleg at the cabin. Throw it down, throw it down!"

Mort drew a deep sigh of reluctance then reached behind him. He dipped his hand into one of his saddlebag pouches and pulled out a whiskey bottle wrapped in burlap. He tossed the bottle to Dutch.

Dutch ripped away the twine and the burlap, popped the cork, and shoved the bottle at Evans.

"Here ya go. Give him plenty, Doc. I purely hate hearin' him sound so miserable."

While Doc fed Waylon more whiskey, most of which appeared to ooze back out between his lips and dribble down his chin and his neck, Fay glanced at the others. To a man, they all stared back at her. There was a darkness in their eyes that made her insides shrivel. Those stark, depraved gazes bore right through her torn black jacket, through her torn brown dress with white polka dots, and froze her right down to her toes.

Later, when they were mounted and riding again, climbing a low bench with a wind building enough that Fay thought it would cover her and her fellow captive's conversation, she leaned out slightly from her saddle to say, "I think we have trouble, Doc."

"What was your first clue?" Evans quipped.

"I think Dude and Thorn are considering a mutiny."

Evans glanced over his shoulder at the other

outlaws following from thirty feet behind him, Fay, and Dutch.

"The Mexican--the one they call Carlos--as well."

"Really?"

"Those three seem to be in cahoots. The way they look at each other when Dutch is talking. I think the others are with Dutch, but they don't seem quite as hard-headed as those three—Dude, Thorn, and Carlos."

Fay cast her own quick look over her shoulder. Those three—Dude, Thorn, and the Mexican, Carlos—rode as a single group, slightly apart from the others. She turned her head forward again and stared over her horse's poll.

She spoke again to Evans. "As a gambling man, what would you bet is going to happen?"

"As a gambling man, I'd have already cashed in my chips and taken a cute little doxie back to her crib." Evans gave a sardonic chuckle.

Fay gave him a look.

The doctor sheepishly cleared his throat. "I think it's just a matter of time before we get caught in a whipsaw, as your dear husband would say in his rustically eloquent fashion."

"All right," Fay said tolerantly. "Would you mind telling me what Ben would mean by that…?"

Evans removed his glasses and moved the

dust around with his fingers as he swayed with the movements of his mouse-brown dun. He glanced at Fay, and narrowed one eye against the sun. "Let me boil it down to this. We'd best come up with a plan. And soon. If that kid doesn't expire first, which is entirely possible, Dude and his two compatriots are gonna get tired of the slow ride an' lock horns with Dutch."

"Yes," Fay said grimly. "Either way, we're doomed."

"Exactly."

"What do you propose we do?"

"I don't know." Evans glanced over his shoulder again, then stretched his lips back from his teeth in a pronounced wince. "I haven't got that far."

Chapter 7

Stillman hunkered low against his bay's neck as the wind beat against him. He pulled his hat brim low so it wasn't whipped from his head.

Sweets's hooves hammered the trail angling south of Clantick. Stillman glanced over his shoulder to see his two spare mounts galloping along behind, the bridle ribbons of the first one, a blue roan, tied to Sweets's tail. The ribbons of the second one, a steeldust with one pale blue eye and one copper brown eye, were tied to the tail of the roan.

Both rangy long-legged mounts, six-hands-high, were built for long distances. And they led well.

Stillman had rented both mounts from Auld's Livery& Feed Barn previously for long, hard rides across vast distances, which was really about the only kind of ride, once he left town, he'd ever known in Montana. Hill County was a big county in a vast territory. One thing separating this ride from the others, however, was that he would recognize no jurisdictional boundaries. He rarely did, anyway. There were too few lawmen in this neck of the territory. One couldn't vacate a hot trail because he'd come to some invisible line, and allow bad men to continue running off their leashes.

But this time there would be no question for one very important reason.

His wife and one of his closest friends could be in a lot of trouble.

Could be...

He kept reminding himself of that as the bay chewed up the miles. There might be a reasonable explanation, beyond a holdup, for O'Sullivan being late pulling the stage into Chadwick Station. The sheriff could very well meet the coach along the stage trail he was following. If O'Sullivan had pulled into Chadwick and then continued northward, Stillman had no way of knowing. No telegraph wires had been strung between the stations, so information between stations had either to be carried by the stage itself or by courier riders dispatched by each isolated outpost.

That he would meet Fay's coach, and that nothing was amiss, was probably a faint hope, but it was all Stillman had. He hoped like hell they hadn't run into trouble.

He arrived at the first relay station south of Clantick, at the very southern edge of the Two Bear Mountains, an hour after he'd left town. The husband and wife who ran the place, Ed and Lilly Solomon, had received word via courier rider from the next station south that the stage was missing.

So far, the Solomons hadn't heard anything more. Stillman had expected as much, though hearing the actual words was like a hand twisting the knife already embedded in his belly. The longer the coach was missing, the larger the possibility it had run into trouble.

Likely hold-up trouble.

He paused at the next station south for fifteen minutes. He wanted to give his horses another short rest as well as water and a few oats.

He let the relay agent, Ma Sorenson, who ran the station with her three "boys" (the youngest was thirty-nine) pour him a cup of coffee and build him a roast beef sandwich to eat later. Like the Solomons, Ma had been given word via hard-riding horseback courier from the next station to the south, Billy Chadwick's station, of possible trouble with the stage.

"I'm worried sick, Ben, and I know you are,

too," Ma said, handing the sandwich and a few extra trail supplies up to Stillman, once he'd forked the saddle again and had his two spare mounts lined out behind him.

Stillman didn't know how to respond. He was afraid if he said anything except, "Thanks, Ma," the knot of terror and worry would bubble up from his throat and come out as an undignified and embarrassing bellowing yowl.

Choking down his emotion, he yelled, "Hi-yah-hh, you broomtail cayuses!" and spurred Sweets off down the trail to the south, the two spares lunging into instant gallops behind him.

He rode another hard five miles before crossing the broad Missouri River via ferry operated by a taciturn, one-legged former cavalry sergeant named James Calhoun, who had a beard that drooped down past his U.S. cavalry belt buckle. The tight-lipped ferryman lived on the Missouri's southern bank in a crude, earthen-roofed shack with his full-blood Gros Ventre wife and several children of various ages. Calhoun also raised horses he bred up from wild stock he'd captured in the Two Bear and the Little Rocky Mountains. This evening, his two pole corrals teemed with whinnying broncs in the process of being broken so they could be sold as remounts to the cavalry.

Of course, Calhoun had also received word

about the coach's disappearance.

In typical Calhoun fashion, all he said was, staring out across the darkening brown water: "Too bad about the stage."

Stillman rode another mile south of the river before it got too dark to continue.

He desperately wanted to push on, but he knew he had to stop. The trail for the next several miles went through rugged country, following a twisting creek between high, forested ridges. Often, rocks from the ridges rolled onto the trail, or blowdowns fell across it. He wouldn't be able to see such obstacles in the dark of that narrow, meandering canyon often hidden from star- and moonlight. He couldn't risk injuring the horses and having to go it on foot.

In the chilly darkness around the snapping fire over which he brewed coffee, he nibbled Ma's sandwich. He knew it would have been right tasty, in typical Ma fashion, at any other time. Tonight, however, it tasted as tough and dry as an old boot. He forced himself to eat a third of it, because he needed sustenance, but his belly threatened rebellion. He drank coffee and smoked a few quirleys. He tried to catch a few winks, but each time he dozed, his dreams woke him, his heart racing.

Dawn seemed to take days, the constellations

crawling across the heavens slowing to near stops at times.

At least his horses were getting a good rest. Having been cooped up in Auld's stable, they were eager to strike out on the trail again at first light. Stillman was glad that so far none had become sick on the green grass they'd been eating after having had little more on their menus besides hay and oats, maybe parched corn.

Midmorning, he pulled into Chadwick's station comprised of a humble log, L-shaped shack, a small barn and two corrals, and a small log blacksmith shack.

As he drew Sweets to a halt in the middle of the yard, he saw the fresh team waiting for the stage. The horses must have known they were supposed to be chewing up the trail, because all six were milling raucously around the corral, manes buffeting and reflecting the buttery sunshine. They seemed as restless as Stillman, who found himself looking around for the stage despite knowing he wouldn't find it here.

When the door to the cabin opened, he held his breath, knowing he was going to get another piece of news. He wasn't sure he wanted to hear it. As soon as he saw Billy Chadwick's face—as the old man, clad in a blue flannel shirt under a broadcloth vest and wearing his usual immigrant hat—walked out onto the stoop fronting the cabin, the lawman was sure he didn't want to hear what the station manager had to say.

Chadwick was a calm, thoughtful man in his late sixties. Like most other station managers in this neck of the woods, he'd done many things in his life, but old age had led him here to this remote station south of the big river. He ran the station with his half-breed son, J.J., a tall, slender quiet, and thoughtful young man, with long hair and wire-rimmed glasses.

J.J., short for the Gros Ventre name Stillman couldn't pronounce, was just then sitting in a rocking chair on the stoop, smoking a pipe. He dressed much like his father—in simple unadorned clothes-- and he even looked a little like his father, except for the dark skin, of course, and the dark brown of his hair hanging in twin braids past his shoulders.

Billy Chadwick had short gray hair and a trimmed gray beard. He spat chaw to one side as he walked out to Stillman, striding slowly, taking his time, a strange frown—or was it a wince expressing the dread of what he was going to say?—creasing his fine-boned face.

"Ben," he said.

"What is it?"

Chadwick gazed up at him.

"Just tell me, dammit, Billy."

Chadwick glanced over his shoulder at the younger man on the porch, who was no longer rocking but staring expressionlessly over the pine pole rail toward the two men in the yard.

"Dammit, Billy," Stillman said, his heart hammering painfully against his breastbone, "just tell me."

"It's in the canyon, Ben. J.J. found it yesterday, after he and Burt Conway rode up from Rocky Ford. Conway followed the robbers' tracks."

Chadwick absently ran a large, bony hand down Sweets's neck as he continued staring bleakly up at the sheriff. Tears glazed the older man's eyes, and a flush of emotion rose in his cheeks. "They ran the damn team an' the coach into the canyon. The whole kit an' caboodle. Burned it, to boot!"

"Christ," Stillman choked out.

Moving slowly, stiffly, feeling as though his body suddenly weighed four hundred pounds, he clambered down from Sweets's back. He placed his hands atop his saddle and stared off into the distance, a wave of raw emotion washing over him. His throat was dry and his knees shook.

"Christ," he said again. Turning to Billy, it took him nearly a minute to ask his next question: "Every…everybody on it? All the passengers?"

"I don't know. Judging by the smell, I'd say so."
Stillman looked up at him.

"J.J. wouldn't go down to look at it. Bad medicine down there. I can't go down because I'm too damn old. You might be too damn old, too, Ben. It's a steep drop."

However old he was, Stillman had just got a whole lot older.

He pushed away from the saddle, trying to steady himself. Somehow, he had to get a look at the stage. He shook like a leaf in the wind. His heart ached with every heavy beat.

He drew a deep breath. "I'd best mosey."

He lifted his left foot, tried to poke that boot through the stirrup but missed. The foot dropped back to the ground, and he fell against his horse.

"Here, here," Billy said, and placed a steadying hand on Stillman's shoulder.

"Here," another voice said—softer, lower.

Stillman turned to see J.J. walking toward him from the cabin. The young man held a steaming coffee cup. J.J.'s worn stockman's boots thudded softly on the hard-packed ground of the station yard. His braids swayed against his chest. He stopped before Stillman, held the cup out to him.

"Have some of this," J.J. said, his face expressionless, though his brown eyes were grave behind his spectacles. "Do you good, Sheriff."

Stillman looked at the cup, almost didn't take it. He wanted to get moving. But the coffee might brace him, though he doubted anything was powerful enough to prepare him for what he would probably find in that canyon.

He took the cup from J.J., lifted it to his lips. He took a couple of big sips, swallowing the strong, hot coffee, wincing against the burn down his throat and into his chest. He took two more big sips, dropping the level of the coffee by half, then handed the cup back to J.J.

"Thanks."

J.J. nodded and stepped back.

Billy said, "They headed west, Ben. The hold-up men. One of them must have been hauled off on a travois. J.J. said he and Conway found tracks heading southwest."

Stillman frowned, staring off. He was trying to absorb the information. His brain worked sluggishly, like a rusty gear on an old locomotive.

Turning to the older man, he said, "Conway went after them, you said?"

"Yes."

"All right." Stillman turned, grabbed the saddle horn, and made a try for the stirrup. This time he made it, and clambered up into the saddle. He looked at Billy. "How far south?"

"'Bout six miles, near that horseshoe bend in

Bull Canyon. You'll see the scuffs on the trail. You want me to ride out with you, Ben?"

"No need."

"I don't mind."

"I'll go alone." He looked at the older man again. "I'd rather do it alone, Billy."

Billy nodded. "Go with God, Ben," Billy told him, staring gravely up at him.

Stillman reined Sweets around. "Thanks."

He touched spurs to the gelding's loins. The bay lunged off across the yard and onto the southern trail, the roan and the steeldust galloping along behind. The horses were tired, but they had enough bottom for the pace Stillman set for them. At least, they'd have to have it.

A couple of miles south of the station, Stillman gave the horses a short blow while switching his saddle to the roan's back. He gave each mount a little water. He drank a few swallows himself, then mounted up and continued following the trail south through the rolling prairie, climbing the grassy swells of the hogback buttes and plunging down their southern slopes.

The horses' hooves lifted a staccato drumming in his ears.

The wind burned against his face, though he was only half aware of anything but grief growing like a cancer inside him. He rode crouched low in the saddle, jaws hard, his mind strangely numb. He felt unmoored from his mind, as though he'd been clubbed in the head.

He had no idea how long he'd been riding before he came to the violent scuffs marking the trail beneath the roan's hooves.

Chapter 8

As he reached the deep scuff marks, he reined the horses to a halt and dismounted.

He inspected the tracks for a time, getting a sense of what had happened here. He dropped to a knee to run his right index finger over the print of a woman's shoe.

Fay.

He turned to the west, where Bull Canyon swung toward him from the east. The canyon had been cut by an ancient river now only wet during springtime, when the snow melted off the mountains around the basin.

Stillman's knees quavered. He felt the urge to hurry after the killers, yet he also felt something holding him back from investigating the canyon.

He looked around a little more, saw the travois tracks Billy Chadwick had spoken about. The twin furrows angled toward the southwest. A half-dozen-plus riders had accompanied the horse and rider pulling the travois.

Why had they needed the travois?

Obviously, someone had been injured. Likely, one of the cutthroats.

Stillman shrugged off the question. He'd find the answer to it later.

He turned to the west. Now he had to take a look at that damned canyon.

He swung back up onto the roan's back and rode to the west, the canyon opening wider and wider before him. He drew rein at the lip of the cut and gazed reluctantly down toward the canyon floor.

At first, he didn't see the stage. Then he saw the long black lump of what could only be the coach and the six-horse hitch lying a little north of where he sat. All three horses with him lifted their noses to the breeze and whickered. Like Stillman himself did, they smelled the scorched-death smells issuing from the deep ravine—dead and burned humans and horses. Charred wood, leather, and luggage.

Stillman rode north along the canyon's lip, looking for a way into the cut. A way down that wouldn't kill him, that was.

Finally, he saw a switch-backing game trail dropping off the tableland, between two shad-bark shrubs. In the gap between the shrubs he saw the split, triangular indentations of deer prints and the black beans of deer scat.

With a heavy sigh, he swung down from the roan's back, wrapped the reins around the horn, pulled his hat tight on his head, and strode forward between the shrubs. He took the two-foot drop from the ledge to the slope, and he gave a grunt when his right boot landed.

Tugging on his hat brim again, nervously, he continued down the ridge, following the slender trail that formed a narrow but traversable shelf extending slightly out from the slope itself.

As he followed the trail, he glanced to his left, at the burned stage and team lying away from the wall of the canyon.

They formed a charred black heap, the front of the stage lying sideways atop both of the two rearmost horses, the wheelers. At least, that's how it appeared. Everything was so badly burned, it was impossible to tell.

The burned brush and grass extended for about fifty feet beyond the wreckage. No smoke still emitted from the wreckage. The fire hadn't burned long. There wasn't enough fuel down there, for there grew mostly just sand and gravel and little patches of grass and sagebrush.

Even following the game trail, the drop was

steep. The short brome grass and needle grass made the footing slippery. Some cedars and juneberry shrubs grew along the declivity, and he grabbed these to slow his momentum or to stop an involuntary slide.

He fell to a knee once, and watched a couple of rocks tumble straight down the ridge to the bottom, clanking together as they rolled to a stop on the canyon floor, a few feet to the left of the coach's rear right-side wheel. The wheel lay on its side away from the coach, and as fire-blackened as the rest of the wreckage.

When he gained the bottom of the canyon, stiff-legged, he walked to the stage, tying his neckerchief across his mouth and nose against the stench of burned flesh and hide. He walked slowly around the wreck. The carriage's roof had shattered in the plunge and lay a little behind and to one side of the rest of the vehicle. Beneath the ashes of burned brush, Stillman could make out three charred bodies, two together, one thrown wide.

While the bodies were charred, the fire hadn't entirely burned away their clothes. Stillman could tell they were all male. He identified the driver, Rocky O'Sullivan, by the man's boots and a gold ring on his little finger, an unusual affectation for a man so otherwise unpretentious.

Neither of the other two appeared to be wearing a three-piece suit, as Evans would have worn. They both wore leather shell belts and holsters. Evans never went heeled. One of the dead men, the larger of the two, was likely the shotgun messenger, Dave Morley. The other man might have been one of the other passengers, killed during the hold-up.

Stillman did not think it was Evans.

It certainly wasn't Fay.

He walked around slowly, carefully, and thoroughly surveying the canyon around the wreck. A body might have flown out during the plunge and be lying some distance away.

Finding no sign of either Fay or the doctor, the knot in Stillman's gut eased slightly.

At least they weren't amongst the dead here.

Where were they?

Had they managed to get away? Likely not. The outlaws must have taken them.

Why?

There were few answers to the lawman's question. What he did have was at least a little hope they were still alive.

He retraced his steps up the canyon wall. By the time he gained the crest of the ridge where the horses now grazed contentedly several yards away from the lip and the stench coming from the cut, Stillman was thoroughly winded. He turned toward the canyon, dropped to his butt, which was raw from the long, hard ride—a ride the likes of which he hadn't been on in many years—and dangled his legs over the ridge wall.

His legs ached, too.

The ache in his mind was worse.

What kind of hell were Fay and Clyde Evans going through? He had to go after them, rescue them from their captors—if they were still alive, that was. He would punish the killers to the full extent of the law, if not with lead.

Soon—very soon—they would know the full extent of Stillman's wrath.

His thinking was interrupted by the growing din of several horses approaching from behind. He turned to see a group of riders turning off the northern trail and galloping at him.

His own horses turned toward the riders, anxiously switching their tails. The roan whinnied a greeting. It was answered in kind by one of the horses of the approaching riders.

Milliron men, Stillman guessed, gaining his feet and turning to face the newcomers.

When they drew close enough for him to recognize Phil Triber himself leading the pack on a tall cream gelding, he knew his guess had been a good one. Flanking Triber slightly was his mousy son, Cole. The four riders behind both Tribers were ranch hands, judging by their standard stockmen's attire, including billowy neckerchiefs and batwings chaps.

A tall man a little older than Stillman, Triber still had more brown than gray in his hair and long sideburns. He wore a long black duster belted at his waist, and a tall black Stetson. His son was considerably shorter than he, and as they moved still closer, Stillman saw a scar on the young man's left cheek.

Cole Triber had acquired the tattoo during a three-year prison sentence in Deer Lodge. Drunk one night in a saloon in Big Sandy, the closest town to the Milliron headquarters, he'd cut a deputy town marshal's throat with a broken whiskey bottle. He'd receive a sentence of only three years because of whose son he was.

In his mid-twenties now, Cole still appeared to be the spoiled, smug, plump-faced, devil's spawn Stillman had always known him to be. The sheriff had barred him from Clantick two years ago after a doxie had been killed in a brothel down by the Milk River. Cole had murdered the girl in a drunken rage, but no eyewitnesses would testify against him, so Stillman had had no choice but to turn him loose...with orders never to show his little rat face in Clantick ever again.

Not even on a supply run.

As he and his men reined up before Stillman, their horses blowing after a hard ride, Phil Triber said, "Cyrus Green sent word from town the stage has been hit."

The hand must have sent a telegram to Big Sandy, Stillman thought. A fast courier had been dispatched to deliver the news to the Milliron headquarters.

"Like I told Green," Stillman said, "I'll handle it."

Triber booted his cream up to Stillman and leaned out from his saddle to peer into the canyon. "That's it down there, huh?" He turned to Stillman. "You been down there?"

"Yes."

"The lockbox is gone, of course."

"Of course."

"What about your wife?"

"She's not in the canyon, so they must have her."

"We'll help you run them down, Sheriff."

"No." Stillman stripped the saddle and blanket from the roan and slung them up onto Sweets's back. Turning to Triber, scowling at him angrily, Stillman said, "Like I told your man in town, I'll handle it."

He leaned down to tighten the latigo strap.

"You're denying the help of me and my men?" Triber's long, clean-shaven features sandwiched between long, neat sideburns were creased with exasperation. "Why?"

"Because I neither like nor trust you, Triber. Not you, your son, or your men. I'm going alone."

"Taking this a little personally—aren't you, Ben? I know they have your wife and friend, if he's not in the canyon, but they also have my money."

Triber's use of his first name rankled Stillman beyond the man's mere presence here. Given their contentious history, they weren't even close to being on a first-name basis. Triber had used his name to show his disrespect of him—pure and simple. As though the sheriff were the rancher's underling.

"Yes, I am taking it personally." Stillman swung up onto Sweets's back and felt his eyes cross with fury as he turned back to Triber. "Now, butt out of my business. I'll get your money back after I have my wife and the doctor back. I'm going to warn you only one more time, Phil—go home and stay the hell out of my way!"

"Hey!" Cole Triber spoke for the first time, pinching his mean little eyes up at Stillman. Like an angry coyote, he spat out: "You can't talk to my pa that way, Stillman!"

"Shut your damned mouth, boy!" Triber flung his left arm out and slammed the back of that hand against his son's face.

Cole cried out as he flew backward, then rolled down his horse's left hip to the ground. His horse spooked, turned, and ran.

Stillman chuffed a caustic laugh as he swung Sweets to the west and put the steel to him.

Chapter 9

"Let's stop here for a bit," Dutch said. "Take a little break."

He led his horse off the narrow trail they'd been following—an old Indian hunting trail, Fay figured—and swung down from his saddle.

"We're stopping again, Dutch?" asked the Mexican, Carlos, reining up behind the outlaw leader and the travois he was pulling. "We just stopped an hour ago."

The man named Carlos was flanked by Dude and Thorn. All three stared incredulously at Dutch, whose fleshy, craggy face began reddening with anger, and his blue eyes sparked bridled fury. "Yeah, well, we're gonna stop again. We'll stop for a half hour, build us a coffee fire. I could do with a cup of coffee, and I don't think it would hurt you fellas, neither."

The other four men flanking Dude, Thorn,

and Carlos didn't say anything. Dude, Thorn, and Carlos shared conspiratorial glances. The white-haired Thorn turned to Dutch and gave a short, caustic laugh. "Dutch, you're turnin' a two-day ride into double that!"

"Why are you in such a damn big hurry to get to the cabin?" Dutch wanted to know. "Once we get up there, all you'll do is complain about how bored you are! Can't wait to hit the trail again!"

Dude sighed and swung down from his horse's back. Holding the bridle ribbons in one gloved hand, he stepped up to Dutch, who stood a good six inches shorter than he. "I tell you what, Dutch—why don't the rest of us ride ahead to the cabin? There's no point in that kid slowin' us all down." He jerked his chin to indicate the injured Waylon on the travois. "Now, I understand how you wanna go easy on him, but…"

Dude stopped when an especially hot and violent fire glinted in Dutch's eyes. The man's beard-stubbled jowls seemed to swell, turning as red as his face. "You wanna pull out on me, that it?" His hand went to one of the big Colts he wore in holsters strapped to his thick waist. "I suppose you'd like to take the money, too, huh?"

Dude threw up his hands, let them drop to his sides. "I don't see any reason why not. Hell, we'll leave you with your and Waylon's cuts!"

Dutch glared up at him, one bright eye narrowed.

Dude didn't say anything for a moment. He seemed mesmerized by the older, shorter man. Finally, he said haltingly, "Look, Dutch…it ain't like we're tryin' to pull a double-cross or nothin' like that…"

"A double-cross, huh?" Dutch said.

If his face could have turned any redder behind his thin, gray beard, it did. His eyes sparked with mistrust.

"Dutch," Thorn said from astride his horse behind Dude, "he said we ain't tryin' to pull a double-cross! That is not what we're tryin' to do here, Dutch. He just said--"

One of the other four men riding up from behind him and Carlos said, "What's this about a double-cross?"

This, from a man whom Fay had heard called Gunther. Mort Gunther. He was thick and stocky, maybe in his early thirties. He wore a wolf vest and a ragged bowler hat, and he had a star tattooed on his thick, brown neck. His right hand hovered very close to the ivory-gripped revolver holstered and thonged on his wool-clad right thigh.

Fay turned to Evans, and they shared a dark look.

Was this about to become the blowup they'd

been dreading?

"Stand down, Mort," Carlos said. "Nobody said anything about a double-cross."

"Well, I sure as heard the word!" Utah, whom Fay had been introduced to in the stage station in Rocky Ford—along with Clem and the now-deceased Fritz--had spoken up. He sat his sorrel pony directly behind Thorn. "I heard it way back here!"

Fay felt her belly tighten as, from her own saddle, Doc Evans sitting his horse to her left, she stared at the toughnuts to her right gathered in a semi-circle around Dutch and Waylon. No one said anything for a time. Then Dude, staring down at Dutch, who glared pugnaciously, suspiciously up at him, said, "There ain't gonna be no double-cross. There never was gonna be no double-cross!"

"That's good," Dutch said, keeping his right hand clamped around the grips of his holstered Colt. "I'm glad to hear that, Dude. When you wanna try one, you go ahead…but expect a bellyful of lead for your trouble." He blinked exaggeratedly, and narrowed both eyes. "You understand me, Dude?"

Dude held up his hands in supplication. "Yeah, yeah, Dutch." He wagged his head in defeat. "I understand."

Dutch looked around him at Thorn and Car-los.

"How 'bout you two? You understand? We're gonna take it easy on account of my boy. Now, if that means we're a little later than expected gettin' back to the cabin, that's how it's gonna be, see?"

"All we're worried about is gettin' run down by a posse," Thorn said. "That's all, Dutch. No double-cross, fer pity's sake!"

"Well, now…that's what I was wantin' to hear," Dutch said. He pointed a finger at the mule on which were strapped the canvas panniers con-taining the money they'd taken off the stage. "Because I'm the one who made the contact an' got us that fifty thousand dollars—the biggest damn haul we've ever taken down at one time!"

He poked his thumb against his chest. "Me. Ole Dutch! Me alone. Now I run things, see? None of you would have near the success you have without me. Ole Dutch! I get no thanks for it, but I organize things an' I run the show, sure enough I do.

"For a few little jobs up north over the sum-mers, you unwashed heathens get to spend the winter down in Old May-hee-ko, dancin' with your darn tails up! On account o' me. Ole Dutch! Don't you forget that. I don't expect no thank you's, and don't want none. But I do not want you to forgit what I done for you boys!

"If I say we're gonna ride slow to save my boy, then, why, that's what we're gonna do. If a posse catches up to us, we fight 'em together. We travel together, like a family. With the loot! Now, I do so desperately hope it ain't too inconvenient for you boys to ride slow to save my boy!"

Fay had worried the man was going to have a stroke before he could finish his tirade.

The younger cutthroats gazed down, some flushing a little. To a man, they looked like admonished schoolboys, cutting quick, furtive glances at one another.

Finally, Dutch removed his hand from his holstered six-shooter.

"Now, then," he said, jerking his buckskin vest down and drawing a deep breath through his nose, composing himself. "You fellas get to gatherin' some dry wood. Carlos, you and Gunther dig a pit an' make the coffee. Thorn, you an' Dude keep a sharp watch on our back trail. But first, unsaddle these damn hosses an' give these cayuses and that mule a good rubdown an' a rest, maybe a few vittles. We got time. We got plenty of time! Utah—are you an' Clem sober yet?"

The men dismounted and sullenly began unsaddling their horses and the mule.

As he started to unstrap the travois from his zebra dun, which he'd led into a patch of shade beneath a large cedar, Dutch glanced over his shoulder at Fay and Evans. "You two see to my poor boy's comfort, ya hear? You see to it good, or else…"

Lying atop the travois, tucked into his blankets, Waylon coughed and said, weakly, "Pa…?"

Dutch whipped his shocked gaze at the young man. "Waylon? Waylon, boy?" His face brightening with delight, Dutch pinched his trousers up at the thighs and dropped to a knee beside the travois. "Waylon, boy? Waylon? You awake?"

Fay and Evans shared a glance then walked to the travois.

"P-Paw," Waylon said, opening his eyes about half-way, bloody spittle again flecking his lips.

"I'm here, son. I'm here, Waylon," Dutch said, running a gloved hand through the boy's thick, sweaty hair. "What do you need, boy? What can I get you?"

"I'm…I'm…k-k-kinda hungry."

Dutch looked up at Evans, smiling broadly, his eyes wide with surprise. "He's hungry, Doc!" He turned to the other men still unrigging their horses and glancing at him skeptically, with muted interest. "Hey, fellas—he's hungry. Waylon's hungry!"

Returning his gaze to the doctor, he asked, "That's a good sign—ain't it, Doc?"

"It's a good sign," Evans said.

"Stay right here," Dutch told his son, as though Waylon could get up and walk away from his travois.

Dutch stepped over him and hurried to the saddlebags still draped over his dun's hind end. He returned with a handful of beef jerky and a baking powder biscuit from breakfast that morning, and handed one of the jerky bits to the young man.

"Here you go, here you go—eat up, boy!"

Dutch laughed with relief, as though everything would be all right now.

Waylon ate several very small bits of jerky, and then Dutch hurried to fetch his canteen and gave the boy some water.

Fay stood next to Evans, gazing down at the boy hopefully. He did look better, she thought. There was a little more color in his cheeks than yesterday. Wasn't there? Or was she only imagining…?

She felt a little guilty. The only reason she felt hopeful about the young man's health was because it meant she might be able to keep hers, as well.

But, then, why should she feel guilty about that?

"Here's a biscuit, boy," Dutch said, when Waylon had eaten enough jerky and water. "Why don't you chow down on that? Help you get your strength back."

Waylon grimaced, shook his head, and held a hand up close to his chest, waggling his fingers in the negative. "Nah…I think I've had enough for now, Pa."

"That's probably enough, Dutch," Evans said. "A little is good. Too much might make him sick."

"All right, all right," Dutch said. "Here, you take the rest of this, Doc." He handed the doctor the rest of the jerky and the biscuit. "In case he wants more. Me, I gotta go take a little walk in the woods."

He gave a dry snort.

When Dutch had waddled off to answer nature's call, pulling up his sagging canvas britches, Waylon looked up at Evans and said, "Am I gonna make it, Doc?"

Fay looked at the doctor. He returned her glance with a grim one of his own.

Evans crouched over the boy, drawing the blankets up close against his neck. "You'll be fine."

"Ah, hell." Waylon winced against another pain spasm and swallowed. "I know I ain't gonna be fine. Leastways, not anytime soon. I'd just like to know if I'm gonna make it."

"You'd have a better chance if we'd taken you to Rocky Ford, to the doctor there. As it is, this rough ride isn't doing you one bit of good. But it's a good sign that you're hungry. And if we don't have too much farther to go, you might be just fine once your ribs have healed. And once you heal internally, as well."

Waylon frowned. "In…internally…?"

"You've been expector…or, rather, you've been spitting up a little blood. That tells me a lung must be pierced. I'm just not sure how badly and if the rib is still poking into it."

"Is…is that b-bad?"

"The rib? Yes. But, hey—you've made it this far, and you were hungry." Evans squeezed the young man's shoulder. "That's a good sign."

Again, Waylon frowned at the doctor. "Why are you bein' good to me, Doc?"

Evans turned a vaguely sheepish look over his shoulder at Fay then smiled down at Waylon, giving his shoulder another squeeze. "Because I'm a doctor. I took an oath to be good to the sick and the injured."

Waylon gave a wan smile, nodded. His eyelids fluttered down over his eyes and then his mouth opened, and he appeared to be sleeping again.

Evans rose to stand beside Fay.

Fay glanced at where the others were now gathering wood or building a fire or filling a coffee pot, muttering discontentedly among themselves. Turning back to the doctor but keeping her voice low, she said, "Is it really a good sign, Doc?"

Evans raised and lowered a shoulder. "Maybe, maybe not." He drew a deep breath, thumbed his dusty spectacles up his nose as he looked at the cutthroats milling around them. "After that nasty little display between Dutch and those three malcontents, however, I think we'd best start planning an escape."

"Those three are a powder keg," Fay agreed, glancing at where Dude, Thorn, and Carlos were talking amongst themselves near a couple of half-dead cedars.

They each held a few deadfall branches in their hands, to make it look like they were gathering wood rather than what they were probably actually doing--plotting a double-cross on Dutch and his allies within the gang. Thorn just then glanced over his shoulder at Evans and Fay, frowning as he spoke to the other two men.

Fay quickly looked away from him. So did Evans.

"A powder keg with a lit fuse," she amended her previous observation.

"Indeed."

"Any ideas, Doc?"

"Well, at least they haven't tied us. We're free to move around."

"I don't think they fear either one of us."

"Yes, yes...we have that in our favor. However..." Evans punctuated the comment with a dark chuckle.

"However what?"

"There may be no reason to fear us. If we hop on a couple of horses and try to gallop away, they'll shoot us down like chicken-thieving dogs. We can't run away on foot, because, since they have the horses as well as the guns, we wouldn't make it fifty feet."

Fay hiked up the hem of her brown dress and toed the dirt with the tip of her black leather shoe. Again speaking in a whisper, she said, "We could try to slip away tonight...saddle a couple of horses..."

"Dutch will post guards again, like last night. They'll see or hear us."

"Well, I guess we could grab a gun apiece and start spraying lead...?" Fay's tone betrayed how insane she knew the suggestion was, that she was grabbing at straws.

"I already tried that."

"Yes. How is your stomach, Doc?"

"Still hurts."

"I'm sorry."

"Don't be." Evans removed his glasses to smear dirt on the lenses with his fingers, squinting as he peered around in desperation. "It'll feel like a love pat in comparison to what we have coming if we can't figure a way out of this mess."

Fay looked down at the slumbering Waylon. "I hope you can keep him alive, Doc. For our sake, I hope he doesn't die before"--she looked to the north and choked on a sob--"Ben finds us."

"Yes," Evans said, donning his glasses and stretching his own gaze to the north, the direction from which help would come, if it came. With customary drollness, he added, "If your husband is going to find us, I'd rather it be while we're still alive so I can buy him a drink for his efforts."

Chapter 10

Stillman stared into the darkness beyond his fire's glow.

He held a cup of coffee in his gloved hands. It no longer steamed. The mud had gone cold a long time ago. He'd taken only a couple of sips before his mind had wandered far beyond the coffee.

It had wandered to Fay and Evans, wherever they were, whatever condition they were in. During his long ride, trailing two spare horses, he'd expected to find their bodies along the trail. Every unidentified shape he saw and which bore the slightest resemblance to a human, he'd thought was either his wife or the doctor until a closer inspection had proven him wonderfully wrong.

Still, he'd expected and still expected to find them dead. Maybe it was a trick of his own mind to do so. That way, the impact of actually finding one or both of them in that condition wouldn't be such a horrific blow.

Of course, it would be. Finding either one of them would be a sledge-hammer to his heart. He didn't know if he could go on afterwards. He would. He didn't know how he would, but he would. It was best not leap ahead, though. He had to slow his mind down and take the trek one step at a time. He couldn't function efficiently or effectively if his mind was a rat's nest of confusion.

In the back of his mind, he wondered if it was worth it. Loving someone. The pain of having them die was so horrific, maybe it was better not to have loved them at all. Of course, if he hadn't fallen in love with Fay, he wouldn't have little Ben. But maybe he would have been better off without either of them.

God, the worry! The wretchedness he felt now certainly couldn't be worth all the joy that had come before.

Had he been happier alone?

Of course not.

He shook his head, drew a breath. His mind was revolving, rotating, swirling, churned by the wooden stick of his anxiety. He couldn't sleep. All he could do was sit here and endure his mind chasing itself in circles, like a wounded coyote.

When he'd stopped for the night just after

dark, he'd taken his time tending the horses—unsaddling them, staking them to a picket line he'd tied between two trees at his camp's perimeter, feeding them, watering them...

He'd gathered wood, built a coffee fire. He'd eaten the rest of Ma's sandwich, curiously finding himself hungry despite his terror and the grisly conjuring of his mind regarding his wife and what the outlaws might have done to her, were doing to her, would do to her. He found himself feeling sheepish about enjoying the sandwich, incredulous that he could still enjoy food while harboring the prospect of Fay's death.

But, then, if he did find her dead, he would have to continue to eat if he wanted to continue to live, and of course he would because he still had little Ben to raise. Alone. Still, he had the boy to raise, and raise him he would, alone. He would continue to eat, and even with Fay dead, he would enjoy food.

Odd.

Again he shook his head, trying again to clear his mind. He sipped the coffee. It was cold and acrid on his tongue. He spat it out, emptied the cup, set it down, and reached for his rifle then stayed the motion.

He'd been going to empty and clean it, but he'd already done that. As soon as he'd finished the sandwich and a cup of coffee, he'd emptied, taken apart both the Henry and his Colt, and given each a thorough cleaning before reloading them, filling all six chambers of the Colt, depositing fifteen .44 cartridges into the Henry's tube.

Both guns were clean and ready to go.

"Dammit," he muttered to himself.

Looking around he saw two eyes regarding him from the darkness over his right shoulder. They belonged to his bay, Sweets. They were two nickel-sized orbs glowing like pennies in the firelight. The horse regarded him curiously, maybe even a little sympathetically, Stillman silently opined.

He and the horse had been together several years now, and they couldn't help reading the other's mind, sensing what the other was thinking, feeling. Stillman usually knew what the horse was thinking and feeling, and he truly believed the horse had such insight into its rider, as well.

As if to corroborate his view, Sweets lowered his head slightly, flicked one ear forward, and gave a soft whicker from deep in his chest. A comforting sound in the heavy night fairly throbbing with the lawman's torment. Knowingly or unknowingly, the horse knew what Stillman was going through. Sweets wanted to lend comfort.

Stillman gave the bay a weak, affectionate smile. "Thanks, boy. I appreciate that."

The horse lifted its head sharply with a soft, startled chuff. It turned to stare behind it, to Stillman's right. It twitched both ears and gave a low, warning whicker. The other two horses looked in the same direction, issuing soft, inquiring sounds.

Instantly, the Henry was in Stillman's hands. He rose from the log he'd been perched on and stepped farther away from the fire. Slowly pumping a cartridge into the rifle's chamber, he took two more steps away from the fire, gazing into the darkness around him.

What'd you fellas hear?

Stillman stood silently staring for over a minute. All three horses had turned their heads as though on the same swivel to stare straight off to the south, straight out away from the lawman. Sweets whinnied. The sudden, loud sound gave Stillman a start, made his heart pump faster.

Then he heard something--the faint snap of a twig under a stealthy foot.

Straight out away from him, maybe fifty, sixty yards.

Animal? Or human?

He hunkered on his haunches, holding the Henry low so that the glow of the sliver moon and the stars wouldn't reflect off the barrel or the brass breech.

He waited.

Animal or human?

He waited.

Another twig snapped. This snap was louder than the previous one.

Again, Stillman's heart increased its pace. That snap had told him there were humans on the lurk—at least one, anyway. No animal—predator or otherwise—would have made a sound that loud on so quiet a night.

A soft whistle came from Stillman's left.

Now he could hear the slow, steady movements of the man straight before him, moving to Stillman's left from roughly a hundred feet away and down a slight grade peppered with ash and box elders mixed with pines.

To the south lay Wolf Creek, along which he'd camped. The man was moving in response to the whistle Stillman had heard on his left, to the west.

Slowly, the lawman rose.

Holding the Henry low by his side, he moved in a northwesterly direction, stepping as quietly as he could. He stopped several times, shouldering up to trees, which he hoped would conceal his own silhouette.

Who was out there? It had to be close to midnight. Certainly not hunters.

Whoever was out there was here because of him. He could be their only reason.

He considered triggering off a shot but nixed the idea. There was a possibility, however faint, that Fay or Evans or both had broken away from their captors and were trying to find him, or seeking the help of whomever might have built the fire. Probably not, but the slim possibility made him hold his fire.

He'd let his stalkers make the first move.

He moved quickly forward then dropped to his haunches, pressing his back against the lodge-pole pine. A gun flashed, barked. The bullet hissed through the air to Stillman's left, nearly grazing his left shoulder.

The shooter had seen him move, and Stillman had nearly taken a blue whistler to his brisket.

He dropped to his knees, snapped the Henry to his shoulder, aimed at where the gun flash still blazed on his retinas, and sent two crashing rounds into the night.

The first slug thumped into a tree. The second one made a softer crunching sound and evoked a man's shocked grunt.

The man cursed.

"I'm hit," he said, his voice loud in the quiet night. "Val, I'm hit!"

Running footsteps and crackling brush sounded

to Stillman's left. Val was on the run.

Stillman cocked another round into the Henry's action and fired toward the sounds of Val's fleeing footsteps. He fired three more times, leading the runner by feel, for he couldn't see anything but the dark tangle of branches ahead of him.

Powder smoke wreathed his head and peppered his nose. He peered through it, seeing nothing, hearing only more wildly running footsteps that dwindled gradually.

He lowered the Henry and cursed.

A moment later, the drumming of hooves rose beyond the trees. The drumming faded quickly to silence as Val made his escape.

The man Stillman had hit was groaning ahead and on his right.

Ejecting his last spent cartridge and seating a fresh one, he moved forward, heading toward the groans of the wounded man. He aimed the Henry straight out from his right hip, keeping his index finger curled tightly around the trigger, ready to shoot if he saw the injured man move, or the flash of starlight off a moving rifle barrel. Judging by the strangled, gurgling sounds the wounded man was making, he wasn't capable of renewing his attack.

Stillman walked quickly between two box

elders standing only a few feet apart, aiming the Henry straight before him. He heard the man's ragged breathing and low groaning but it took several seconds for Stillman to see him.

The man sat on the ground, leaning back against a tree directly behind the box elder on the lawman's right. Stillman saw the twin reflections of starlight off the man's eyes. Knowing the man could be holding a cocked pistol, ready to fire, Stillman stepped quickly to him and rammed the Henry against his chest, quickly scanning the man for a gun.

Seeing none, but hearing the man give a yowl of pain as the Henry's barrel prodded him, Stillman pulled the rifle away.

"Who're you?"

"Go to hell," the man said thickly, as though drunk. He wasn't drunk, though. He was dying.

He knew it.

"You killed me, you devil, Stillman."

Stillman dropped to a knee beside the man to study him closely. He scowled, incredulous.

The man before him was one of the hands Stillman had seen with Triber.

"What in the hell are you doing out here, trying to pot-shoot me?" Stillman asked, his voice hard. "Your boss send you?"

The man didn't say anything. In fact, he fell

totally silent. He just sat there against the tree, not moving. His eyes were steady, unblinking reflections of the starlight. Stillman could no longer hear him breathing.

Slowly, the man slid sideways, his back raking against the tree, until he lay on his side on the ground, legs slightly curled toward his belly.

"I'll be damned," Stillman said softly to himself, since he was now the only man here. At least, he thought he was. If Triber had sent more than this man and Val, they probably would have made their presence known by now.

Slowly, Stillman rose, wincing at the creaking of his aged knees, and stared straight out to the north, where Triber must be camped.

"Why in the hell did you send two men to trim my wick, Triber?" Stillman gave a wry snort. "That's no way to treat your favorite country sheriff. No way at all…"

The lawman doubted the dead man and Val would have tried to kill him without having been ordered to do so.

Stillman gave the dead man a kick, just to make sure he was really dead. Satisfied the Milliron man was already saddling a cloud, he made his way back to his fire. He reloaded the Henry from his cartridge belt, leaned the rifle against a tree, within an easy grab, and refilled his coffee cup.

He sat on the log he'd occupied before, staring into the night.

He took one or two sips of the coffee then promptly forgot about it again.

Chapter 11

Earlier that day, Dutch took his time with their mid-afternoon break. It was almost as though he was taunting the others in his gang, flaunting his position of power, which, apparently, he viewed as rock solid. As though he were still the alpha wolf he might have been twenty years ago, and he wanted to make sure the others knew it.

He could take as much time as he wanted, and there wasn't a damned thing the others could do about it.

He leisurely sipped his coffee and packed and smoked his pipe, lounging back on one elbow. He produced a liniment tin out of his saddlebags, held it up for the others to see, chuckled drolly and rubbed his behind. He turned and ambled off into the brush to apply the substance to his old, aching backside while H.G. Thorn, Dude, and Carlos muttered and grumbled and spat and cursed their impatience.

The others—Clem, Gunther, Utah, and Scrim McAllister—didn't say anything, but Fay could tell they were feeling impatient, as well. So far, however, those four were sticking with Dutch. They'd seen how easily he'd killed Fritz, and they weren't going to mess with him.

On the other hand, Fay didn't think they had the gall to mess with Dude, Thorn, and Carlos, either. They seemed to sort of cower into themselves, sharing furtive glances and hiding their taut, anxious expressions behind their coffee cups, or covering them with feigned yawns and by dragging hands down their unshaven cheeks.

Fay was only too well aware that these men—mulish, arbitrary, violent, and not very bright—could easily be sparked into action against one another. Not only were they at odds regarding the mulish, arbitrary, violent, and not very-bright-Dutch—there were the two panniers bulging with money.

Fifty thousand dollars' worth, according to what Dutch had said, crowing about his accomplishment.

Fay sensed the money was a cancer growing inside these men's heads, festering. To a man, she'd noticed them all cutting occasional, sharp-eyed, greedy glances at the two pouches, which

Dutch usually kept near to hand, as he did his rifle. He also, Fay noticed, kept the keeper thongs free from over the hammers of his twin Colts, always ready for a quick grab if needed.

Fay took a sip of her own coffee, swallowed, drew a deep breath, trying to calm the raw, nervous ache inside her. Not only did she have to endure the excruciating tension among the men who held her life and that of Evans in their hands, she had to put up with their ogling her, as well. Just as she caught them steeling sharp looks at the money, she also caught them—all of them, even the four lesser lights of the gang—staring at her intermittently with flat, devious gazes.

She knew what they were thinking about. And it chilled her right down to her toes.

Evans was right. They had to get away from these men. And soon. If they waited much more than a day, it would be too late. In the event of Waylon's dying, or the powder keg of the gang imploding, turning on its gray-bearded leader, the doctor would have it far easier than she. They'd likely kill him fast.

As for her? They'd take their own sweet time with her.

When Dutch returned to the fire, tucking his shirt into his pants, he announced, as though a king to his minions, that it was time to pack up and head out. "Enough lazing about the fire, you worthless saddle tramps," he intoned heartily, clapping his hands together, a big grin of mockery glinting in his eyes. "Saddle them cayuses and let's pull them picket pins! You wanna lay around here all day? Me—I'm lookin' forward to my soft bed at the cabin. Hah!"

Fay and Evans helped Dutch strap Waylon's travois back to Dutch's mount. Someone kicked dirt on the fire, and each man returned his coffee cup to his war pouch. They leathered their horses as well as the mule, and in a few minutes they were off, heading slowly, purposefully southwest to the Highwood Mountains growing before them, shaped like a giant top hat rising up out of the rolling green tableland.

A thunderstorm just then passed over the range—a large, purple mushroom cloud sparking with witches' fingers of lightning. A pale gown of rain or hail billowed above the formation. Fay listened to the low, distant rumble of thunder and couldn't help feeling as though it were the dislocated voices of her and Clyde Evans' mingles fates.

The gang rode for only a few more hours before, at dusk, Dutch called a halt for the night. He seemed to delight in the dourness of his underlings, the obvious frustration at the slow pace stealing over their faces—even the faces of the four he seemed to have a stronger hold on.

Again, Fay and the doctor shared a brief, conspiratorial glance, silently warning each other: "Soon."

But Fay saw little to no opportunity. She was under close scrutiny by all the men, and Evans was busy administering to Waylon, with Dutch hovering over him, urging him, prodding him, threatening him to heal his injured son.

Fay was given the task of building the fire and cooking supper, using airtight tins from the men's warbags to concoct a hearty stew. She also made baking powder biscuits, which she'd never done in a Dutch oven over a fire before, but she didn't burn them too badly.

Only one man complained. That man, of course, was Dude, who tossed his biscuit into the fire. "She's fun to look at, but she ain't much of a cook, is she?" he remarked when everyone else was swabbing their nearly empty plates with the last of their own biscuits.

He lounged on the far side of the fire from her and Evans. He carelessly tossed his plate across the fire to her. It landed near her right elbow, making her jump, then fume. Glaring through the dancing flames, Dude said, "You better be better at dish washin' than you are at cookin'."

"Shut up, Dude," Dutch said, still shoveling stew into his mouth. "She did right well with the stew."

"My biscuit was burnt on the bottom," Dude said, wrinkling his nostrils at Fay. He slid his belligerent gaze to Dutch. "It was burned on the bottom."

"Mine, too," allowed Thorn, sitting next to Dude. Carlos sat on Dude's other side.

Utah took a bite of his own biscuit and said, chewing the mouthful, "She done better than you do when you cook."

Dude glared at him. "When I want any crap out of you, Utah, I'll stomp on your head."

Several others laughed at this sally.

"Shut up, now," Dutch said, tossing his own plate to Fay and picking up his coffee cup. "Mind your manners—all of you."

Tensely, Fay rose to gather the dirty dishes. She tried to keep her eyes away from Dude, but she could feel his stare on her, like rays of a fire branding her.

"I don't see the point of havin' a purty woman in the camp if we can't have a little fun with her," Dude said, his gaze traveling over her body in a way that would have earned most men a hard slap across the face.

Evans jumped in with: "If anyone touches a

hair on her head, Dutch, I'm done tending this boy." He glanced down at Waylon, who looked at least half-asleep though his eyes were partway open. Evans had been rewrapping his ribs.

"I'll handle it, Doc." Dutch glared at Dude through the steam rising from his cup. "What did I just tell you?"

"I just don't understand it, Dutch," Dude said. "Why can't we have a go at her?"

"Because we're men, not alley cats!" Dutch said, his eyes flashing with building frustration. "Besides," he added, chuckling, "your face ain't even healed yet, an' here you're wantin' to try her again. Hah!"

Moving around the fire, Fay took a plate and cup from Utah. She walked slowly, purposefully gathering the dishes, though she wanted to hurry over to the stream where, in relative privacy, she would clean the plates, cups, and forks in the cold spring water. Where Dude's and the other men's eyes would not be ogling her with their goatish depravity, making her feel naked and as vulnerable as a small child.

In the corner of her eye, she saw Dude curl his upper lip at the older man and say with unbridled mockery, "Just 'cause you can't, don't mean we shouldn't."

Fay had just picked up the last plate and cup.

She was balancing the precarious pile against her chest when she halted and cast her anxious gaze to Dutch. Evans stared at him, too, between the edgy, nervous glances the doctor was casting at Fay.

Dutch dropped his cup. In a blur of motion too fast for Fay to follow, one of his Colts was in his hand. The barrel blossomed rose-red fire.

Dude yowled as the tin cup, which he'd been holding in his left hand, flew into the darkness behind him. He leaped to his feet, clutching his left hand in his right one, wincing and gritting his teeth, gazing down at the bloody hand, also glistening with the hot coffee he'd been drinking.

The thunder of the Colt's hollow blast rolled away in the night, echoing.

Clutching his injured hand, Dude glared at Dutch. "You old devil!" He cursed, groaned, then held up his hand. The top half of his fourth finger had been shot off, and dark-red blood ran in two streams down toward his open palm. "Look what you did to my hand!"

Dutch glared at him, one eye shrewdly narrowed, through the powder smoke wafting around his head.

The others now sat at attention, gazing in wide-eyed exasperation from Dude to Dutch then back again.

Silence, save for the crackling of the fire and the faint gurgling of the coffee pot hanging over it, settled over the camp. What Fay could hear most clearly was the thunder of her own pulse in her ears as she stared at the two men locking glares from opposite sides of the fire.

"That," Dutch said finally with crisp, quiet menace, "is the end of the conversation." He holstered his six-gun and glanced at Fay. "Mrs. Stillman, let me apologize for that man's behavior. Please don't let him reflect poorly on the rest of us." He cast his angry, reproving glare back to Dude. "'Cause he don't!"

Fay glanced at Evans again. She'd dropped the dishes when Dutch had triggered the bullet into Dude's cup. Now she gathered them up again as calmly as she could and strode stiffly off into the darkness beyond the fire, heading for the creek angling around the southeastern edge of the camp.

"I'll help with those," Evans said, rising from his position beside Waylon.

"Where you goin' Doc?" Dutch asked.

"I'm going to help Mrs. Stillman with the dishes," Evans told the man firmly as he followed Fay into the trees and brush. "We won't be long."

"Yeah, well, you make it fast, an' I'll be watchin'!" Dutch yelled. "No funny business with you, either, Doc!" He cackled a ribald laugh.

Only silence from the others.

"You all right?" Evans asked as Fay reached the edge of the stream murmuring softly, its black water reflecting light from the velvet sky in which the stars shone like diamond pinpoints.

"No! Are you?" Fay dropped the pans, cups, and forks with a loud clatter, and knelt beside the sliding water churning softly around half-submerged rocks. She gave a sarcastic chuff.

Evans fells to his knees beside her. He took one of the plates and dunked it in the stream, absently grabbing a handful of sand and gravel and scrubbing the plate. "I think it's time."

"What?"

"It's time to make a run for it."

"What? Now?"

"I don't think we have a choice. Those men are turning on each other, and you're going to get caught in the whipsaw."

"You mean we are."

"You, most of all." Evans glanced over his shoulder and splashed water over his plate. "I want you to go. Now. Make a run for it. I'll stay here and make enough noise to cover your escape."

Fay looked at him in shock. "Not without you, Doc."

Gritting his teeth, but keeping his voice low so it couldn't be heard above the water he was splashing over the plate, he said, "Cross the creek and run like hell, Fay. Head up that intersecting canyon. It's your only chance. I will buy you some time."

She just stared at him, her mind racing, amazed at his courage. She was ashamed to acknowledge here and now that she'd always seen Evans as a weak, bitter man enslaved by his own worst impulses. But here he was offering—no, insisting—that he sacrifice his life for hers.

He reached out and squeezed her arm. "You have more to live for than I do. I'm a scoundrel. You have Ben, little Ben…a good life. What do I have?" He scoffed. "I have my whiskey and my books, a flea-bit dog, a parlor girl when I have the money."

Choking back a sob, Fay threw herself against him. She wrapped her arms around his neck. "You are all of that." She wheezed out a phlegmy laugh. "But we love you, Doc." She pulled away, stared into his eyes. "I love you. And I am not going anywhere without you."

Starlight shimmered in Evans's eyes, glazed with emotion. A tear broke away and dribbled down his cheek. He just stared at her, eyes glistening behind his glasses. Fay knew his heart, which he loved to claim was as cold as granite, was swelling inside him.

"Doc!" Dutch cried behind them. They both jumped with starts. "Doc! Come quick—it's Waylon!"

They turned to see the old man standing silhouetted against the fire, thirty feet behind them and between two pines. He beckoned sharply. "He's chokin', Doc. I think he's chokin' on his own blood!"

Evans looked again at Fay. He grimaced, shook his head reprovingly. She read his mind. This might have been her only chance, and she'd tossed it away. That was all right. She couldn't leave him behind. Doing so would have been worse torture than staying and facing what would happen to them here.

"Doc, dammit, get back here and help this boy!" Dutch yelled, his voice quaking with emotion.

"Coming," Evans said, continuing to stare at Fay. Louder, he said, "I'm coming!"

He rose and walked back to the camp.

Leaving the eating utensils beside the stream, Fay followed him back to the flickering firelight and the dark shadows of the men hunkered around it.

Chapter 12

With a weary grunt, Stillman hefted the dead Milliron rider over the back of the man's horse, which he'd found tethered to a tree a hundred yards from where he'd drilled the bushwhacker. He tied the body securely, using rope from his saddlebags, then, holding the reins of the man's horse, swung up onto Sweets's back.

It was early, only a thin gray light hovering like fog in the trees around him. The ashes from the previous night's fire lay cold in the stone ring. He hadn't built up the fire this morning. No time even for a cup of coffee. As long as there was a little light to illuminate the killers' trail, he would ride.

Leading the dead man's horse, he booted Sweets northwest through the forest, the hooves of all four horses thumping loudly in the early-morning silence interrupted occasionally by the demonic screech of a still-hunting owl and the shrill cry of a terror-stricken rabbit bleating out its last breaths on this worldly plain as it became the owl's breakfast.

The lawman's two spare horses followed of their own accord now, not needing to be led. Horses being the most social of animals, they didn't want to be left behind.

Stillman stopped at the edge of the trees and stared out across the rolling, brown and green prairie sweeping off toward the north. Buttes and mesas poked up darkly, lightening gradually as the gray dawn thickened by the minute.

Stillman studied that dim, vast sweep of land, wondering where the dead man's boss, Phil Triber, was camped with his son and his three other hands. By now—likely several hours ago—that third hand would have told Triber the grisly tale of what had transpired here.

"Why did you want me dead, you son of a buck?" Stillman growled, his frosty blue eyes studying his back trail from beneath his Stetson's brim.

He'd known Triber and his men had been following him from roughly a half-mile away. He'd glassed his back trail several times the previous day, and he'd spied the six riders.

They'd been too far away to see clearly, even through the field glasses, but Triber himself was unmistakable, dressed in that black coat and black hat and riding that tall cream horse. The other men, including his son, had been following him, the group shaped in a ragged V, sort of like a mother goose and her goslings, Stillman had drolly, silently opined.

Stillman had figured the rancher would dog his trail, wanting to retrieve his money. But the lawman hadn't expected the man to try to kill him. Why not let Stillman run the robbers down? If Stillman proved incapable, then Triber could move in and make his own play.

Instead, the rancher had sent two men to drill the sheriff. They wouldn't have taken such a drastic measure on their own. Not Phil Triber's hands.

Why?

Stillman caressed his chin with the thumb and index finger of his right hand.

"How much money are we talkin' about, you old devil?" he asked aloud, narrowing his eyes as he studied those gradually lightening, widely scattered bluffs and mesas to the north. "And what's it for…?"

No time to worry about it now. He'd just have to keep an even sharper eye on his back trail than he had yesterday, lest a bullet should come flying in from it and drill him between his shoulder blades.

He swung down from Sweets's back and led the dead man's horse, a smoky gray gelding, several feet to the north. Then he removed his glove and slapped his hand sharply against the horse's rump. He watched the mount gallop off with its stiffening package, and message, in care of Phil Triber. The rancher and his men were now on Stillman's mental "Wanted" list.

Triber would answer for that misdeed, sure enough. Even a man of the rancher's stature wasn't immune to Deer Lodge. Not when he tried to kill Ben Stillman.

But, first…

Stillman heaved himself onto Sweets's back, trying to ignore the rawness in his backside and the stiffness in his shoulders. He swung the horse to the south, quickly picked up the twin furrows the travois had made a dozen hours ago, and booted the fresh gelding into a lope. At the pace his quarry was traveling, which was slow, and as many times as they'd been stopping, he had a feeling he'd overtake them soon.

The prospect was bittersweet. He wanted to catch up to them, of course, but he wasn't sure he wanted to know what conditions his wife and Doc Evans were in. Even though he had not yet found their bodies along the trail, he knew there was a good chance they were dead.

He couldn't figure out why they'd been taken in the first place. At least, he couldn't figure out why Fay had been taken. Evans had probably been grabbed to tend whoever was being carried on travois.

But Fay...?

There was only one reason he could think of. He scrubbed his mind of it as soon as the seed began to sprout again, as it had so many times before, without him so much consciously noticing it as feeling the burn of the prospect deep in his belly, starting from just behind his heart.

He kept up his usual hard pace despite the fatigue and soreness he felt in every bone and muscle. At least he kept it up until, glassing his trail an hour after sunrise, he spied Triber's bunch coming on at an even faster place, closing gradually on him from behind.

He'd stopped on the south side of a low, long-sloping rise, the crest of which was peppered with pines and deciduous trees. Having left his three horses below the crest, he stared through his field glasses.

He lay belly down, his hat resting on the ground beside him. His jaws hardened as he watched the six riders close on him from two hundred yards away. Crouched over the saddles, old Triber himself in the lead, they galloped hard, hat brims wind-basted against their foreheads.

They traversed a long swale carpeted in shin-high blond grass splashed with sage and wild-flowers, their horses kicking up gouts of sod and sending them arcing off behind them.

Stillman cursed. He not only resented the rancher for the attempt on his life, but for this current delay.

He grabbed his hat and crabbed several feet back down the rise. When he was out of sight from the other side, he rose, set the hat on his head, and strode quickly to the horses. He returned the field glasses to his saddlebags and shucked his Henry from its scabbard.

Levering a round into the action, he headed back up the slope, dropped to his knees, then his side, resting on his elbow. He stayed just beneath the crest, listening to the growing din of the approaching riders. When he could hear the rasping breaths of the horses and feel the reverberations of their hooves in the ground beneath him, he rose to a knee and lifted the Henry.

He stared down the slope toward the north.

Phil Triber was fifty yards away and coming hard, flanked by the others spread out to both sides. Triber saw him as soon as Stillman had shown himself. The venal old rancher lifted his head so sharply, the wind blew his hat off.

His eyes nearly popped out of his skull as he yelled with a start: "Whoahhh!"

He started to draw sharply back on the reins when Stillman pressed the Henry's butt plate to his shoulder and blew a fist-sized gob of sod out of the ground near the horse's still-scissoring left front hoof.

The cream whinnied shrilly, showing its teeth like an angry dog. It lurched back on its rear legs, both front hooves coming off the ground. As its rear hooves slid up beneath its belly, the horse leaned precariously back over its left hip, throwing its rider from the saddle.

Cursing, Triber hit the ground and rolled as the horse struck the turf only inches away from the rolling rancher.

Stillman levered another round into the Henry's magazine, punched another forty-four-caliber bullet into the ground—this time in front of Cole Triber's black-and-white pinto.

That horse pitched as well, but Cole maintained his hold on the reins and his position on the saddle, casting his exasperated gaze to Stillman, who was racking another round into the Henry's chamber, then firing that round into the ground as well.

He levered and fired until he'd blown up five tufts of sod in front of the Milliron men, most of whom were busily checking down their curveting, screaming horses while clumsily trying to draw the six-shooters from their holsters.

"Keep those shooting irons leathered!" Stillman advised, aiming down the Henry's smoking barrel once more.

All five followed his suggestion, returning both hands to their reins.

When they had their horses settled down, or at least stomping nervously in place, blowing and angrily switching their tails, Stillman looked at Phil Triber, lying on the ground, glaring up the slope at the lawman.

Triber rested on his side, his head downhill from his booted feet. The man's short, gray hair was mussed, and his lean, deeply lined, weather-darkened face flushed with fury. He had one hand on his own revolver holstered high on his right hip, but he left the hogleg in the leather.

Stillman saw he had all five men's attention. Good.

Keeping the Henry extended from his right shoulder, he said, "Go home, Triber. I'll deal with you later. If I had time, I'd arrest you all right now for attempted murder. As it stands, I don't have time. If I see you on my back trail again, you'll get what that bushwhacking rider got last night, and there won't be any due process. None at all."

He drew a breath, gritted his teeth, and locked glares with Triber. "You better understand me, you son of Satan. My wife's life is at stake here. I don't give a damn about your money, but I'll be looking into it later—why it means so damn much to you, what it's for. As for now, I'm out to get my wife and friend back, and, since their lives are worth more than ten of each of yours, I won't be this civil with you again. If I see you again, I'll kill you. And your son. And I'll dump you both in the same ravine."

Triber just glared at him, lips stretched back from his teeth.

The others stared, as well, from where they sat their finally settled-down mounts.

Cole Triber's mean eyes glared up the slope at Stillman, an evil little grin twisting his plump-lipped mouth. Stillman noticed that his old man had busted his nose the day before, for it was swollen and dark, and both the young man's eyes were black. But it didn't seem to have taken much starch out of the young firebrand's shorts.

Cole might have been on his heels at the moment, but the fight was still in him. Stillman just hoped his old man was smarter than his son was, and obeyed Stillman's warning.

The sheriff hadn't been blowing smoke. If he saw them on his back trail again, he'd kill them.

If they caught up to the outlaws before Stillman did—and in their haste to get Triber's money—they'd likely get Fay and Evans killed.

Tiber cared about nothing but his money.

Stillman wouldn't risk his wife's life. Not for Triber. Not for any man.

He lowered the Henry, turned, and walked back down the slope to his horses.

***

Cole Triber stepped down from his pinto's back and walked over to where his father lay on the ground, still glaring up the slope to where Stillman had been standing until a few seconds ago.

Cole extended his gloved hand to the old man. "Let me help you up, Pop."

Phil Triber turned his stony gaze on him. His gray eyes were flat and dark.

The elder Triber extended his own gloved hand, and Cole pulled the older man to his feet. No sooner had the rancher got his boots settled than he whipped his right arm back then forward, burying his fist in Cole's midsection.

Cole jackknifed as the air was punched from his lungs. He dropped to his knees, gasping like a landed fish. He saw his father's shadow slide on the ground beside him.

Phil Triber jerked his son's head up by his thick, dark-brown hair, and glared down at him, his gray eyes now black as coals. He pulled Cole's hair savagely; tears of pain glittered in the younger man's eyes.

"Pa!" he complained. "Jesus, Pa!"

Phil Triber crouched, shoving his craggy, long, severely featured face close to his son's. "This is all your doin'—you know that, don't you?"

"Yes!"

"Every bit of it!"

"Yes!" Cole yowled, stretching his lips back from his teeth, the top of his head feeling as though it had been doused with coal oil and set aflame. "Let go, Pa!"

"This wouldn't have happened if you hadn't killed that girl," the elder Triber bellowed. "You been home from then pen not yet a year, an' you go to Big Sandy an' you get to drinkin' and you get crazy-wild, and you kill that girl."

"Pa, please—dammit!"

"Dammit, what?" Triber spat out, his spit smelling of the chaw he always chewed spraying Cole's face. "Are you sayin' this hurts so much you can't take it? My pullin' your hair. Does it hurt bad, Cole?"

Cole reached up to wrap both his hands around his father's slender but iron-like wrist.

He felt as though his scalp was about to pull free from his skull. Tears of pain dribbled down his cheeks. "Yes!"

Phil released Cole's hair and continued glaring at him. "It ain't nothin' like the pain of goin' back to prison! For the rest of your no-good life this time!"

"Christ!" Cole yelled, lowering his head to the ground, pressing both his gloved hands to his scalp, trying to rub away the burning pain.

"Now we gotta kill that son of a buck! 'Cause I already tried it once, and those two fools fouled it up!" Tiber glared at Val Moony, one of the other two men, including the dead man, Dale Culpepper, whom he'd sent to trim Stillman's wick the night before.

Moony stood with the other two hands in a ragged circle around the two Tribers. Holding their horses' reins, they looked hang-dog, sullen, incredulous. Having the elder Triber's rage directed at him caused Moony, a boot-stupid man but supposedly one good with a shooting iron, which was why Triber had hired him, to blanch and shrug his shoulders.

"I do apologize, Mr. Triber."

"'I do apologize, Mr. Triber,'" the older man mocked him.

"Mr. Triber, he was...well, Stillman was savvier than I expected for a man his age. I mean, ridin' as hard as he did, I figured he'd be plum dead to the world last night."

"Yeah, well, it turned out the only one who now is dead to the world is Culpepper. And Stillman knows I sent you boys to kill him!"

Moony winced and gazed off into the distance.

Triber drew a deep, calming breath. "Well, we got no choice now." He eyed each man standing around him. "We can't let Stillman get back to Clantick alive. He has to die out here. Right along with those idiots who held up the stage and stole my money. Stillman's gotta be crow bait, you understand?"

Cole had lifted his head. He sat back on his heels, still caressing his scalp with one hand, fingering his hat with the other. "What about his wife, Pa? And the sawbones…?"

Phil Triber stood staring off at the top of the slope. "I don't care about neither of them. I don't give a damn about anything but that money. We have to get it back. That's a good chunk of my fortune. I sold my chunk of a gold mine for that money."

He returned his incriminating gaze to his son. "And those hardtails have it. They wouldn't have it if I hadn't needed it to clean up your mess!"

"I know, Pa," Cole said, looking miserable,

wagging his head. "How many times can I tell you I'm sorry?"

"Too late for that." Triber swung around and began walking, limping slightly on his injured leg, toward his horse grazing several feet down the slope. The saddle hung at its side. "We got a lawman to kill and my money to retrieve. Come on, you men. Get mounted!"

Cole stared at the old man's board-straight back.

Val Moony hunkered beside Cole, poked his hat brim up off his forehead, and cast the younger Triber a sympathetic gaze. "Jesus, the old man really has a temper, don't he?"

"And he wonders where I got mine."

"You all right?"

"Hell, yeah." Cole smiled and stared after the old man again, who was straightening and cinching his saddle. His smile broadened into a grin of devious delight. "I got that old devil right where I want him, Val, my friend!"

Chapter 13

Something closed over Fay's nose and mouth, choking off her breath.

Panic fired through her. Lifting her head from her saddle, she gave an involuntary scream of terror, which the hand effectively muffled so that it sounded like a half-born grunt.

"Shh!" an urgent voice said in her ear, the hand clamping down tighter against her mouth. "It's Doc."

Fay turned her head to see the doctor kneeling beside her, where she'd been lying with her head against the underside of her saddle. She blinked, trying to get her bearings. Her heart was slowing, her panic waning.

The darkness of night pressed close around her. The fire had burned down to flickering umber coals. The iron spider and the tripod with which she'd cooked supper earlier, were silhouetted against the pale stones of the fire ring.

In the darkness of the deep night, roofed by a velvet black sky smeared with stars, she saw the shapes of several of the outlaws slumped nearby, wrapped in their bedrolls. Their mingled snores resonated.

Evans removed his hand from her mouth and whispered very quietly into her left ear, "Waylon died."

Fay's heart thumped. She drew a shallow breath, her pulse striking up another frenetic rhythm. She stared at the doctor in mute shock.

Evans nodded. His light brown eyes reflected the firelight, but his large pupils were cast with foreboding.

Fay just stared at him. The worst had happened.

And she wasn't prepared.

"We have to make our move," Evans whispered again softly in her ear. "But we have to move slowly and be very, very quiet."

Fay drew a breath, suppressed a horrified shudder, and nodded. She followed the doctor's glance to where Dutch sat against a tree to her left. The old man's head was tipped back, and he was snoring.

His son's head lay on his lap, the blanket-wrapped body unmoving. When Fay had finally drifted to sleep, the last thing she'd seen was Dutch cradling his son's head like that.

The doctor had finally managed to get Waylon settled down. He'd been choking on his blood, but the doctor had given him something from his kit to ease the convulsions. He'd also adjusted the bandages wrapped tightly around his chest.

Waylon had fallen asleep in his father's lap, Dutch moaning and sobbing and smoothing the boy's hair back from his sweat-beaded face.

Fay had known he was going to die. Still, she was so exhausted from the hard ride and worry, she'd fallen asleep against her saddle.

She watched in horror as Evans stole quietly over to Dutch. The old man's rifle leaned against the tree he slept against.

Oh, god, she almost said aloud.

Evans' picked up the rifle slowly, quietly. She saw him stretching his lips back from his teeth as he stared down at the slumbering, snoring old man.

If Evans woke Dutch, he and Fay were dead.

Stiffly, trembling, Fay rose. Evans sidled up to her, spoke again into her ear: "There are four men on watch."

Fay nodded. She remembered Dutch telling the others that he wanted four men on watch at all times—one for each direction, in case a posse out of Rocky Ford caught up to them. Where those four pickets were now was anyone's guess. It was too dark for Fay to see more than a few feet around her.

In a soft, breathy whisper, she asked, "What are we going to do, Doc?"

Evans looked around. Nervously, he rubbed his free hand across his broadcloth-clad left thigh.

Suddenly, Dutch's eyes opened and he stared straight up at Fay. She slapped both hands to her mouth, squelching a gasp.

Dutch said, "Agnes, honey, our boy's asleep. Did you put up the chickens?"

Fay glanced at Evans. He stared down, wide-eyed, at Dutch. Dutch stared up at Fay, as though awaiting an answer.

One of the men behind her stirred.

Her heart flip-flopped.

"Dutch, dammit," the man rasped, raising his voice. "Stop talkin' like a crazy man and go back to sleep!"

Fay was too frightened to turn and look at the man who'd spoken. She heard him groan. She heard blankets rustle. He must have snuggled back down in his bedroll. A few seconds later, his snores resumed. Dutch kept his eyes on Fay, but then opened and closed his mouth and rested his head back against the tree.

He closed his eyes. Then he was snoring again, more softly than before, parting his lips as he inhaled, making them flutter when he exhaled.

Fay was too afraid to move, to look at the man behind her. Apparently, he hadn't seen her and the doctor. Their shadows must have merged with the darkness pressing in against the camp.

She let out a slow, nearly silent breath of relief.

Evans took her hand in his own, canted his head to one side, apparently choosing at random a direction in which to flee.

"Slow…and…quiet," he said in her ear.

She glanced down at her shoes. She'd taken them off when she'd lain down earlier. She considered them now, decided to leave them. She'd move more quietly without them.

She squeezed Evans's hand as she followed him barefoot through pines and aspens, around shrub tangles. As they walked, setting each foot down carefully, Fay searched around for the pickets. Somehow, she and the doctor had to slip between them.

She thought she could hear the nervous beating of Evans's heart beneath the hammering of her own in her ears. Their hands, clamped together, were greasy with sweat.

One slow, quiet step at a time…

The ground dropped slowly. She remembered

they'd camped on a high bench.

She wasn't sure how far they'd walked when cigarette smoke peppered her nostrils. Evans smelled it, too. He stopped.

Low voices rose from ahead and to the right. Evans glanced at Fay. His glasses winked in the star shine and in the light of a new moon rising in the southeast.

At least two of the men had moved together and were smoking, conversing. One laughed. The other snorted. They continued talking in hushed tones.

They were breaking the rules. Dutch had told them to stay separated, not to "stand out there chinnin' or smokin', fer godsakes—a good tracker will see the glow or smell the smoke, ya damn dunderheads."

That's why they were keeping their voices low, sheepish as ill-behaving children.

Evans squeezed Fay's hand reassuringly. He gave her a flicker of a hopeful smile. At least they knew where two of the pickets were. That left only two others to worry about. Two being together had opened a larger gap for the fleeing captives to slip through. They just needed to slip through the right gap, though there was no way of telling if it was to these two pickets' right or their left.

Evans chose the left.

He led Fay around a large pine, around a brush snag, over a deadfall pine. They moved exceedingly slowly—almost painfully slowly, terrified of making a sound.

Still, grass and pine needles crackled beneath their feet. Occasionally, one of them stepped on a pine cone, and they both winced at the soft crunching sound that, to their ears, sounded as loud as two symbols crashing together.

The ground began sloping more sharply down. Neither Fay nor Evans had been ready for the abrupt drop. Evans lunged forward and Fay did, as well, running into him when he stopped and set his feet beneath him again. Fay grunted as their bodies collided.

As she staggered, her left foot came down on a branch, snapping it.

In the silence of the still night, the sound had sounded like the crack of a small-caliber pistol.

She and Evans stopped, looked at each other, eyes wide with horror.

Evans thumbed his sagging spectacles up on his nose, then turned his head forward. They were both going to take another step when a man's voice called, "Who's out there?"

Fay and the doctor froze.

The voice had come from behind them, off

their right flank. The man had spoken as loudly as two people conversing in a quiet parlor. Still, the voice echoed inside of Fay's head, as though he'd bellowed his query.

Evans slid his head up close to Fay's and said softly, so that it was hardly even a whisper, "Keep moving." He nudged her forward.

"No."

"Who's there?" the man called again, louder this time.

Evans raised the rifle. "Keep moving. I'll catch up."

He gave her a more insistent shove. She continued walking down the slope, reaching out to each side, brushing her hands along the rough sides of trees for balance. As she continued moving, wincing as brush crackled and prickled beneath her bare feet, she heard the soft, metallic rasp of a rifle slowly being cocked.

Doc was getting the Winchester ready.

Vaguely, she wondered if he could shoot. She'd never seen him fire a gun. She couldn't remember ever seeing one in his house. He was more of a book man, the doc was...

Vaguely, she hoped he didn't shoot himself in the foot.

She gasped when another voice yelled from slightly farther away, "They're gone! Doc and the woman are gone!"

The man near Evans shouted, "They're down here!"

Up the dark slope beyond Evans, a gun flashed and wailed. The rifle flashed and wailed again. That bullet snarled through the air to Fay's right and smacked into a tree downslope from her.

Another gun flashed. This one was between Fay and the outlaw who'd triggered the first two shots. It was Evans. She saw flames stab from the Winchester's maw, silhouetting the crouched doctor against them.

A man shrieked. There came the crackling thud of a body hitting the ground.

Running footfalls sounded up the slope. Fay saw a shadow moving quickly toward her. Evans's glasses glinted in the starlight. He nearly fell as he stopped before her, his half-boots sliding on the grassy declivity.

"Go!" he said, his voice pinched and panicked. "Keep going, Fay!"

He brushed passed her and continued down the slope. She followed, so terrified now that she was moving too quickly for the terrain. She tripped over something, and fell. Evans gave a wail as he fell too, and rolled ahead of her down the slope, crashing through the brush, cursing.

"You all right, Doc?"

Men behind her shouted. Boots thudded as

they scrambled through the woods and brush, racing toward the fleeing captives.

Fay heard Dutch cursing loudly back by the fire. Cursing and sobbing. He'd awakened to find his son dead in his lap.

"Where are they—you see 'em?" a man's urgent voice cried in the distance.

Looking over her shoulder, Fay saw another man standing maybe thirty feet behind her—a slender silhouette with starlight reflecting off the barrel of the gun in his hands. The man who'd shouted was running toward the near man. The running man gave a startled yell. There was a thud and violent thrashing, as though the second man had tripped and fallen.

"You see 'em?" he cried again, gaining his feet.

"I don't see 'em." The nearest man spat angrily. "But they killed Clem."

The others were running for the two men who'd spoken. All except Dutch, it seemed. Fay could hear the old outlaw leader back in the camp, wailing and sobbing.

She crawled down the slope toward where Evans was gaining his knees after his tumble.

"You all right, Doc?"

"Yeah." Evans picked up the rifle. "Shit!"

"Evans voice was shaky. One of the bows of his spectacles and slipped off his ear. Now he tucked the bow behind his right ear and slowly levered another cartridge into the Winchester's chamber. "You keep goin'," he said. "I got one of those devils. Lucky shot, but maybe it's my lucky night!"

"Doc--"

"I killed one. No problem. I'll kill mo--"

"No, Doc!"

"Dammit, Fay," Evans said. She saw the line of his teeth in the darkness. "Do as I say—now, go!"

He'd spoken too loudly. Up the slope behind them, one of the killers had heard.

"They're down here!"

Chapter 14

Up the slope behind Fay and Evans, a gun flashed and roared.

The bullet slammed into a gnarled cedar to Fay's left. She stifled a startled yell.

"You're not Jesse James, Doc!" She grabbed his arm and turned him around. "You're coming with me!"

Another bullet curled the air off Evan's right ear. "All right—if you insist!"

Fay took off running. Muttering curses as bullets slashed the air around them, Evans followed.

A man bellowed behind them, "They're down there!"

They ran hard down the slope that gradually grew less steep and contained fewer obstacles. Fay's heart shriveled at the din of gunfire rising behind them. A few of the bullets screeched through the air around them, some snapping through the brush to each side.

Behind Fay, Evans fell. He cursed as he rolled into Fay, cutting her legs out from under her. Then they were both rolling, one atop the other. They rolled into high grass, which slowed them down, and they rolled up against a boulder.

Up the slope behind them, the shooting continued. Running footfalls thudded.

Fay glanced back to see the flashes. Some of the men appeared to be shooting from stationary positions on the black slope while at least two ran toward her and Evans, sporadically triggering guns that flashed in the darkness.

Keeping low, Fay looked at Evans. "You all right, Doc?"

"I'm growing less and less fond of that question." Evans scrubbed his shirtsleeve across his mouth and gained his knees, also keeping his head down. He spat dirt from his lips and turned to her. "I'm gonna make my stand right now. You keep running. I'll get one or two, and--"

"No!"

She glanced around. Finding a blown down branch behind them, she picked it up, drew it back behind her right shoulder, and heaved it forward with a grunt. It flew out across the belly of the slope, to her and Evan's right.

It dropped with a thud and crackle of grass.

It must have dislodged a few rocks, because it kicked up a stony clattering sound.

"You hear that?" asked one of the men behind them.

"That way!" yelled another.

Shadows of the outlaws angled off toward the branch.

Evans turned to her, one brow arched. "Where'd you learn to throw like that?"

"Come on, Doc!" she rasped, tugging on his arm.

They rose as one and scrambled off through the tall grass, heading across the belly of the slope, in the opposite direction from where the two cutthroats had just run. She heard Evans tight on her heels. Their running was smoother here, for there was only grass. The farther they ran, the thinner the grass grew.

Fay angled down the slope.

Behind her, she heard the two men shouting, probably realizing by now they'd been tricked.

Fay kept running. She heard Evans running behind her, his breath raking in and out of his lungs. He sounded weary. He carried the rifle in one hand.

They gained the floor of the valley running along the base of the slope. A broad, pale piece of ground, lower than that which she ran on, stretched out to the left. Fay headed toward the ravine. She began breathing hard, weakening from exhaustion. Sweat bathed her. The night air cooled it.

She stopped at the ravine's edge.

She couldn't see very far along its route, but it seemed about fifty feet at its deepest and roughly a hundred yards wide. It appeared to run for quite a distance, angling through buttes rising on either side of it. A murky dark line of brush along the far side probably concealed the creek that had cut the shallow canyon.

She turned to look behind her. Evans ran toward her, dragging the toes of his boots. His knees looked as though they were threatening to buckle. He carried the rifle by its barrel, dragging the rear stock along the ground.

He drew up to her, breathless, and dropped to his knees. "You throw like a boy, and you run like a damned deer!"

Out of breath herself, Fay leaned forward, hands on her knees. "I always run fast when someone's shooting at me."

"Oh?" Evans dropped his head to the ground, drawing in deep draughts of air. "This happen a lot, does it? If so, remind me never to share a stage with you again."

"Don't worry—I don't think I'll ever ride another stagecoach again in my life."

"Good idea." Evans sat up, leaned back on his heels. He glanced behind. "I don't hear anything."

Fay straightened and gazed in the direction from which they'd come. "Eerily silent, isn't it?"

"That's a good word. You can bet they're trying to pick up our trail."

"You can bet when they do, they'll be coming. They can't let us get away. We're the only two people who know who they are and where they're heading."

Evans eyed her drolly. "You're beautiful, you can throw and run, and you're sharp as a tack. How did Ben get so lucky?"

"I don't know, but if he doesn't come for us soon, I'm going to divorce him."

"You could marry me." Evans grinned.

Fay gave a caustic chuff. She tugged on Evans's arm. "Come on, Doc. We can't sit here. We have to keep moving, find a place to hide down there in that ravine. It'll be light in a bit."

Evans sighed. "What I wouldn't give for a drink and a good cigar."

"Doc!" Again, Fay tugged on his arm.

"All right, all right. I retract the marriage proposal. I see now that Ben is most certainly henpecked."

Fay turned, stepped off the bank into the ravine. She followed a game trail down through the brush lining the edge of the cut, then began walking down the cut itself. There were boulders and the skeletal visages of fallen trees here, likely washed down the cut by previous spring floods, offering more cover if she and Evans needed it.

When they'd walked a couple of hundred yards west along the ravine's sandy bottom, Fay stopped suddenly.

Evans stopped, too, frowning at her, again thumbing his glasses up his nose. "What is it?"

"Listen."

Fay stared back the way they'd come.

Then Evans heard it, too—the thudding of horse hooves. Men's voices sounded, too.

"Come on, Doc!"

Fay tugged on Evans's sleeve. She looked around for a slight break in the shrubs lining the creek. Finding one, she crouched and pushed into it. She grimaced as the branches grabbed her hair and the sleeves and torn skirt of her ragged dress.

"Where are you going?"

"Hiding! Follow me, Doc!"

"Ah, hell." Evans pushed through the brush behind her.

When she was roughly ten feet inside the shrubs, Fay turned to face the open ravine and dropped to her knees. Evans did the same, wincing as a thorny branch tore the sleeve of his broadcloth coat.

"For chrissakes!"

"Shhh!"

"This coat was new!"

"Will you please be quiet!"

The hoof thuds grew louder. The outlaws had saddled horses to come looking for her and Evans. That's why they'd gone quiet for a time. But they couldn't track in the dark. Even with the new moon and the stars, they couldn't see well enough to spot foot prints.

Besides, since Fay was barefoot, she probably hadn't left much of a trail. The doctor might have, but again, the killers would have to look closely by the light of day to follow them.

Fay glanced around. Since the big dipper lay straight away from her, west was on her left, east on her right. She peered through the brush to the east. The stars appeared to be dimming over there. The sky might even be lightening slightly.

Day would be here in a couple of hours.

Hoof thuds grew in the east. Three horseback riders slid into view beyond the brush, moving from Fay's right to her left. The men were trotting their mounts, spread out about ten feet apart, looking around.

Her heartbeat quickened...

"You fellas see anything?" one asked the other.

"Nah," said one leaning away from his saddle to study the ground. "Still too dark."

"We have to find them," a third one said. "They've seen us!"

"I know, I know!"

"Why don't you two fellas shut up and keep lookin'. We'll find 'em. They can't be far. They're on foot, fer chrissakes!"

"They could be anywhere down here," one complained as they passed Fay and Evans's position in the brush. She recognized the voice of the Mexican, Carlos.

"We'll get better light soon," the middle rider said, then gigged his horse on ahead of the others. Fay thought she recognized the abominable Dude's voice. "Then we'll have 'em! Ole Dutch ain't gonna keep me away from Stillman's wife any longer. No, sir!"

When they'd all ridden off to the west, Evans let out a held breath and lowered his head over the rifle he held in both hands across his belly.

"Damn," he said. "Now what do we do? They're on horseback. We're on foot. No food." He chuffed, raked a hand down his face. "I sure could stand a drink…"

"You and me both, Doc." Fay slid a stray lock of tangled hair behind her ear. "If we get out of this,

I'll stand you one. Maybe even two."

"I sure wish your husband would get here."

"He's looking for us. I know he is. He's worried. I know that, too. I can feel how worried he is. He'll get here soon, Doc." Fay wrapped her arm around the doctor's shoulders and pressed her cheek against his arm. "We just have to buy ourselves some time until he does."

"How are we going to do that? My earlier shot was lucky. I can't normally hit the broad side of a barn with one of these things." He indicated the rifle. "From inside the barn!"

Fay was about to respond, but she closed her mouth suddenly and snapped her head to the left. Again came the sound of an approaching horse and rider. They were heading back this way.

No. Not they.

There seemed to be only one man riding back toward the east.

Evans had heard the sounds, as well. He stared through the brush toward the open canyon. In the starlight, Fay saw a bead of sweat trickle down the side of his face. She was sweating too, though it was not a warm night—was even a little on the cool side.

Evans leaned forward a bit, peering to the left.

He drew his head back and said very quietly, "One's returning, and he's going to pass very close."

Evans stared at Fay.

Her heartbeat quickened again. She felt the pulse in her temples. She read the doctor's mind.

A horse.

They could really use a horse.

She shook her head slowly. No, she thought. No, we can't chance it.

Another bead of sweat popped out on the doctor's mustached face. It glistened in the starlight.

The hoof thuds grew slowly louder. The three searchers must have split up to more thoroughly scrutinize the brush.

Sliding his mouth up close to Fay's ear, Evans said, "I'm gonna try to jump the devil when he's out front of us. You stay here."

Fay grabbed his arm. It was an automatic gesture. She dug her fingers into his flesh. She stared at him, terror chilling her blood.

What if he didn't make it?

Evans peeled her hand off his arm, then crawled slowly forward through the slight gap in the brush they'd followed a few minutes earlier. He dragged the rifle in his right hand. Fay watched him, imagining what might happen in a few seconds.

She leaned forward and crawled slowly behind the doctor. He glanced over his shoulder at her, frowning.

She waved a hand, silently telling him to keep moving. She was coming whether he wanted her to or not.

They crouched side by side in the thick shrubs, within inches of the open ravine. Fay saw the horse and rider walking slowly toward her and the doctor, on their left.

The man and horse were so close, she could hear the horse breathing now, occasionally tossing the bit in its teeth. The saddle squawked. The rider stared into the bushes. In about ten seconds he would be staring right at Fay and the doctor.

Okay, Doc—he we go. I hope you know what you're doing, because I sure don't!

She had decided to follow his lead, offer help if he needed it.

When the rider was nearly straight before Fay and the doc, Evans bulled forward, rising up out of the brush like a half-wild steer. He grabbed the rifle by its barrel and started to raise it.

The rider saw him. Fay saw the Mexican's eyes widen beneath the broad brim of his hat. The white line of his teeth shone beneath his drooping mustache.

"Mierda!" he said.

A half-second later, the stock of Evans's rifle slammed into his face.

Carlos grunted and tumbled straight back off

his horse's rump. He dropped the rifle he'd been holding. The horse whinnied and jerked sideways with a start.

"Grab the reins!" Evans yelled.

Fay lunged out of the brush and reached for the reins just as the horse swung its head away from her. She missed the ribbons and fell to her knees.

In the periphery of her vision, she saw the doctor walk over to the man who'd tumbled off his horse and lay writhing on the ground.

"No—no, wait!" Carlos pleaded.

There was a loud, crunching thud, almost like the sound of a rock slammed against tree, and a brief chuff of expelled air as the Mexican fell back against the ground. Fay lunged for the reins again and caught them just as the horse was about to dip its hindquarters and high-tail it.

She held the reins firmly, let the horse pull her to her feet. The horse tried to run, but then Evans was beside her, grabbing the reins in front of her and pulling back against her, checking the horse down to a stop.

"Hurry!" Evans was breathing hard. His voice quavered anxiously. He and Fay heard the other two outlaws galloping toward them, shouting.

Clambering into the saddle, Evans then extended his hand to her. Awkwardly, poking her

bare left foot into the stirrup and hopping ridic-
ulously on her bare right one, and with Evans's
help, Fay managed to get seated atop the horse,
just behind the doctor and the saddle.

"Okay, Doc," Fay cried raggedly, her heart
shrinking as guns flashed and popped in the
west. "Let's go!"

Evans looked wildly around, the horse shift-
ing nervously beneath them. "Which way?"

"Any way away from them!" Fay shouted as a
bullet buzzed perilously close to her head before
thudding into the ground to her right, making
the horse whinny.

"All right," Evans said, turning the horse
around. "Hold on tight!"

He put the horse straight into the brush and
batted his heels against its ribs.

Chapter 15

Stillman halted Sweets at the base of a low bench.

He studied the twin furrows the travois had carved in the turf below him. They trailed straight up the side of the bench and into the rocks and pines at the top, maybe two hundred feet away from his current position.

He'd been tracking men long enough to know the tracks he currently stared at were a good twelve hours old. He could distinguish the age of tracks by their darkness or lightness, by the small erosions of wind and time, and by how damp or dry they were.

Also, the horse apple he'd sniffed a ways back had not owned the verdant pungency of a recent dropping; it had crumbled when he'd mashed it been his fingers, meaning it had dried for more than a few hours.

The outlaws had traveled through here last

evening. They'd probably camped at the top of the bench and pulled out this morning. Stillman wanted to ride straight up to the top of the bench and continue along the killers' trail...his wife and Evans's trail...but something told him to proceed with caution.

His desperate sense of urgency resisted that inner urging, but he was too seasoned to give in to it. He had to proceed with caution, which meant he'd have to quarter around to the left and climb the bench from the east side, where there were more trees and outcroppings to conceal his approach. The gang might be waiting for him up there.

Why they would have lingered here, he had no idea. Other than to scour him from their trail...

He hipped around in his saddle to peruse his back trail. He'd left his two spare horses a couple of hours ago, successfully discouraging them to follow. He'd known he was closing on the gang, and he wanted to do so as quietly as possible.

The two spare mounts would have been overly eye-catching to someone glassing him from a distance. He'd last seen both horses idly grazing on a gentle slope near a creek. He'd pick them up on his way back to Clantick or send someone out to fetch them. They were Auld's property, but Stillman couldn't worry about the horses now.

He saw no sign of Triber's bunch. He'd have bet double eagles to navy beans they were following, but at least they weren't being obvious about it, and they weren't close. They were probably going to let the lawman make his own play on the gang, and move in when and if he failed.

Which was reasonable, he supposed. Still, Triber was going to pay for trying to kill him. As most men would, Stillman took umbrage with someone attempting to kill him. The man's arrogance was boundless, and it was time to check him down.

The sheriff neck-reined Sweets to the left and nudged him into a trot. As it was, he was exposed out here. There was little cover. There had been little cover for the past mile or so—all open ground carpeted in tawny grass. Someone glassing him from the south would have seen him, but there was no way to avoid that possibility. He could do as much as he could to avoid getting picked off by a rifleman positioned atop the bench, however.

He was in the first broken hills of the Highwoods. The hat-shaped eastern face loomed beyond the bench. He followed the base of the bench for a quarter-mile then reined the horse to the right.

He and the bay lunged up the slope, weaving

around scattered pines and occasional aspens and outcroppings of granite exposed by the weathering away of the thin soil. It was steeper here than where the outlaws had climbed the rise. Sweets lunged with his hind legs, lurching off his rear hooves, loosing sand and gravel behind him.

Roughly halfway to the top, which was covered with thicker forest than what he'd found on the east side, Stillman reined the horse to a halt. He swung down from his saddle. He staggered a little, throwing his arms out for balance. He pinched the bridge of his nose between his thumb and index finger, shook his head to clear it. He felt drunk, though he hadn't had a drop, even if he'd had a drop to take, which he'd didn't.

Deep fatigue burned into him. He was now running on desperation. Eventually, his energy reserves would run out, leaving him high and dry.

In the meantime, he had to keep pushing ahead...

He ground-reined the bay, shucked his Henry from the leather, levered a cartridge into the chamber, off-cocked the hammer, and continued climbing tow the ridge crest on foot.

A bullet slammed into the rock he'd just passed on his right.

The rifle's screeching hiccup reached his ears an eye wink later.

Stillman threw himself to his left, hit the ground, and rolled up behind another rock.

The crack of the bullet meeting with the rock continued to ring in his ears. Sweets whickered edgily, tossing his head.

Inwardly, Stillman cursed. Unfortunately, he'd been right in his suspicions about someone lingering atop the rise. But for all his savvy, he hadn't avoided him.

He doffed his hat, pressed his back up against the rock, then edged a cautious glance around his cover's right side. He saw the rifle barrel laid across the top of a rock near the crest of the forested rise. He pulled his head back behind his own covering rock just in time to avoid a third eye socket. The bullet slammed resoundingly into the face of his covering, gravestone-shaped rock.

Again, the rifle screeched wickedly, its echoes rolling out over the plain behind him.

Stillman jerked his rifle up over his own rock and sent two rounds hurtling at his assailant. Through his own wafting powder smoke, he saw the man pull his rifle down behind his own rock. Beneath the Henry's cashing reports, he heard a shrill curse.

Stillman lowered the Henry and scrambled from behind his cover, running as fast as his weary legs would carry him across the shoulder of the rise, weaving between small pines, cedars, and more rocks. He ran hard, his boots slipping on patches of slide rock, spurs ringing.

The shooter opened up on him, triggering three fast rounds.

The bullets spanged off the rocks around him, one clipping his boot heel, another snapping a branch from a wind-twisted cedar.

He dropped behind a rock thirty or forty yards from where he'd first encountered the shooter. He aimed the Henry over the rock, but could no longer see his assailant. The man didn't appear to be where he'd been a few moments before.

Stillman hefted the Henry, gained his feet, and made a mad dash—or what for him was a mad dash--straight up the rise and into the trees at its crest. He pulled up behind a pine and dropped to a knee. He wheezed as he sucked air into his lungs and blew it out, sucked another breath, blew it out...

His heart was racing, hiccupping.

For god's sake, don't have a heart attack now, Stillman, you old goat...

When he'd got some of his wind back, he quickly brushed sweat from his eyes with his gloved hand and edged a look around the right side of the pine and into the trees beyond. The shooter was moving toward him through the shadowy woods, the ground between trees dappled with golden sunshine.

Stillman couldn't see his quarry very well. The man was a hatted shadow holding a rifle, moving slowly as he stole quietly at Stillman from the eastern end of the rise.

The man aimed his rifle in Stillman's general direction, knowing his target would be over here somewhere, trying to get around him.

The sheriff pulled his head and rifle back behind the pine.

He pushed himself to his feet with a soft grunt then stepped around the tree's left side. Just then a squirrel began chittering nastily. The man gave a startled grunt and whipped to his left, away from Stillman.

"Hold it," the lawman said, loudly levering a fresh round into the Henry's chamber.

The man gave another startled grunt and whipped around toward Stillman. Stillman angled the Henry low and fired.

"Ach!" the rifleman cried as he stumbled backward then dropped to his knees.

Grimacing, he let the Spencer repeater sag in his hands. He grabbed his right leg with that hand and cursed sharply.

He was older than Stillman. A stocky, potbellied man in a buckskin vest over a red-and-black checked shirt and battered gray sombrero. He wore a thin, gray beard on his pale and puffy, red-splotched face. Two Colts were holstered on his hips.

Stillman scowled at him dubiously. "Dutch?" He stepped slowly forward, ejecting the spent shell from the Henry's breech and seating a fresh one in the chamber. "Dutch Wayne?"

The groaning man only vaguely resembled the man Stillman remembered. But, then, the years will that to a body...

The old outlaw sagged backward onto his butt and extended both legs before him. He clamped his right hand over the bloody wound in his right thigh.

"You shot me, you son of a buck, Stillman," Dutch Wayne complained between grunts and frenetic breaths. "Blew a hole right through my damn leg! Now how in the hell am I supposed to..." He let his voice trail off. His face crumpled and suddenly he was sobbing, tears rolling down his cheeks. "My boy's dead, an'...an'...ah, hell everything's gone to hell!"

He punched the ground with his fist.

Stillman glanced around warily. He doubted anyone else was here, because he'd likely have known about it before now.

Still, he kept an eye on the trees and brush around him as he moved slowly up to stand over old Dutch Wayne, an outlaw Stillman had arrested at least twice in his distant, deputy U.S. marshal's past.

Gritting his teeth angrily, he glared down at the yammering old man and said, "Where is my wife, Dutch? Where's Doc Evans? Stop your damned caterwauling and answer me before I blow a damned hole through your fool head!"

"I don't know!"

"What do you mean, you don't know? I assume you're part of the bunch that took her!"

"She ran off! Her an' the sawbones!" Dutch tipped his head back and loosed a mewling wail at the breeze-jostled crowns of the pines. "After my boy died!"

He cried openly, with the abandon of the truly bereaved.

"My boy, Waylon—he's dead, an' I killed him!" the man bawled.

"I don't care about your son, you two-bit son of Satan! Where is my wife!"

Dutch punched the ground again. "Dammit, I told you, I don't know!" He waved his left arm, waggling his fingers. "They ran off last night and the boys went after 'em. I don't know why they ain't back yet. I'd have thought they'd have found 'em by now, but they ain't back yet, so I don't know nothin' about it!"

Stillman squatted before the man. "They ran off last night. My wife and the doctor?"

"That's what I said! Oh, just shoot me, Ben! Shoot me an' put me out of my misery!"

"I'd love to do just that—believe me, Dutch." Stillman wasn't lying. Now he had a wounded prisoner on his hands, and he desperately needed to get his wife and friend back from the cutthroats who'd gone after them.

Stillman looked at the blood bubbling up from the wound in the old man's leg and inwardly cursed. He untied the soiled red neckerchief from around the outlaw's neck and wrapped it around his bloody thigh. Dutch threw his head back and sucked air through his teeth from the pain.

"When did Fay and Evans run off, and in which direction did they head?"

"Hell, I don't know. I looked down, and my boy wasn't breathin' no more. An' he was just starin' up at me, an' he was sorta smilin' at me..." More sobs bubbled up from the man's sharply rising and falling chest. "I heard the men yellin' that they was gone, but I was more concerned about my boy. My only boy, Ben! I killed him!"

"Why'd you kill him?"

"I didn't mean to! I killed old Fritz 'cause he got

too damn big for his britches! The hitch spooked and jerked the coach, an' Waylon fell from the roof onto the damn strongbox!"

Dutch lowered his head, bawling. "He was broken up somethin' awful inside." The old outlaw looked up at Stillman; his face was a puffy red ball of sorrow and rage. "I told Evans he'd better keep my boy alive or I'd kill him, dammit! He'd die, too!"

Stillman pulled both the pistols from the old man's holsters and shoved them behind his own cartridge belt. He broke the man's rifle over a rock and tossed both pieces into the brush, as well.

He checked to make sure Dutch wasn't packing any other weapons, and found only a skinning knife, which he tossed away. Doubting he was going to get much more clarity out of the caterwauling old reprobate, he hurried off to the east to fetch his horse.

When he rode Sweets back into the woods atop the rise, he found Dutch standing over a freshly mounded grave beyond the remains of the killers' campfire. The old man leaned on a branch he was using for a crutch, his right leg hanging limp and a little out to one side.

Stillman swung down from the saddle and began scouring the area for tracks, trying to get a handle on which direction Fay and Evans had headed when they'd fled the camp.

Absently, he asked, "Where's the loot, Dutch?"

Dutch turned awkwardly to scowl curiously at Stillman. "Huh—what?"

"The loot. From the stage. Triber's money. Where is it?"

The lines of Dutch's scowl cut deeper lines across his puffy, red-splotched, gray-bearded face. "How'd you know it was Triber's money?"

Stillman turned to him, his own scowl cutting into his own wind- and sun-burned features. "How did you know it was Triber's money?"

Dutch gave a crooked, foxy grin. "Oh…me…I got my ways of knowin' such things."

"Yeah, well, Triber's gonna be here soon, so you'd better have a good story for him. Better yet, you'd better have his money, or I don't doubt the old bastard will draw an' quarter you."

Dutch frowned, fear in his eyes. "Whadoya mean? Triber's here, too?"

"He will be soon. He trailed me out from Chadwick Station." Stillman couldn't help taking devilish pleasure in the old man's sudden fear. "He's madder'n an old wet hen."

"They took the money!" Dutch waved his arm. "The boys took the money an' left me with nothin'. They said they'd come back here when they found your wife an' the sawbones, but they're prolly long gone by now, leavin' me high an' dry and penniless an' bereft after all I done for 'em!"

So far, the tracks were telling Stillman that his wife and the doctor and their pursuers had lit out to the west. His business was done here.

"You're on your own, Dutch." Stillman would take him into custody later, after he'd found his wife and his friend. "Good luck."

Stillman reined Sweets around.

"Wait!" Dutch limped, grunting and wincing, toward Stillman. "You can't leave me here alone, Ben. You gotta take me with you!"

"No time, Dutch."

"I got my horse!" Dutch pointed to his left, where three horses stood tethered to a long rope line tied between two trees. "I'll throw a saddle on him. You can't leave me here, Ben. Not without my weapons! You got my guns. Them boys—they took everything! All I got is a few beans and a canteen with a little water. They left me here to grieve all by my lonesome!"

"You're wounded, Dutch. Sit tight. I'll pick you up on my way back."

Limping badly, pathetically, Dutch reached out to pick up his saddle. He didn't make it. He yelped as he fell and rolled in the dirt by the fire, sobbing.

"Oh, hell!" Stillman swung down from Sweets's back.

Even in such a desperate situation, he couldn't in good conscious leave a defenseless, wounded old man here to fend for himself. If Triber didn't kill the old outlaw, some wild animal likely would. Not that it wasn't better than what the old devil deserved…

With a disgusted chuff, Stillman picked up the old man's saddle.

Chapter 16

"My boy!" Dutch sobbed. "My boy, my boy, my boy…"

"Shut up, Dutch."

Stillman led Sweets down the slope west of the killers' camp. Dutch rode along behind him, leaning forward in his saddle, clamping one hand over his bullet-torn thigh.

With his other hand, he held the reins of his zebra dun. He also held a red handkerchief with white polka dots over his mouth. He wheezed and whined and sobbed into it, between loud, phlegmy honks as he blew his nose and bawled.

"My boy is dead, damn you, Sheriff!"

Stillman's gaze studied the ground, following the bent brush showing where several people had passed only a few hours before. He'd found the body of one of the robbers a few minutes ago, farther up the slope. He'd been drilled through the forehead with either a .44 or a .45 round.

"I don't care, Dutch."

"My boy is dead! He's all I had! Agnes left us when Waylon was just a tyke, an' he was all I had!"

"Well, I see you brought him up right, anyway. You oughta be proud, Dutch. Real proud."

"He's all I had, damn you! I'm all alone now. I'll die alone!"

Stillman gave a sardonic snort and wheeled. He stomped back to the old man riding the horse following Sweets. He clamped a hand over the man's right knee, just below the wound.

Dutch drew his chin up sharply and sucked a pained breath through his gritted, coffee-colored teeth.

Stillman glared up at him. "I don't care about your boy. As far as I'm concerned, he got what he deserved. I am wishing right now I hadn't just wounded you but blown your damned head off, because now I have to put up with your infernal caterwauling!"

He released the man's leg.

Dutch lowered his head. It hung as though in shame, though Stillman knew there was no shame in Dutch Wayne. He was a life-long outlaw who'd once been a killer of some repute—handy with six-gun. He'd been in and out of Deer Lodge for the past thirty years, and two of those times had been of Stillman's doing.

"My boy, my boy, my boy…" the old man wheezed quietly.

"You keep your damned voice down or I will drag you out of the saddle and leave you behind… with a bullet in your damned outlaw head!" Stillman warned. "I am not fooling around here, Dutch. When it comes to your life or my wife's life, you know whose I'll pick. Now, shut up!"

"I'll be quiet, I'll be quiet," Dutch said with some chagrin, though Stillman knew the sentiment wasn't genuine. "Don't leave me behind, Ben. I killed my boy an' I fear his ghost. I purely do. Not that I don't deserve his wrath…but I'm scared. An' you know what's worse?"

Dutch tipped his wretched, sorrowful gaze to the sheriff standing beside him. "I fear death!"

Stillman would be damned if that bit of sentiment wasn't genuine, after all.

"Surely I'll burn in hell for my sins," Dutch continued. "I fear it somethin' awful, Ben. All the men I've killed…" He reached out and grabbed the front of Stillman's shirt. "Just don't leave me alone…to die alone…"

Stillman removed the man's hand from his shirt and got back to the subject most pressing on his mind. "Did my wife or the doctor get a gun?"

"Huh?"

Stillman jerked his glance up the slope. "That dead man up there. I assume he's one of your gang. I assume your own men didn't shoot him. Did Evans or my wife get their hands on a gun?"

"Oh." Dutch frowned down at his saddle horn, pondering the question. "That must be what happened to my rifle. They took it. It was leanin' beside the tree I was sleepin' against, but when--"

"So they have your rifle."

"They must."

Stillman frowned curiously. "Whose rifle were you using when you tried to pot shoot me?"

"My dear boy, Waylon's, old Spencer. I gave it to him for his thirteenth birthday. Do you know, Ben, he could shoot a rabbit, just a small one, from a hundred yards away with that old rifle…"

Stillman swung around and continued following the sign down the slope, heading toward a shallow canyon. A faint hope rose in him. At least Fay and the doctor had a weapon. With a weapon, they might have a chance.

He'd followed the sign of two people on foot— one barefoot and who was most likely his wife, judging by the small size of the feet—and several horseback riders into the ravine running along the base of the rise the killers had camped on. He'd stepped into his saddle and was trotting along beside the thick brush following the course of an unseen creek bed, when Dutch said, "I just want you to know, Sheriff, I kept 'em off of her."

Stillman swung a sharp look over his shoulder.

"You know," Dutch said with a wolfish half-grin, slitting his eyes obsequiously. "I didn't let 'em get after her, like men would. Oh, they wanted to. She's a righty purty woman, Ben. But I ain't that kind." He pursed his lips and shook his head. "Never been that kind. I won't ever let a man who rides with me do a woman that way."

Stillman gave a caustic chuff. "If you think you're gonna get some medal from me, Dutch, you're going to be waiting a long time." He turned his head back forward, his belly feeling like a tightly wound ball. "Now, shut your damned trap!"

"That's the thanks I get?"

"That's the thanks you get, Dutch. If it weren't for you and those coyotes riding with you, she wouldn't be where she is right now. Neither would Evans."

He slowed his horse to more closely study the sign on the ground before him.

Dutch rode up on his right. "I'm sorry, Ben. Purely, I am. I wish we hadn't done it. I wish I hadn't done a lot of the things I've done in my life."

Stillman eyed him skeptically. Again, he'd be

damned if the old fool didn't mean it. "Well," the lawman said. "I reckon that's something, anyway."

"Can we stop and take a rest? This leg is really grievin' me."

"You can stop anytime you want, Dutch."

"Ah, hell," the old scoundrel complained.

He really did seem to be having a crisis of conscience. No doubt because of his son. The boy's death had taken the starch out of his shorts. Under the circumstances, Stillman couldn't work up much sympathy. Maybe a little. But very little.

He drew back on Sweets's reins and heard a grunt slip out through his compressed lips. Narrowing his eyes, he studied something on the ground maybe forty feet ahead.

"What is it?" Dutch asked, halting his dun to Stillman's right.

The lawman's pulse drummed. What lay on the ground was a body. That was the only thing it could be. Had the coyotes caught up to their prey?

"Hi-yahh!" He spurred the bay into a lunging, wild-assed gallop.

When he checked the horse down a few seconds later, relief washed over him. He was staring down at a man lying belly down in the blond grass. Not Fay. Not Evans, either.

As Dutch rode up behind him, Stillman swung down from Sweets's back. He kicked the body onto its back, and a round-faced Mexican with a dark-brown mustache stared up at him through half-closed lids. The man's left temple had been smashed in. The weapon that had accomplished the grisly task lay to the dead man's left.

"That's my rifle," Dutch said.

Stillman picked it up by its barrel and inspected the rear stock. It was cracked and bloody, and a small tuft of black hair clung to the blood.

"No way to treat a good rifle," Dutch said.

"Who is this man?" Stillman asked him.

"Carlos Alcazar. Mescin. I never did like him, but I've never trusted any Mescin. I thought I was doin' him a favor, bringin' him into the group, but—"

"So he's one of your men."

"Was." Dutch gave an amused chuff. "He must have tried tangling with your wife. Dude tried her, too, and ended up with some nasty scratches on his face for his trouble."

Stillman choked down his rage at the man's flippant manner. Dutch was an old fool; he was trying to be amusing, although if he kept it up, he was going to be rewarded with a smashed head, like Carlos Alcazar.

Fay and Evans were fighting, though, Stillman thought. That meant they had a chance.

He glanced around.

Where in the hell were they?

"Musta gone across the creek," Dutch said.

Stillman was studying the ground, trying to read the tangle of overlaid tracks. He looked at Dutch, frowning. Dutch nodded toward the brush. "See how them branches are broken? Looks like they went straight through them shrubs. On a horse, most like."

Stillman walked over to the brush. Dutch was right. Several horses and riders had plowed through the brush.

Pushing branches aside, he walked a few feet into the dense chokecherries and hawthorn shrubs. He stopped and plucked a piece of brown cloth off a thorny branch. The cloth was about two inches long by one inch wide. Stillman could see the curve of a single white polka dot.

Fay had a light brown summer dress with white polka dots.

He shoved the cloth into a pocket of his denims and hurried back to his horse.

"You were right, Dutch," he said, swinging into the leather. "They must have taken Alcazar's horse and bulled through the brush." He had a feeling their pursuers weren't far behind them.

"See?" Dutch said. "Now, ain't you glad you brought me along?"

Stillman only grunted then spurred Sweets into the brush, following the disheveled path of flattened and broken branches. He crossed the creek, which was only a few inches deep and maybe ten feet wide, and spurred the bay into the buttes beyond it.

***

At the same time, Fay held her hand against the snout of the strawberry roan she and Evans had appropriated from Carlos. She shoved the horse's head low, so it couldn't be seen over the top of the boulder before her. She clamped her hand over the horse's nostrils, trying to keep it from neighing or whickering.

As she did, she edged a look over the top of the rock. Her heart was raced and hiccupped in her chest.

She heard the riders moving along the wash before her, heading toward the crease between buttes she and the doctor were hiding in. The crease intersected with the cut of a creek just beyond.

She and Evans had spied the riders a minute ago, heading toward them along the creek. She hadn't thought they'd spied her and Evans, though, so instead of trying to make a run for it and risk being seen, she and the doctor had hidden behind the boulder in this narrow wash, which was part of a small devil's playground of washes they'd found themselves in when they'd galloped blindly away from their pursuers.

She stared at the brown water of the creek rippling before her, sending little white stitches of froth up around half-submerged stones. A few willows and cattails stippled both banks of the creek, offering moderate cover. Red-winged blackbirds gave their ratcheting cries from weed tips, curiously cocking their heads at the human interlopers. She and Evans had followed the creek, riding right down the middle of it, through the water, making it harder for Dutch's men to follow them.

The prey had outfoxed their stalkers. At least, for a time.

Whether the killers would remain befuddled was an open question.

She heard them now approaching on the bank running along the far side of the creek. They were following the same creek she and the doctor had, knowing their quarry had ridden in this westerly direction from the rise they'd camped on and fled from. They were looking for the sign that would betray their prey's location, stubbornly clinging to her and Evans's trail.

She heard two of them talking in angry tones, but she couldn't hear exactly what they were saying above the din of the blackbirds and the rippling water. When they came into view, riding from her left to her right, trotting their horses and peering around, frowning beneath their hat brims, she jerked her head behind the boulder.

"Oh..." Evans grunted behind her.

She turned to him, frowning with annoyance and placing a finger to her lips, shushing the man. He sat on the ground, both legs partly extended before him, clamping his left hand over his bloody left calf.

When the killers had pursued them through the brush along the creek several hours ago, the doctor had taken a bullet. It was only a flesh wound, the bullet having plowed all the way through, but Fay had discovered to her dismay that the doctor made a considerably worse patient than he did a sawbones.

Evans caught her admonishing signal and flushed sheepishly.

As the riders clomped past the mouth of Fay and Evans's intersecting ravine, on the other side of the creek, one of them raised his voice in frustration: "I say we forget about 'em an' get back to ole Dutch an' the money. We're wastin' too much time out here, an' that old coot's liable to run off with the loot!"

Another man responded with: "If we leave 'em, then we..." His voice trailed off as the fast clomping of the horses' hooves dwindled into the distance.

Fay heaved a relieved sigh and turned an angry scowl on the doctor. "Dammit, Doc—can't you keep quiet for even a few precious seconds?"

"I apologize," Evans said in exasperation. "But this bullet wound hurts considerably!" He gritted his teeth as he clamped his hand tighter over the wound, which Fay had helped him wrap with a length of cloth she'd ripped from her skirt.

"It's going to hurt a lot worse if you get another one!"

Evans looked at her sharply through his dusty glasses. He was about to give a sharp retort but instead, he snorted with laughter. Fay slapped her hand to her mouth, muffling her own amused chuff. For some reason, the comment struck her as funny, as it had the sawbones.

Suddenly they were both holding each other, trying to muffle each other's hysterical guffaws as the horse, which Fay had released, watched them dubiously, slanting its ears forward and back. The humans doubled over in laughter, mirth erupting from them on a geyser propelled by long pent up anxiety and sheer terror.

Fay kept hearing her own ridiculous words echoing around inside her head—"It's going to hurt a lot worse if you get another one!"--and she kept seeing Evans's initial reaction to it, and laughed harder and harder.

Finally, thank god, their laughter dwindled to a slow boil which continued for another minute. That died then, as well, and they both slumped against the side of the ravine, aching and exhausted, but somehow buoyed, as well.

Nothing like a good laugh to lighten the load, Fay thought.

"Well," Evans said, catching his breath, "that took the pain away, however briefly." He looked at Fay and chuckled, his old laughter threatening to swamp him again. "It's back again now, though, of course. The pain, I mean. Oh, mercy!"

"Do all doctors make such lousy patients?"

"I don't know," Evans said. "I've never doctored a fellow medico. Never have been able to stand the sight of my own blood, however. I can look at bowls of someone else's, but even when I just nick myself shaving, I get queasy." He paused, drawing another breath to replenish that he'd spent laughing so hard. "I suspect it's a fear of death I've never looked at all that closely. Haven't wanted to, nor have I had to…till now."

He looked off with a philosophical air.

Fay leaned over to kiss his cheek. She patted his knee. "We'll make it, Doc. Did you hear them? I think they're getting tired of looking for us. If we can stay ahead of them for another hour or two, we may be in the clear."

"Where in the hell are we, anyway? With all the hard riding and tension, I've completely lost my bearings."

"I don't know, but…I think we'd better get out of this creek bed, and fast!"

Evans looked at her sharply. "Why? Are they returning?"

Fay pointed a finger at the sky. "No, but a storm's coming. And a bad one, judging by those black clouds."

Evans followed her gaze toward the twisted, dark-purple mass sliding over them, blocking out the sun and silencing the birds. His jaw dropped. "Oh, dear!"

Just then, thunder peeled loudly, making the ground shiver.

"My sentiments, exactly!" Fay said. "Come on, Doc." She tugged on his arm. "We don't want to be in this ravine when those clouds open up!"

Chapter 17

Stillman cursed loudly as he glared up at the swollen, tongue-shaped mass of plum-colored clouds looming over him, swooping at him from the northwest.

Lightning flickered inside the ominous mass. Thunder rumbled. A pale curtain of rain and probably hail hung beneath the storm's belly. Already Stillman could smell the brimstone and the cool rain, feel the first chill drops splattering against his face.

"That's a bad one for sure," Dutch said, also staring up at the storm. "We'd best head to high ground fast, Ben. If this gully fills up…"

Stillman was already looking around for shelter. He and Dutch had followed the gang's horse tracks into this natural corridor between a haystack butte on their left and a slanting, high-walled mesa on their right. A dry creek bed ran down the middle of the cut. At least, it was dry for now. When that storm opened its floodgates, the creek bed would become a raging torrent.

Stillman nudged Sweets ahead as he swept his gaze from right to left, looking for some sort of shelter above the creek bed. The horse was nervous. It could smell the storm, and it could hear it even better than Stillman could. Sweets didn't like it one bit.

Stillman continued forward, following a dog-leg bend in the cut. Ahead and on his right, he spied a narrow black line on the side of the mesa, maybe a hundred feet up from the base. A cavern?

Only one way to find out.

He booted Sweets into a lope. The beast caromed around two boulders and a snag of june-berry and wild raspberry, and then Stillman put the mount up the sloping western ridge. He drew to a halt on a natural shelf. A mild relief touched him.

Sure enough. A cavern had been weathered into the wall on his right. Roughly forty feet wide, it appeared tall enough for the horses. There was even some dry brush and a dead, lightning-struck cottonwood in a slight notch to the right of the formation, offering wood for a fire.

If Stillman could reach it before the rain did.

He glanced behind.

Dutch leaned forward in his saddle as his own horse climbed the ridge. He grimaced against the pain in his wounded leg. Beyond Dutch, the storm was overtaking them, the wind building and tucking their horse's tails up against their bellies. It blew Dutch's hat off his head and bounced it along the ground, the old outlaw cursing as he watched, unable to go after it.

Snugging his own hat down tighter on his head, Stillman swung himself from the bay's back and led the mount up the ridge. He and the horse slipped on the loose clay and gravel, Stillman falling to his knees twice, Sweets once, before they gained the shelf beyond which yawned the cavern. He led Sweets into the cave, having to tug on the reins of his wary mount.

When he finally got the horse inside, he took a quick look around, glad not to see the glowing eyes of a disgruntled wildcat or a wolf, possibly even a grizzly bear, gazing at him from the cave's murky darkness.

He dropped Sweets's reins and ran down the slope to where Dutch sat in his saddle, crouched against the wind and the rain that was starting in earnest now, thunder clapping overhead like the cymbals of angry gods.

The old man hung his head in defeat, wincing against the pain in his leg.

"Come on, Dutch—climb down from there and get inside!"

"Ah, hell," the old man grumbled, leaning toward Stillman.

Inertia had set in. He looked drawn and pale, only half conscious.

The sheriff helped Dutch out of the saddle. After slipping and falling several times, Stillman finally got him into the cavern. The old outlaw dropped to his knees beside Sweets who was whickering and sidestepping anxiously as the storm bore down.

Stillman ran back outside and, after another desperate struggle, led Dutch's mount into the cave.

Stillman dropped to his knees beside Dutch, exhausted. Fatigue was an anvil on his shoulders. His heart raced; he couldn't seem to rake in enough air to satisfy his weary lungs. He ached in every joint. His aches ached!

Still, glancing outside, seeing the rain falling at a slant, he knew he had to get out there and gather some wood. He needed coffee. A few beans wouldn't hurt, either. He had beans and bacon in his war sack, and he had touched neither yet.

Gritting his teeth, he hurried outside and into the gap beside the cavern. The notch was sheltered somewhat from the storm, so Stillman was able to gather a couple of armloads of dead cottonwood branches before they got too wet to burn. He crouched over the wood, shielding it from the rain with his body. When he'd brought a second load into the cavern, he dropped it against the eastern wall, a good fifteen feet away from the entrance, out of reach of the storm's lash.

He fell to his knees again in exhaustion.

After another short breather, he broke up the wood as best he could, separating smaller branches and dead leaves from the larger branches he'd add to the tinder later. He placed a small pile of the makings on the cavern floor, struck a lucifer to life on his shell bet, and touched the flame to the dry leaves and wood slivers. He blocked the fledgling flames from the wind and rain blowing past the cavern and whipping the horses' tails sideways.

Still, it took him several tries to nourish a flame large enough to add kindling to the tinder.

Finally several flames licked up from the wood. They were large and hardy enough to hold their own against the wind slithering around Stillman.

He straightened his back and turned to where Dutch sat slumped against the west wall, across from Stillman. The horses stood side by side near the cavern opening. The cave was roughly thirty feet deep, the ceiling tapering sharply downward near the back wall, only a few feet from Stillman.

The old outlaw sat with his legs stretched straight out before him, gloved hands resting in his lap. His hat was gone, but it had matted his short, gray hair to his head, a half rooster tail rising at the very crest of his skull.

He appeared even more depleted than Stillman felt. His upper right thigh was all blood. The blood nearly hid the neckerchief Stillman had tied around it.

He seemed to be staring at Stillman, but the lawman didn't think the man was really looking at him. He seemed to be staring right through him.

"I'll get some coffee going in a minute, Dutch. Maybe cook some beans."

He'd had to speak loudly to be heard against the wind and thunder. Dutch stared at him obliquely. Stillman couldn't tell if the man had heard him or not.

The outlaw curled his upper lip in a foxy smile. "I got me a secret."

Stillman added a little more wood to the fire.

"I said I got me a secret, Ben," Dutch said louder, his voice so raspy, he was hard to understand. "About the loot."

Stillman glanced at him, one brow arched.

Again, the man's upper lip rose in a knowing grin. "Triber's son put me up to it."

"His son?"

"That's right. I seen him in Great Falls. In the Omega." Dutch spat into the dirt of the cavern floor. "He told me about the loot the old man had comin' on the next stage from Billings. From Billings, the stage was faster than the train. Besides, no one's held up that line in years, 'cept for the mail pouch once or twice."

"Why'd he put you up to it? Robbing his old man, I mean."

Dutch shrugged. "I don't know. My guess is the kid killed somebody, like he's known to do. Ain't that what got him shipped down to Deer Lodge? My guess is the old man had to pay somebody off, like he's had to do before." He paused, worked his tongue around inside his cheek. "Just figured I'd tell ya. Now, only you an' me know." He gave a devious wink.

Stillman turned back to the fire. He waited until the flames had grown a little stronger then added more fuel.

When the fire was going well enough on its own, he filled his coffee pot from his canteen, which was still nearly full from when he'd filled it at a creek. He'd taken time to drink very little water and to eat very little food, and he knew that was a big cause of his fatigue.

He was running almost solely on worry and desperation.

When he had the coffee steaming over the fire on his iron spider, he rose to his feet and walked to the cave entrance. He stared out into the storm that had filled the cut between the mesa and the next butte to the south.

It was almost as dark as dusk, and the rain fell in buffeting sheets. The wind howled maniacally. Gazing down the slope before him, he saw that the dry wash was already filled with muddy water churning down the drainage from his right to his left, littered with deadfall and dead leaves.

He muttered an oath under his breath as the horrific consequence of the storm whispered maliciously in his ear. The torrent had without a doubt already covered the tracks of the horse he'd been following. Those tracks had been a bridge to his wife and to Evans. That bridge was gone now, washed away by the storm.

How would he ever find her now?

His heart a heavy stone in his chest, he walked back to the fire. The pot was boiling, water bubbling up around the lid and from the spout.

He used a scrap of burlap to pull the pot off the spider, and added a couple handfuls of Arbuckles from his burlap sack to the water. He set the pot back on the spider, then removed it again when it returned to a boil. He added a little water from his canteen to the coffee, to settle the grounds, then poured himself a cup of the scalding black brew.

He looked over at Dutch sitting across the fire from him, leaning back against the opposite wall.

"Coffee's ready."

He didn't know why he was offering the man coffee. The man might have, however indirectly, killed his wife and his friend. If not for Dutch Wayne, Fay would not be in the position she was in now—on the run for her life, or, if the killers had caught up to her and the doctor, dead.

What Stillman should do, what he felt he had every right to do, was drill a .44 round through Dutch's head. He didn't know what compelled him to call once more, "Dutch—coffee?"

Dutch's eyes seemed to focus. His lips were parted. His chest rose and fell slowly. Even more slowly, he shook his head and blinked once.

"Nah," he said with more volume than he appeared capable of. "I'm just gonna sit here. Listen to the rain." He turned his head to stare out into the storm. "Somethin' kinda peaceful about it."

Stillman sipped his coffee. He took no comfort from the storm. It only added to his frustration.

"Hey, Ben?" Dutch called above the wind and the pounding rain.

Sitting back against the cave wall, on the opposite side of the fire from the old outlaw, Stillman looked at the man through the steam rising from his cup.

"You believe in hell, Ben?"

Stillman pondered the question briefly, then looked at Dutch again and nodded. He'd never taken the notion seriously before, but now he did. What he was going through right now could only be the product of some devil's high jinks—whether a human devil or otherwise.

"Yes, I do, Dutch." Stillman sipped his coffee, swallowed, and stared out into the storm again. "Yes. I sure do."

He was still staring out into the storm, which was dwindling as it rolled off to the southeast, when he heard a strange sound.

Sweets had heard it, too. The bay lowered his head and laid back his ears, sliding his snout toward where Dutch sat back against the cave wall opposite Stillman.

The old man's eyes were closed. His lips were slightly parted. His chest rose heavily. He made a gurgling sound that Stillman could hear clearly now that the rain had lessened considerably.

The old man's lips fluttered.

He drew a breath, making a strangling sound.

Suddenly, his eyes opened very wide. So wide

that for a few seconds Stillman thought his eyeballs would pop out of his skull. Dutch sat straight up against the wall. He looked as though he'd just seen something he could in no way wrap his mind around.

"Agnes, honey!" Dutch cried. "Please don't leave me, honey! Them others didn't mean nothin' to me. Think of our boy!"

On the tail end of the wail, Dutch's mouth closed. His eyelids shut halfway. He sagged back against the cave wall, then slid slowly down the wall to his left shoulder. Stillman could see his half-open eyes staring opaquely at the blood that had pooled on the ground around him.

Both horses lifted their heads and whinnied a shrill death dirge.

Chapter 18

Riding double on the Mexican's roan, Fay and Evans crouched against the building wind and the rain starting to slash at their faces.

Fay rode in the saddle, Evans crouched behind her, arms wrapped around her waist, clinging to her desperately as the horse lunged ahead, frightened by the thunder that rumbled more loudly with each clap.

Lightning sparked over a forested ridge to Fay's right. A pine standing at the very top of the ridge exploded, sending sparks flying. Slashed in half by the bayonet-like lightning, the tree folded down over itself, the top half crashing to the ground and sending up even more sparks that quickly flickered out as the pale curtain of rain hammered it.

The tree must have been a good mile away, but the northern wind carried to Fay's nose the burned-hair smell of brimstone.

"It's getting closer," Evans yelled above the thunder.

Fay drew back on the horse's reins.

"Why are we stopping?" Evans asked.

"Look!"

"Huh?"

Fay pointed with her left hand. "There!"

A log cabin sat in a horseshoe-shaped notch in the wall of the forested mountain to her left. Evans removed his rain-splattered spectacles and used his thumb and index finger to smear the water around on each lens as he and Fay studied what appeared to be a small ranch.

A barn, another outbuilding, and a couple of corrals flanked the cabin. It was a small, humble place, but apparently it was occupied. Wind tore at the smoke issuing from the brick chimney running up the cabin's right wall. A lamp glowed wanly in a window.

Fay glanced over her shoulder at the doctor. "Think they'll take us in?"

"Won't know until we ask."

Evans looked to the north. The storm pounded closer and closer, the purple mass of clouds closing over them. At the moment, it was only sprinkling, but that pale curtain sliding over the forested northern ridge portended a gully washer.

Fay batted her bare heels against the horse's ribs and swung it toward the cabin, hunched low in the stormy murk, increasing wind nibbling at the wooden shakes of its roof. As she and the doctor approached to within fifty yards, she spied movement in the sashed window to the right of the door.

A sallow curtain slid to one side then dropped back into place.

When the Mexican's strawberry roan had taken two more trotting strides, the cabin's front door opened. A big man ducked low to come through it.

When he rose to his full height on the front stoop, holding a double-barrel shotgun in his right hand, Fay saw that he was a very big man, indeed. He was at least a whole head taller than Ben, she absently opined. He had thick, curly, red-blond hair with a shaggy, matching beard. He wore high-topped lace boots with the cuffs of his buckskin trousers stuffed inside, and a red plaid shirt and suspenders.

A woman hovered behind him. Much shorter than the man, she had to lean out to each side to see around him. Her head didn't even come up to his broad shoulders.

Apprehension rose in Fay. She knew that re-mote-living people—and this place was definitely remote, the closest town most likely Big Sandy, thirty or forty miles northwest—could be suspicious of strangers. Downright unreasonable. She knew from stories Ben had told her that when it came to strangers wandering up to such folks' places, a danger such hermetic folks might shoot first and ask questions later was always present.

An added caution here resided in the man confronting them from the porch of his cabin being large and imposing, not to mention he just now raised the big shotgun and rested the barrel in the open palm of his large left hand, poking his right finger through the trigger guard.

Fay stopped the horse, watching the man skeptically, ready to swing the mount around and hightail it if he started to lift the shotgun.

The man stepped out from under the porch roof, arched a shaggy brow as he glanced at the sky, then came on down the steps and walked slowly to where Fay and Evans sat the strawberry roan. The man didn't say anything, just narrowed his piercing, lake-blue eyes pointedly, his mouth forming a straight, grim slash inside his shaggy beard.

Fay hesitated, said, "H-hello…" She winced as the intensifying rain slashed against her from her left side.

"We need help," Evan said over her right shoulder. "Men are after us, and I've been shot!"

Inwardly, Fay winced. Leave it to the good doctor to get to the point of the matter…

The information didn't seem to surprise the big man standing before her, holding the shotgun across his chest. He glanced behind them, as though he might see the pursuing riders, then returned his vaguely questioning gaze to Fay.

"It could be dangerous," Fay warned the man, beginning to have second thoughts about stopping here. "Taking us in, I mean. They might follow, but…we could use the help. Like the doc said—"

"I've been shot," Evans finished for her. "And as you can see…" He glanced at the sky through spectacles beaded with rain.

The woman, who had gone back into the cabin, now remerged, running, holding a large trade blanket, shaking it out as she approached the newcomers. She shoved the big man aside, ramming him hard with her shoulder, though her push hardly seemed to faze him.

Holding up the blanket to Fay, she said, "You're soaking wet! Let's get you inside!"

The little, gray-haired woman's eyes were soft and sympathetic, comforting. Fay lifted her right leg over the saddle horn and dropped to the bare ground. Instantly, the little woman wrapped the blanket around her shoulders then, with one hand firming on her arm, began leading her to the cabin.

As she did, Fay glanced behind to see the big man lowering the shotgun with one hand, then using his other hand to help the wounded Evans dismount from the strawberry roan. When both men were on the ground, Fay saw that the top of Evans's head rose little higher than the big man's shoulder.

The big man looked suddenly docile enough, however. While his bearded face was broad and half-wild-looking, he wrapped a thick arm around the doctor's waist and slowly, gently guided the sawbones across the wet yard to the cabin.

The bird-like old woman led Fay up the steps and into the cabin, saying, "Oh, it's so wet! The storm came up awfully fast! Here, you dry off with the towel, honey. I'll fetch you something clean and warm to wear! I have coffee on the fire!"

As the woman disappeared through a curtained doorway in the rear wall of what appeared the living area of the small, wooden-floored shack, Fay realized she'd spoken in the lilting accent of a Scandinavian. Fay held the blanket tightly around her. She moved to one side as the big man stooped through the doorway behind the limping, shuffling Evans.

"Here, Doc." Fay pulled a hide-bottom chair out from the table in the cabin's kitchen area, to the right of the living area. "Sit down here, and take some weight off that leg."

The doctor groaned as he eased himself into the chair.

The big man closed the door and turned to Fay and the doctor, scowling. "Men are after you, you say, ja?" He lowered his shaggy head to peer through the window right of the door. "A few years ago I would have said Injuns, but the army rounded up all the Gros Ventre and put them on the reservation. They used to give me holy hell, though, I tell you!"

He, too, spoke with a Scandinavian accent. His was thicker than the woman's.

"Oh, Rasmus, stop your yammering!" the old lady castigated the big man as she pushed back through the curtained doorway. She held a small pile of clothes in her hands—some white ladies' underwear and a maroon cambric dress with white lace.

"Here," she said as she shoved the clothes at Fay. "These might fit your pretty little body. They belonged to the teacher who stayed with us a couple of years ago. She was about your size. She left when she married Hjalmar Rasmussen, and I keep forgetting to take these clothes over to her at their Double-Tree Ranch. You can go in there and change, and I will have a hot cup of coffee waiting for you!"

She glanced at the curtained doorway through which she'd just emerged.

"Oh, Mrs...."

"Stryk," the woman said, smiling broadly, with old-country affability. "I am Hilda and this is Rasmus. Don't let his size scare you. I am the one who had to shoot our old dog when he got so full of the arthritis he couldn't get up anymore. Rasmus's heart is too tender!"

She leaned back and cackled out a delighted laugh.

"That is very generous of you, Mrs. Stryk, but—"

"Hilda!"

"That is very generous of you, Hilda, but first I must warn you that by taking us in, your lives might be in danger."

"That's what she said outside, Momma," Rasmus said, glancing at the doctor, then frowning down at his wife. Turning his startlingly blue eyes on Fay, he said, "Don't worry, little lady. You are here now. You are safe."

"Thank you so much..."

"What happened? Who is after you?"

"I'm Fay Stillman, Sheriff Ben Stillman's wife.

This is Doctor Evans. We're both from Clantick. The doctor and I were on the stage back to Clantick from Rocky Ford when we were held up. We were taken hostage, but we got away, and..."

She let her voice trail off as she glanced down at the doctor, who had pulled up his wet trouser leg to examine his bloody calf. "The doc was shot when were making our escape on that horse out there."

Hilda gasped as she stared down at Evans in shock. "Uftah!"

"The stage was held up, you say?" said Rasmus. "The one from Rocky Ford?"

"Yes. The driver and the shotgun messenger were killed."

"No!" intoned Hilda, slapping her hand to her mouth.

"They killed Rocky O'Sullivan?" asked Rasmus.

"And Dave Morley, that's right," Fay said. "Both of them."

"Devils!" Hilda hissed.

"Ahhh, no," Rasmus complained, wagging his big head grievously. "Poor ole Rocky. Dave—he has a wife and little ones. Who were these men who killed that old Irishman and Morley?"

"Dutch Wayne's bunch." Evans spoke for the first time.

"Dutch Wayne, Dutch Wayne." Rasmus cupped a hand to his chin, pensively studying the floor.

"I've heard that name…but a long time ago…"

"He's not as young as he used to be," Evans drolly quipped. "Listen," he said, smiling a little sheepishly up at Rasmus, "you wouldn't have a shot or two of who-hit-John lying around, would you, Mr. Stryk? I could use something with some teeth in it to take the sting out of this nip."

"No!" Hilda hissed again, narrowing her light-brown eyes as she glared up at her husband. "I haven't let this big scoundrel have a single teaspoon of the devil's spirits in the past twenty years. Not since—"

"Now, Hilda. Now, Hilda, let's not get into my past transgressions," Rasmus urged, holding up both of his dinner plate-sized hands in submission. He grinned at Evans. "I got somethin' even better out in the springhouse."

He grabbed a greased canvas rain slicker off a peg by the door. "I'll take your horse to the stable where those cutthroats won't see him if they ride up to the place, and I'll fetch you a bottle of my chokecherry wine. I started it last fall—a good crop of berries last summer — an' I been lookin' for a good cause to pop the cork. No better occasion than unexpected company—eh, Momma?"

Hilda hissed at him. Ignoring his wife, Rasmus shrugged into the slicker, winked cunningly at Evans, and went out.

☆☆

Fay lifted the delicate little wine glass to her lips and sipped the chokecherry wine.

It was good and sweet, like a fine liqueur. It soothed the damp chill in her bones. Still, a shiver swept through her from time to time as she sat in the cabin's parlor area, in an armchair near the rain-streaked window.

A fire snapped in the hearth. She held the blanket around her shoulders to help ward off the stubborn cold only partly due to the weather.

Fear enhanced her chill.

Six men, including Dutch, were still after her and Evans. However, she hadn't seen Dutch among their pursuers. The rain would slow the five men down, but the storm itself was beginning to taper off now, a couple of hours after she and Evans had arrived at the cabin.

That meant Dutch's men would take to the trail again. Unless the rain had successfully discouraged them, and they'd decided to end their hunt, take their money to their Highwood Mountain cabin and wait for their own trail to cool, or go to Great Falls or Helena and waste it on whiskey, women, and cards.

Would they do that?

She'd heard one of them make such a suggestion

when she and the doc were cowering behind the boulder earlier in the morning.

"Don't worry, Mrs. Stillman," Rasmus Stryk said from the kitchen table. "The rain wiped out your trail, most like. They won't follow you here. Even if they did, I wouldn't let nothin' bad happen to you and the doctor. You are safe here. No man messes with Rasmus Stryk. Not unless he wants to face one of these."

He held up one of his clenched, ham-sized fists, and grinned.

"And not if he wants to face ole Astrid over there." He glanced at the shotgun mounted on pegs above the door.

"He named the gun after his grandmother back in Norway," said his wife, Hilda, snickering over the rim of her own wine glass.

She sat in a small, ornately scrolled and embroidered armchair on the other side of the fireplace from Fay. She'd decided having guests was occasion enough to celebrate with some of her husband's otherwise forbidden wine.

Rasmus chuckled and sipped from his own wine glass, which had delicate little gold bird etchings on the side, above the slender stem. The glass looked hardly larger than a thimble in his huge hand.

"That gun resembles my dear old bestemor,

she does—Hilda! Long and skinny, dressed in black, and"—Rasmus grinned broadly, his blue eyes twinkling delightedly—"deadlier than the waters off Sogn Fjord!"

He looked at the doctor sitting across the table from him and winked. He raised his glass in salute, and drank.

"Oh, Rasmus!" his wife said, shaking her withered head, her hair pulled back in a tight, silver bun. "How you do go on!"

She was embroidering a kitchen towel secured to a wooden hoop, working crouched over the cloth, needles and pinking shears in her lap. Her wine glass stood on the table beside her.

Rasmus and the doctor played cribbage while sipping their wine. Fay had helped Mrs. Stryk bandage the doctor's calf. Evans had grown as white as freshly fallen snow as he'd grimaced at the ragged wound, which hadn't looked all that bad once they'd wiped the blood away.

Fay had said as much, to which the doctor had grunted and, gritting his teeth, said, "It hurts like a..." Remembering his place here as a guest, and that ladies were present, he revised the rest of the sentence to: "It hurts like the blazes."

He had glanced at Fay and pursed his lips, sheepish.

"Here, Doc," Rasmus had said, lifting the heavy

stone wine jug, and tipping it over the doctor's nearly empty glass. "Have a little more wine. It will file the teeth off that wolverine chewing on your leg!"

He'd laughed bawdily.

Now the men played quietly, desultorily, the doctor looking ridiculous but warm in a pair of Rasmus' buckskin trousers and wool shirt, the cuffs and sleeves of which he'd had to roll several times. His own wet clothes were drying along with Fay's by the fire.

Mrs. Stryk crouched over her embroidery, adroitly working her needles and shears. A roast from a steer Rasmus had recently butchered cooked in the range with garden carrots, onions, and potatoes, its succulent aromas filling the cabin.

The fire sputtered and crackled.

Outside, as the afternoon dimmed to early evening, the storm rolled into the distance. Rain dripped slowly from the eaves.

Fay sat in the window, staring out in dread of seeing her captors again.

"Not to worry, little lady," Rasmus told her from the table, offering a reassuring smile. "You are safe here. Everyone is safe here with Rasmus and Hilda!"

Chapter 19

The wine tempered Fay's fear enough that she managed to enjoy Hilda Stryk's delightful supper as twilight turned the windows blue. She even indulged in a slice of peach pie capped with a dollop of buttery, freshly whipped cream for dessert.

Judging by his grunts and groans of culinary delight as He hunched over his plate and shoveled the food into his mouth without hardly ever looking up from his toil, the doctor enjoyed the meal, too. He thrilled Hilda by accepting without argument a second piece of her delicious pie, which, like Fay, he washed down with a second cup of hot, black coffee.

The wine, the food, and the coffee as well as Rasmus and Hilda Stryk's easy, affable company improved Fay's mood to the point that she found herself during the evening sometimes nearly forgetting the perilous predicament she and the doctor had been in only a few hours ago. The rain had likely wiped out all trace of their trail.

Of course, she and the doctor were not out of the woods yet. She still wasn't back home with her husband and little boy.

But as the evening passed without further danger rearing its ugly head, her safe return to Clantick seemed more and more imminent.

Rasmus Stryk had assured her and the doctor that as soon as he finished his chores the next morning, he'd hitch his stout Percheron, Rolaag, to the traces of Hilda's buggy, and chaperone her and the doctor to Big Sandy. There they could pick up the train heading north, or wait for Ben to catch up to them.

Fay never doubted her husband was looking for her and Evans. Just as the weather had foiled their outlaw captors, it had most likely stymied Ben's own efforts at tracking her and the doctor. But she felt more and more optimistic as the evening wore on and the little Stryk cabin ensconced her in the warm congeniality and safety of hearth and home that she would soon be reunited with her own husband and child, in their own home.

While Rasmus excused himself to tend his barn chores, and the doctor lay down in the guest room at the cabin's rear, resting his wounded leg, Fay helped Hilda wash and dry the dishes. She took comfort in the domestic duties.

Still, she glanced out the cabin's front windows from time to time, watching for Dutch's men, though it had grown so dark she probably wouldn't have been able to see them until they'd ridden up to the cabin.

The thought gave her another chill. She reminded herself that the outlaws wouldn't be out looking for her and Evans in the dark. Especially with no trail to follow even by starlight.

She was glad when Rasmus returned from the barn. She found great comfort in his big, burly presence. Such a man, not unlike her husband, was a man to be reckoned with. As long as she and Evans were here on the Stryk ranch, they'd be safe.

She was sure of that.

When the doctor returned to the main part of the cabin after his nap, he and Rasmus broke out the jug of wine again, and resumed their cribbage game. Hilda and Fay sat in the parlor, conversing like any two women during an ordinary visit.

Fay told Hilda about her life with Ben in Clantick, about their little boy, their chickens, her favorite horse, Dorothy, and about the Bible study meetings she attended at Katherine Kemmett's house every Wednesday evening.

As she mentioned Katherine's name, Fay

cast a sly, meaningful glance at the doctor, who returned her look as he moved his pegs in the cribbage board, curling his upper lip in a mock expression of reproof.

Hilda told Fay about her and Rasmus's life out here on their Sawmill Ridge Ranch, where they'd lived for the past thirty years. She spoke fondly and bittersweetly of the three sons they'd raised in this small cabin. One had died in a stampede. One had "gone bad" and they no longer heard from him. The other one, she proudly related, was a stock buyer for a big eastern cattle syndicate in Nevada.

In their first years here, fresh from Norway and with three children coming three years in a row, the Stryks had fought off the Gros Ventres as well as wildfires, droughts, buffalo stampedes, and illness to build up their ranch to a herd of nearly five hundred cattle and up to twenty-five horses.

Rasmus had imported two seed bulls from England. While the bulls were long since dead, their progeny lived on, grazing the grassy slopes of the thousand-acre ranch both of the proud old ranchers had vowed they would be buried on, on either side of their son, Olaf, to keep him company through eternity.

Later, when Rasmus and the doctor had tired

of cribbage, the big rancher plucked his fiddle off the wall and insisted Fay and Hilda dance. Apparently, fiddling and dancing was a common diversion for the pair.

Without hesitation, Hilda set her embroidery aside, fairly leaped out of her chair, and began hop-skipping to and fro, lifting her skirts above her shoes and turning wild circles upon the parlor's braided rug. She clapped, tapped, sashayed and do-si-doed to Rasmus's raucous beat.

She threw her hands out to Fay. The old woman's revelry was catching. Fay rose from her own chair, self-conscious at first but quickly throwing herself into a wild dance around the rug, leaping and wheeling and laughing, enjoying the feel of her hair dancing about her shoulders.

His wounded leg resting on a pillow-padded chair before him, Evans laughed and whooped and clapped his hands in rhythm to Rasmus's fiddling.

The night reminded Fay of barn dances when she was a girl growing up on her family's sprawling ranch near the Powder River. How unexpectedly she'd found such joy here after such terror. She knew she would remember this night, at the tail end of so much trouble, for the rest of her life.

When the two dancers as well as the fiddler finally wound down, Hilda heated wash water on the range for Fay and the doctor, who were both in desperate need of a bath. Sponge baths would do. Evans repaired with his washbowl and a fresh towel to the back bedroom while Fay took her own bath at the kitchen table, after Rasmus and Hilda had retired to their loft bedroom for the night.

Clean and refreshed, Fay dressed in the sleeping gown Hilda had provided, and retired to the parlor sofa to sleep. She was so exhausted and relieved to be free and alive and headed home at last, that not long after she'd snuggled into the two star quilts Hilda had provided as bedding, she drifted into a deep, dreamless sleep.

A horse's loud whinny and the drumming of hooves roused her out of slumber, like two savage hands plucking an innocent fish from a peaceful stream. She sat straight up with a gasp, sure she would see horses and riders bearing down on her, men whooping, guns blasting.

"Oh, dear!" Hilda stood at the kitchen range, forking bacon around in an iron skillet.

Fay's gasp had startled the woman.

Clyde Evans sat at the kitchen table, clad in his dry but rumpled suit clothes. Over a steaming stone mug of coffee, he smiled reassuringly behind his finally clean glasses. "Nothing to worry about, my dear. Rasmus just let his horses out of the barn, is all."

Fay peered out the front window before her. The sounds of running horses, happy to be free of their stalls, came from behind the cabin.

Out front, beyond the flour sack curtained window, lay nothing but the open yard, which lemony rays of the rising sun was just now bathing. After the rain, the grass was a brilliant dark-green. Everything looked freshly cleansed—the trees, shrubs, sage tufts, the sky, rocks, and a forested mountain ridge rising maybe a mile away to the west.

"Whew," Fay said with relief.

"Ja," Hilda said, smiling, one small bony fist on her aproned hip, the other hand working the fork. "All is well. It is a beautiful morning."

Fay smiled as she peered out the window. "It is, isn't it?" she said. "It really is."

Evans slid his chair back and rose. "I'll finish my coffee on the porch so you can dress."

"Thanks, Doc."

When the doctor had stepped out onto the cabin's stoop, Fay tossed the quilts back, feeling as refreshed by her deep night's sleep as the world looked after the rain, and pulled the simple maroon frock over her head. As she tossed her hair out from under the dress's lace-edged collar. The smell of bacon and coffee made her mouth water and her stomach groan.

"As soon as Rasmus returns from the barn, we'll eat," Hilda said. She must have read Fay's mind. "I'll pack you a lunch for the trail, so you won't get hungry on the way to Big Sandy. We don't want you getting any skinnier, or your husband won't recognize you!"

She winked and laughed as she cracked an egg into the bacon pan.

Ben, Fay thought. Little Ben. Heart broke at the prospect of seeing her men again soon...

Fifteen minutes later they were all gathered around the kitchen table, devouring Hilda's delicious breakfast and listening to Rasmus recount a story of a half-wild old stallion he'd used to sire colts for himself and his ranching neighbors, when Fay glanced out the window between Rasmus and Evans. She froze.

She'd been lifting a forkful of egg and bacon to her mouth, but now her hand opened and the fork clattered back onto her plate.

"Oh, my god!"

Evans frowned at her. "What is...?" He'd turned his head to peer over his shoulder and out the window flanking him.

"Ufta namen!" Hilda said, to Fay's left.

"What is it, Momma?" Rasmus asked, also hipping around in his chair to peer out the window behind him.

Fay stared in silent chock through the window. Five horseback riders hurried toward the cabin. Fifty yards away, they were trotting fast. As they approached, Fay recognized all of them.

Dude and Thorn rode in front of the pack. As Dude came closer and closer, those scratch marks Fay had made on his face grew more and more discernible. To Dude's right, H. G. Thorn rode straight-backed and hard-jawed, his white hair bouncing on his shoulders. The others were the big, dull-eyed Mort Gunther; the tall and lean Utah with his long nose and close-set eyes; and the stocky, moon-faced Scrim McAllister riding a wild-eyed steeldust gelding that kept biting its bit.

"Dear, dear, dear, dear..." Evans was muttering under his breath.

Rasmus glanced at him. "Is that them, ja?"

"Ja. I mean, yes," Evans said shaking his head. He added slowly, fatefully, "It...sure...is..."

Rasmus switched his gaze to Fay and arched his brows determinedly. "Don't you worry, little lady. I'll get rid of them. They won't get off those horses..." He rose from his chair and pulled his shotgun down from the pegs over the door. "Leastways, if they do," he added, shuttling his pointed gaze to Fay and then to Evans, "they won't be breathin' by the time they reach the ground!"

"Oh, Rasmus—you be careful!" Hilda hissed.

"I'm just gonna send 'em on their way, Momma." Rasmus broke the shotgun open and peered down both barrels, making sure they were loaded. He snapped the shotgun closed with a resolute click. "When they get a look at my big, ugly hide an' ole Astrid here, they'll decide they got some place else to go fast!"

He chuckled dryly, then glanced at Fay and the doctor again. "You two stay out of sight. Don't let them see you through the windows."

Fay was too paralyzed with fear even to nod.

Rasmus opened the door only far enough to accommodate his body then stepped out onto the stoop, closing the door quickly behind him. Evans rose from the table and limped on his injured right leg to the window's right side, edging a look around the frame. Fay sat in her chair beside Hilda, frozen in place.

She didn't think the outlaws could see into the kitchen through the glass. The sunlight was behind them; it was likely reflecting off the panes.

Fay clutched the edge of the table with both hands. Hilda slid her left hand toward Fay, closed it over the younger woman's right hand, and squeezed it reassuringly.

Fay's heart thudded. She didn't realize she was taking very small, shallow breaths as she stared out the window before her, watching the five killers rein their horses down about fifteen feet out from the stoop. Rasmus stepped into view, moving to the edge of the stoop and then walking slowly down the steps and into the yard.

Dude studied the old man.

Rasmus raised Astrid in both hands, holding the double-barreled shotgun at a slant across his broad chest. He faced the outlaws, all five spread out before him.

Dude smiled as, leaning forward, resting an arm against his saddle horn, he studied the rancher before him. "Damn—you're a big son of a buck, ain't you, Grandpa?"

Rasmus stopped about halfway between the stoop and the five killers, spreading his feet and squaring his shoulders. "What is it you want here, young fella?" he asked in his heavy, lilting brogue.

Ignoring the question, Dude turned to Thorn sitting to his left. "Damn, he's a big son of a buck—ain't he, H.G.?"

"Yeah, yeah," Thorn said, spitting a wad of chaw onto the ground then running his tobacco-stained red shirtsleeve across his mouth. "So he's a big son of a buck. He's a big son of a buck with a big shotgun. Who cares?"

He stared at Rasmus. "We're lookin' for a man and a woman," he said, snapping the words out angrily, his flushed cheeks contrasting with the odd paleness of his hair. "The woman's purty, with curves in all the right places. You wouldn't miss her. The man's about my size and he's wearin' a suit."

"Wears glasses," added Scrim McAllister, pointing at his eyes as if illustration were needed.

Rasmus shook his head resolutely. "Haven't seen neither one. No, sir. Sure haven't."

Dude ridged his brows. "You sure? The way they was headed when we last seen 'em, they likely would have passed by here. I'm purty sure they'd have stopped here, if they seen the cabin."

Fay jerked with a start when Dude suddenly turned his gaze to the cabin, squinting as he stared through the window. His faze fell on Fay. At least, it appeared to fall on her. She suddenly felt crawling sensations all over her body.

Had he seen her?

"Nope, haven't seen 'em," Rasmus insisted.

"You sure, old man?" Dude said, still staring through the window at Fay.

At least, he was staring in her direction. She was almost dead certain he couldn't see her through the window. It was too bright outside, and she was too far away from the glass.

"Yes, I'm sure." Stubbornly, Rasmus wagged his head. Raising the shotgun a little higher in his arms, threateningly, he said, "Now, you five bug-gers ride out of here. You're not welcome here. This is private land, and you're trespassing!"

Fay's heart quivered as it thudded. Don't push too hard, Rasmus, she silently urged the rancher, sensing he was showing off for his audience in the cabin. You don't know what they're capable of. Please, be calm. Be polite. Don't make them angry.

"Buggers?" Thorn jerked his head back, frown-ing, offended. Glancing at Thorn again, he said, "Did he call us 'buggers'?"

Evans glanced darkly at Fay.

She didn't say anything but drew a deep, slow breath to try to calm her heart.

"Oh, Rasmus," she heard Hilda mutter to her-self, bowing her head as though in prayer.

Fay muttered a prayer of her own.

Chapter 20

"Yes, I called you 'buggers'. Now, hang it, you buggers get out of here! I won't tell you again!"

Rasmus had taken one more step forward. He pressed the shotgun's butt plate against his right shoulder and aimed the double-barreled blaster out before him. He sort of waved it around, aiming the gun at each outlaw in turn.

"Wait, wait, wait, wait!" Dude said, chuckling and holding up a placating hand. "Hold on, now, old timer. You be careful with that thing. It's liable to go off!"

"That old bugger is crazy!" intoned Utah in a high-pitched nasally voice that sounded almost a squeal.

"You lower that shotgun, you old devil!" Thorn ordered, pointing a threatening finger at the man.

"I'll lower this shotgun after you're off my land," Rasmus returned. "And not before!"

The outlaws' horses shifted nervously. The killers stared at the big Norwegian, who stared back at them from over the double bores of Astrid, whose hammers he cocked, each in turn. Fay could hear the ratcheting clicks even inside the cabin.

The outlaws were angry. Their eyes were hard, cheeks flushed.

Oh, no, Fay thought. He's pushed them too far. They can't ride away now.

But she was as amazed as she was relieved when Dude said, "All right, all right—we're goin', old-timer. Don't have a fit over it. We were just askin' if you seen them two, is all."

"Old fool!" barked the temperamental Thorn.

"That ain't no way to treat visitors, old man," remonstrated Utah.

McCallister narrowed his little eyes, his plump cheeks sunset red, and said, "Someday you're gonna point that shotgun at the wrong fellas, and they're gonna take that gun away from you and--"

"But first they'll have to get it away from me!" Rasmus bellowed back at them, taking another enraged step forward. He appeared so angry, Fay almost thought he'd leap out of his boots.

Inwardly, she cursed.

Just let them go, Rasmus. Just let them go.

"Come on, fellas," Dude said, reining his horse

around. "We got bigger fish to fry than this old square-head!"

He booted his horse back the way they'd come. One by one, the others turned their glaring eyes from the big Norwegian and booted their own mounts after Dude. McAllister was the last to ride away. He did so while glaring over his shoulder at Rasmus and extending a threatening finger.

Fay held her breath until the five outlaws had ridden out of sight. Then she released it and drew another...another...and another.

They were gone. Thank god.

Rasmus walked back into the cabin. He was grinning like the boy who'd just beat up the schoolyard bully.

"See?" The old Norwegian laughed his thundering laugh. "They didn't want no part of my big, ugly hide. No part of dear Astrid, either. Hah!"

"Oh, Rasmus, you could have got yourself killed!" Hilda had risen from her chair and hurried to the door. Now, glancing cautiously out over the stoop, as if making sure the killers were really gone, she closed the door slowly, latched it quietly, and pressed her back against it.

She ran her sleeve across her wrinkled forehead. "Uftah, Louie—I was worried!"

Rasmus towered over her, placing Astrid back

in her pegs over the door. "What were you worried about, Momma?"

Hilda bunched her lips angrily, drew her thin arm back, then shot it forward, ramming her clenched fist into her husband's belly. She wanted it to look like a serious blow, but Fay knew it hadn't been. Rasmus drew his arms back down, laughing, placing his hands on her forearms, trying to pull her toward him.

Hilda narrowed an eye as she glowered up at him. "You could've got yourself kilt, you big old blowhard Norski devil!"

"Well, I didn't, Momma, I didn't." Rasmus wrapped an arm around her, drew her against him, and pecked the top of her head. "They turned tail, just like I knew they'd do. They were no match for me. By Charlie, I fought the Gros Ventre!"

He looked at Fay and Evans. Fay wondered if her face was as pale as the doctor's. "Did you see them run? They took one look at Astrid there, and oh boy, they remembered they needed to be somewhere else fast!"

Still laughing and crowing, Rasmus pecked his brooding wife's cheek. She gave him another swat, then he and Hilda returned to their places at the table.

Fay stared down at her plate. She'd eaten only

half of her food. While it was delicious, she didn't think she could eat another bite. She'd suddenly lost her appetite. In fact, what she'd already eaten sat like a lead weight in her stomach.

Evans similarly stared at his own plate.

Fay was about to pick up her fork again and try another mouthful, when a low rumble sounded outside. She looked straight across the table at Evans. He stared back at her, his eyes turning bright and glossy behind his glasses.

The rumbling grew louder. This time it was coming from the cabin's north side, to her right.

The hoof thuds grew louder and louder until Fay could feel their reverberations through the floor beneath her feet.

"What now?" Hilda said in exasperation.

Fay sucked a breath when all five outlaws reappeared, galloping around the cabin's front corner and into the yard before her. They swung their mounts away to face the cabin, in roughly the same spot where they'd been before. Dude and Thorn were again in the lead, with Utah, McCallister, and Mort Gunther flanking them.

They blinked in the swirling dust, the upper halves of their faces shaded by their hat brims.

Rasmus cursed loudly in Norwegian and slapped the table. He threw his napkin down and rose from his chair.

"Rasmus!"

"Stay there, Momma. Stay right there!" He reached up and pulled Astrid down from her pegs. "I'll be right back!"

"No," Fay said under her breath, staring in horror through the window. "No, no, no—don't go out there!"

But then she saw the big man stomp down the porch steps, again holding the shotgun high across his chest.

"We seen Carlos's strawberry in the corral, you old bugger!" Dude yelled. "We know the saw-bones and the purty sheriff's wife is here!"

"I told you to get off my land and stay off!" Rasmus bellowed, raising Astrid to his shoulder. "Now there's gonna be hell to pay!"

Before he could get the shotgun leveled, Dude's right hand moved. His revolver glinted in the sunlight.

It flashed a quarter-second before the flat bark reached Fay's ears. She jerked in her chair as though the bullet had struck her. Rasmus jerked, as well, stopping in his tracks about half-way between the stoop and the killers.

They'd all drawn their pistols now.

Thorn extended his six-shooter at Rasmus, narrowed his right eye as he aimed down the barrel, and fired.

Again, Rasmus jerked. He took a halting step backward, Astrid sagging in his hands.

It was as though the killers were taking turns, because Scrim McCallister fired next, then Mort Gunther.

Rasmus howled as bullets punched into his chest. He twisted around, giving his back to the killers, and began staggering toward the cabin. Astrid dropped from his hand.

Fay stared in horror at the blood staining Rasmus's white shirt between his suspenders.

Now it was Utah's turn.

He'd been grinning, holding his pistol barrel-up in front of his face.

He extended it before him, narrowed an eye as he aimed down the barrel. The pistol bucked and roared, orange flames lapping toward Rasmus, who fell forward as though he'd been pushed hard from behind.

"Rasmus!" Hilda screamed.

She'd bounded out of her chair after the first gun blast.

Fay saw her dash across the porch and into her own lead storm, all the outlaws firing at her at the same time. She'd managed to get about three feet from where Rasmus lay writhing on the ground in front of the porch before the first bullets cut into her, making her jerk and shake as though she'd been struck by lightning.

She'd started to crouch over her husband, but the bullets picked her up and threw her backward, twisting her around and throwing her little, spindly, blood-soaked, lifeless body onto the porch.

Grinning evilly, Dude triggered one more bullet into Hilda's back, making her body jerk once more.

Then his eyes, as did those of the other killers, shifted to the cabin.

"Come on!" It was Evans.

Fay had been so shocked and horrified by the killing of Rasmus and Hilda, she hadn't been aware of the doctor moving around the table to stand beside her, tugging on her arm. "Fay, get up. We have to get out of here!"

"Come out, come out, wherever you are!" Dude taunted.

He was still sitting on his horse, as were the others, their beady eyes riveted on the cabin.

"Don't make us come in there," Thorn yelled. "Get your asses out here now!"

Fay climbed to her feet. She felt drunk with anxiety. As Evans pulled her away from the table, she tripped over Hilda's chair. She groaned and dropped to a knee. Evans pulled her to her feet and led her out of the kitchen and into the parlor.

Fay glanced at the front door. It was nearly closed. She vaguely remembered Hilda had jerked it open so violently it had bounced off the wall and swung back into its frame.

"We're done, Doc," Fay said numbly as Evans, who limped and hopped on his bad leg, led her quickly through the curtained doorway at the rear of the parlor. "We're finished. It's over…"

As she followed the doctor into the rear bedroom, the curtain jostled back into place behind her. She shuddered when she heard one of the killers curse loudly. Boots pounded on the stoop.

They were coming in…

"Is there a back door?" Fay asked, looking around the small room that had been built onto the rear of the cabin probably after one of the Stryk sons had been born and more room had been needed.

"No back door." Wincing, Evans had dropped to his knees and was pulling up the braided hemp rug lying on the floor to one side of the small, rumpled bed. "But there is a cellar. It's a chance. Not much of one. But there's a chance they won't find us here…"

As boots stomped around the cabin and the men cursed and called for them, Evans pulled at the iron ring attached to the trap door lying flush with the floor. He grunted. The door rose slightly, thumped back down in its frame.

"Help me!"

Fay dropped to her knees, poked two fingers through the ring. She and the doctor tugged together. The door rose up out of the floor.

They rose with it, straightening their legs, the doctor cursing and groaning against the pain in his wounded calf. The black hole yawned up at them, rife with the smell of earth and cold stone.

The cellar appeared only five or so feet deep. It looked like a shallow grave. There was nothing in it but one moldy onion.

Boots thudded beyond the curtained doorway. They were growing louder fast.

One of the killers stomped toward the bedroom.

"Go, Doc—hurry!" Fay shoved Evans toward the hole.

He dropped his legs into it. "You, too!"

"No time! Go, go, go!"

Chapter 21

Evans dropped into the grave-like hole. He landed with a thud and a shrill groan.

Boots thudded mere feet away from the curtain.

Fay gasped. She and the doctor were seconds away from being discovered.

Dude used the barrel of his Colt .44 to slide the curtain back. He took one step into the room and stopped. He looked around. The room was maybe ten by ten. A small bed lay to the right. To the left was a zinc-topped washstand with a bowl and a pitcher. Beside the stand was a ladder-back chair. A bear skin hung on the wall over the stand. On the floor was a rug.

Dude grimaced with deep frustration. If either of his quarry had ever been in this room, they were gone now.

He swung around and pushed back out

through the curtain.

Fay scrambled out from beneath the bed. Thank god he hadn't looked under there!

She drew back the rug, which she'd quickly flattened over the door just before Dude had stepped into the room. She grunted as she jerked up the trap door.

"Comin', Doc!" she whispered, hearing the outlaws tromping around the cabin, loudly arguing and cursing. It would be only a matter of minutes before another one, giving the cabin a more thorough scouring, investigated this room.

She dragged the rug up over the door, and holding the edge of the door and the rug with one hand, dropped into the hole.

"How in the hell did he not find you?" Evans asked, whispering beside her.

"He didn't think to look under the bed." Standing up in the hole, her head just above the level of the floor and holding the very edge of the door and the rug with both hands, she lowered both the rug and the door over her, wincing, hoping the rug remained in place when she released it. It the rug didn't at least appear to be in a similar position to when Dude had seen it a minute ago, her...and Evans's...goose was cooked.

When the door was only a couple of inches above the floor, using the very tips of her first two fingers, Fay slid the rug a couple of inches from the door. Through the crack, she watched it slide out over the floor. It didn't slide much, but a little. She released the door, and it gave a light thump as it settled into its frame.

Of course, she had no idea how the rug looked now. It probably lay crooked. She hoped that at the very least it concealed the door.

Otherwise, they had no chance at all...

She sat on her butt in the hole, knees drawn to her chest. She couldn't see Evans. It was too dark to see her hand in front of her face. But she could hear the doctor breathing beside her, just off her right shoulder.

Both were so terrified, they didn't say anything.

Above them, the cabin rumbled with harsh foot falls. Fay heard the gang's muffled voices as they argued. Two or three must be looking around outside, because she thought she was hearing only two sets of frenetic footsteps now.

Maybe we're in the clear, she thought. Maybe they'll go away.

Probably not.

They'd clung to her and Evans's trail this long. Why would they give up now?

It must be very important to at least the majority of them that she and Evans be found and killed, so they didn't identify the killers. Probably, to them, it was a matter of their own living or dying. Or being hounded by lawmen and bounty hunters for the rest of their days, always looking over their shoulders...

Evans grunted. He was moving around a little, his breathing growing a little more strained. There came a scratching sound. A match flared to life. Fay saw the flickering flame and smell the rotten egg-like odor of sulfur.

"What're you doing, Doc?"

"Just thought I'd take a little look arou..." Turning, he let his voice trail off. "And I'm glad I did."

"Huh?"

"Look there."

She peered over her right shoulder, toward the match's flickering flame. She could see nothing but shadows. She smelled something, however. Not only the doctor's lucifer. She was smelling smoke.

She lifted her nose toward the door above her head. The smoke grew in intensity. She also smelled kerosene.

A frigid hand of mind-numbing horror spread its tendril-like fingers across her back.

"Oh, my god," she trilled. She snapped her head toward Evans. "Doc! I think...I think..."

Evans had smelled it to. He'd turned toward her, his eyes and his glasses, which reflected the flame's dying light, lifted to the door through which tendrils of smoke now oozed.

"They're burning the cabin," he finished for her.

Panicked, she jerked her hands at the door. "We have to get out of here, Doc. We don't want to burn up in--"

The match blinked out. Evans cursed as it burned his fingers. He grabbed Fay's arm, squeezed. "No, no. Hold on."

"What is it?"

"I'll show you."

Another scratching sound. Another match flared, spreading a weak light around the hole, gently pushing back the stubborn shadows.

Fay's heart raced as images of burning alive in this musty grave swept through her brain, stirring her to panic.

"Look," Evans said.

"At what, Doc?"

"There." Evans crawled away from her, toward what above would be the bedroom's rear wall. Holding the match ahead of him, he glanced back at Fay. "The hole seems to extend out beneath the rear of the cabin."

"So…it's a big hole…?" More smoke began sifting through cracks around the door.

"Might be a tunnel."

"What?"

"Follow me."

"A tunnel to where?"

"We won't know until we've investigated it. Follow me."

Fay turned on her hands and knees and crawled after him, wincing as small pebbles bit into the heels of her hands, into her knees. She glanced behind her, expecting to see flames licking through the trapdoor.

She was so anxious, her arms and legs were as stiff as boards. She knew it was a trick of her panic, but she thought the hole was growing closer and closer around her, closing in on her. She fought the urge to scream and to bolt back to the door.

Only by sheer force of will did she manage to move her arms and legs enough to keep within a few feet of the doctor's half-boots. At the same time, she believed she and the sawbones were going to suffocate as soon as smoke filled up the hole.

She also kept thinking that soon the doctor's feet would stop moving. Soon, he would reach the end of the hole. So far, however, that did not happen. The farther he crawled, her right behind him, the more her fear eased the pressure inside her, the more her curiosity grew.

Where were they going? Where did the tunnel lead?

It had to come to an end sometime. When it did, would it have an exit?

Evans had lit several matches, lighting their way. Then he stopped lighting them. She didn't know if he'd just run out of lucifers, or if he'd just decided to continue crawling in the dark, by feel...

"What is this, Doc?" she said just behind him, breathless, fighting panic, wincing as a sharp chunk of gravel ground into her right knee.

As he crawled, breathing hard, Evan said, "Remember Rasmus talking about his old trouble with the Indians? The Gros Ventres?"

"Yes."

Suddenly he stopped crawling. Fay overtook his feet, then backed off a little.

She could tell he was looking back at her, because when he spoke again, his voice was clearer. "I'm betting this is an escape tunnel he and his sons dug, in case the Indians burned the cabin."

"Like Dude and the other killers are doing right now."

"Exactly. It was a common practice back in the old days, during the time of the Indian trouble.

I've heard of many early settlers outwitting the redskins by escaping through tunnels like this one. Nowadays, they mostly use the tunnels for food storage in the winter."

"If it's an escape tunnel," Fay said, hope rising in her, "then it has to have a back door—right?"

"Yes."

"When do you suppose we'll come to it?"

"We have."

"What?"

Evans grunted. He groaned. Grunted again. There was a slight raking sound.

"What're you doing, Doc?" Fay asked, her impatience growing.

"Trying to open the door." Evans was breathless. "Come up here. Help me."

Fay crawled forward. When her forehead pressed against what felt like his hip, she rose to a kneeling position.

"Raise your hands," he said.

She did.

"Can you feel the door?"

"Yes!" She felt wooden slats pressed against her open hands.

"Brush has probably grown over it. Wait till I count to three then push...hard!"

"Okay."

"One...two...three!"

They both grunted and groaned, pushing with all their strength against the door. Fay heard a creaking, tearing sound as the door began to rise through overgrown sod.

"Ohh!" Fay said, her strength giving out on her.

Evans's did, as well. He blew out a held breath.

Raking air in and out of her lungs, Fay dropped her hands and knees. "It's just too solid, Doc!"

"I know, dammit. I know."

"What if we can't get it open?" Again, fear threatened to overwhelm her.

"We have to."

Evans groaned again as he pressed his hands against the door. Fay couldn't see him in the darkness, but she could hear him, hear the creaking of the wood.

She raised her own hands, pressed their heels firmly against the door, and, pushing up from her knees, put every ounce of her strength against the wood, hearing again the soft tearing sounds of the grass.

A little light began to seep in around the sides of the door, so that she could see Evans's silhouette beside her, pushing up against the door, his teeth making a white line between his stretched lips.

Suddenly, the door flew up away from them.

Fay had been grinding her hands against it, and

then she was pushing only air, lurching upward, as did Evans, propelled by their own momentum as the force pushing against them disappeared.

Fay froze with her hands above her head, staring up out of the tunnel. Sunlight slashed her eyes like bayonets.

She'd glimpsed a man's dark, broad-shouldered figure kneeling before her. As dread began to temper the sudden disorientation she'd felt when the door had disappeared, she heard the unmistakable click of a gun being cocked.

Oh, god—the killers had found them, after all!

The man before her shoved a big cocked Colt toward Evans. He pressed the barrel of the revolver against the doctor's forehead.

Shielding her eyes from the blazing sunlight, Fay squinted up at him. Surely, she must be dreaming.

She blinked, looked again, saw the blue eyes beneath the Stetson, the brushy salt-and-pepper mustache mantling the wide, familiar mouth she'd kissed a thousand times and couldn't wait to kiss again.

No, she was not dreaming.

Her heart ballooned.

"Oh, my god!" she screamed, steepling her fingers before her. "Ben!"

Chapter 22

Keeping his Colt pressed against the forehead of the man in the hole, Stillman slid his gaze to the woman who had just screamed his name.

He froze, his lower jaw dropping in astonishment.

His wife's large brown eyes gazed up at him from around the hand she was holding to shield the sunlight angling into the hole from over Stillman's left shoulder. She was smiling in mute disbelief and rarefied delight. Tears welled in her eyes.

"Fay...?"

"Umm." This from Evans, who stood with his hands raised, palms out, as Stillman continued to hold the Colt against the sawbones' forehead. The doctor used his right hand to nudge the gun away from his head.

The lawman looked at his old friend. "Doc!"

He pulled the gun back, chuckling. "Sorry, Doc. My god! What...?"

He holstered the Colt, then extended his right hand to Evans. The doctor took his hand and, stepping back and setting his feet, the lawman pulled the doctor out of the hole. Laughing, feeling giddy at this unexpected surprise, Stillman gave the man a brusque hug then extended his hand to his wife and pulled her easily up out of the hole and into his arms.

He wrapped his arms around her, squeezed her tight. He didn't know what to say. There were no words for the relief he felt.

Fay wrapped her arms around his neck, hugging him almost savagely. He felt her shuddering as she sobbed.

"My god," he muttered. "My god."

"Oh, Ben."

"Are you all right, honey?" Stillman slid a lock of hair back from her cheek, and looked her over.

She nodded, smiling, tears of joy dribbling down her cheeks.

He spun her around, holding her, delighting in the thudding of her heart against his own. He wished he'd never have to release her.

"How did you find us?" she asked, smiling up at him. "Oh, dear god...not that I'm complaining, mind you—but how did you ever find us, Ben?"

"I heard gunfire, saw the smoke." That was enough of an explanation for now. Suddenly, the burning cabin...the killers...the pressing problems at hand came rushing back at him through the fog of his unexpected joy and relief at finding his wife and friend alive.

He took Fay's hand and led her behind a willow bush that would screen them from view from the ranch yard. The burning cabin lay about sixty yards away.

They were facing the back of the cabin as well as the privy and the woodshed, both only twenty feet away. The barn and corrals were to the right. Horses were running in circles around inside one of the corrals, whinnying in terror at the smoke and flames churning skyward from the burning cabin.

Stillman had heard gunfire roughly a half hour ago, and had raced here to find the cabin on fire. He'd been about to run to the cabin, fearing Fay and Evans might have been trapped inside, when he'd heard a strange sound coming from the ground near where he'd been crouching, staring in horror at the flames, somehow knowing Dutch's men had set the cabin ablaze.

Following the curious sounds, Stillman had found the trapdoor nearly buried under a tangle of sod and brush. By pure luck, he'd opened the door to find his wife and the doctor squinting up at him. Stillman had never been a man who believed in miracles, but maybe he was one now.

He glanced at Fay on one knee beside him. "Are you sure you're all right? They didn't hurt you, honey?"

Fay nodded as she stared, wide-eyed, at the cabin. "I'm fine. Just tired. Terrified." She cupped a hand to her mouth, and tears welled in her eyes. "Oh, god—look what they've done."

She sobbed.

Stillman turned to Evans, who knelt behind them. The doctor had found a branch to lean on. "How 'bout you, Doc? You all right?"

"Never better, Ben," Evans said, his voice toneless, ironic. He gave a weak half-smile then returned his own anxious gaze to the cabin.

"Anyone else inside?" Stillman asked Fay.

"No." She shook her head. "They're both outside. Rasmus and Hilda. Those men shot them down like dogs, Ben. Just shot them like they were rabid dogs when all they did was give me and the doc shelter. They're dead because they helped us!"

Again, she placed her hand over her mouth, trying to control the emotion rolling out of her.

Stillman stared at the cabin, not seeing anything but the flames and the smoke. There didn't seem to be any movement in the yard, but he couldn't see the front of the cabin. If Dutch's men were still there, they were staying out of sight.

He turned to Fay again. "What was that hole you crawled out of?"

"An escape tunnel," Evans said. "The Stryk's must have dug it when the Gros Ventre were running off their leashes."

Stillman heaved a relieved sigh, smiling at the doctor and then again at his wife, squeezing her hand. "I sure am glad they did."

"Oh, Ben!" Fay leaned into him, wrapped her arms around him again, pressed her head against his shoulder. "I just want to go home. I want to see little Ben!"

"I'll get you to Big Sandy, honey. We'll put you on the train."

Fay frowned up at him. "What about you?"

"I'm gonna come back for them." Stillman slid his hard, angry eyes at the cabin. "Those killers aren't getting away with this. Not any of it."

"There's five of 'em, Ben," Evans said, wrinkling his nostrils distastefully. "Five of the nastiest snakes I've ever encountered. Six, if Dutch is still alive."

"Dutch is dead," Stillman said. "But I have his horse. Both mounts are in a creek bed to the north. Not far." He heaved himself to his feet and extended his hand to Fay again. "Come on, honey—let's you get you two out of here."

Fay accepted his hand and rose to her feet.

"Come on, Doc." Stillman noticed the man had a bad leg. "Put your arm around me. Let me help."

Evans wrapped his arm around Stillman, clamping his hand over the lawman's right shoulder, taking some of the weight off his own right leg. As Stillman led him and Fay to the north, their feet crunching dry brown grass, the lawman glanced at Evans grunting along beside him. "What happened, Doc?"

"Took a bullet in my calf. It's nothing, though, Ben. Pain means nothing to me." The doctor smiled ironically at Stillman. "Pain and I are old friends."

Walking along beside them, Fay snorted a caustic laugh.

Stillman laughed, as well. "That's good, Doc. It's good to hear pain an' you get along so well."

"We're on a first-name basis—pain' an' me."

They reached the creek a few minutes later. The sandy bed was mostly dry, with a thin stream of water trickling down its middle. The creek lay down a few feet beneath a cutbank.

Sweets and Dutch's zebra dun were where Stillman had left them—tied to a bald, sun-bleached part of a cottonwood extending from the bank into the creek bed. The lawman had saddled and led the dun for the same reason he'd rented the two livery mounts in Clantick—to cover more ground faster.

He'd left Dutch in the cave in which they'd sought shelter from the storm, deeming the cavern as good a final resting place as Dutch deserved. At least, it was as good a grave as Dutch was going to get, for after the storm had passed, Stillman had wanted to get quickly back to scouring the hills for his wife and friend.

The storm having undoubtedly wiped out all sign—which he had quickly discovered it had—he'd needed to cover a lot of ground fast.

Fortunately, he'd picked up the trail of the five killers a couple of hours after leaving the cave, and it had been those tracks that had led him to the Stryk ranch.

Now he was doubly glad he'd taken the zebra.

He untied the horse's reins from the cottonwood.

"Doc, you climb up on the dun's back. Fay will ride with me. Come on, Doc—easy does it," he said, as he helped the doctor into the saddle.

When Evans was mounted, Stillman turned to Fay. "Come on, honey."

He took her hand and led her down off the cutbank and over to his bay.

A shrill rattling sound rose cut through the warm afternoon air.

"Whoa!" Evans said, jerking back on the suddenly skittish dun's reins. "Snake, Ben—snake!"

Stillman whipped around. The snake must have been sunning itself on a rock near the water. Now the sand rattler was tightly coiled, flicking its button tail and aiming its flat, diamond-shaped head at Evans and the dun.

Stillman's Colt was instantly in his hand, leaping and roaring twice...three times. The first bullet had missed the snake, falling a little short, pluming sand. The second had only nicked the viper. The second one had cut it into two bloody halves, the tail still quivering, its jaws still working, biting at the rock it had fallen on.

Stillman stared out over his Colt's long, smoking barrel at the snake. The echoes of all three reports were still hammering skyward, dwindling. They echoed loudest of all inside Stillman's head.

For he knew the implication.

He cursed and turned toward the ranch. He couldn't see the cabin from this vantage, only black smoke still roiling into the air.

Fay stared at him. Reading his mind, she slapped her hand over her mouth. Her eyes glittered with renewed terror. "Do you think they heard?"

Stillman whipped around. Holding the Colt down low against his leg, he stepped back up onto the cutbank.

He cursed louder when he saw five horseback riders galloping toward him, coming around the west side of the horse corral then making a bee-line to the creek.

"I'll take that as a yes," Evans dryly quipped.

Stillman leaped back into the creek bed. He grabbed Fay around the waist and hoisted her up onto Sweets's back.

She gave a shriek of surprise.

Stillman shoved the bay's reins at her, then slid his Henry from the saddle boot. "You an' the doc hightail it downstream along the creek. Follow it along the base of the mountain. When you come to a tributary, follow that tributary northwest. If I don't catch up to you, that tributary will take you to Big Sandy. Ride and don't stop riding!"

"Ben, no!" Tears streamed down Fay's cheeks.

Enraged and terrified, Stillman leaned forward at the waist, squinting his blue eyes at his wife. "Dammit woman, you do as I say for once in your life, and you do it now—you understand me?" He'd fairly bellowed the words.

Fay choked out another sob, keeping her eyes, swimming in tears, on her husband.

Stillman looked commandingly at Evans.

"Come on, Fay." The doctor booted his horse along the creek bed. "He'll be along soon. You know him. He's too damned contrary to get killed!"

Fay looked once more at her husband, her tear-streaked cheeks red with anger. "Damn you!" Then she reined Sweets around and batted her heels against the bay's ribs.

Stillman ran back to the cutbank. Standing in the creek bed, the bank before him, he stared over the bank toward the burning cabin.

The five killers were closing on him, forming a wedge, two men at the point of the wedge, the other three spread out a little behind. They came at him hard, wind buffeting their hat brims. They'd heard his gunfire and they'd probably seen Fay and Evans ride off on the two horses.

All that lay between his wife and friend and those five proven killers was Stillman himself. Five against one. He had to make his bullets count.

Holding the Henry across his chest, one hand on the cocking lever, he stared at the fast-approaching killers. Anger was a bronco stallion bucking inside him. Those five cutthroats had incurred his wrath, and now they were about feel the full brunt of it.

He stepped up onto the cutbank.

"There!" the lead rider shouted, pointing at Stillman then pulling a pistol from one of the two holsters on his hips. As he drew closer, Stillman saw two scratch marks on his left cheek.

Dude was the one Dutch had told him had gone after Fay, and he wore those two scratches as a testament to his sins. The one galloping along beside him had long, nearly white hair.

Stillman racked a cartridge into the Henry's action. He dropped to a knee, raised the Henry, pressed the butt plate against his shoulder, and aimed.

"Whoa!" Dude yelled, seeing Stillman drawing a bead on him.

He jerked back on his horse's reins as the Henry spoke.

Dude yelled and went flying off his gelding's back, turning in midair to hit the ground on his belly then rolling off to Stillman's left.

Stillman ejected the spent cartridge over his right shoulder, pressed the rifle to his shoulder again, and slid the barrel at the white-haired man who crouched low in his saddle, sort of using his horse's head as a shield.

Stillman hated to do it, but he'd have to shoot the horse.

He aimed at the horse's chest, and fired.

The bullet missed the horse and plunked into

White Hair's left thigh. White Hair grimaced against the pain, then batted his heels even harder against his horse's ribs, spurring the mount mercilessly. He aimed his pistol over his horse's head, and fired—smoke and flames blossoming from the barrel.

The bullet flew over Stillman's head to screech off a rock behind him.

Stillman raised the Henry again, then drew it back down. He didn't have time to take another shot. White Hair was only ten feet away from him, intending to run him over, the eyes of his frightened but hard-charging horse appearing to Stillman as large as two chocolate-brown dinner plates.

Chapter 23

Without a second to spare, Stillman threw himself to the right as White Hair and his hard-charging horse leaped off the cutbank and into the creek bed, swooping through the air where Stillman had been standing less than an eye blink before.

At the same time, yelling like a wounded coyote, White Hair triggered another shot at the lawman. The bullet flew far afield as Stillman hit the gravelly bed of the ravine and rolled.

Sitting up, raising the Henry again, he turned to where White Hair was neck-reining his horse around sharply, bellowing and lifting his pistol toward Stillman. The lawman levered a fresh cartridge into the rifle's chamber, aimed quickly, and fired. That shot missed, for White Hair's horse was still turning, and Stillman's right shoulder ached where it had been introduced to the gravelly creek bed.

White Hair triggered another round at Stillman. The bullet warmed the air off the lawman's left ear. Stillman levered another round, and fired two more times.

Both bullets plowed into White Hair's chest, throwing him straight backward over the angrily arched tail of his horse. The horse gave the man an added kick as it lunged off its rear hooves, and bolted on down the creek bed past Stillman, splashing through the water wending through the middle of the cut.

Guns barked behind the sheriff. Two bullets tore into the lip of the cutbank, only inches away from their target. Stillman drew his head down, swept a wing of salt-and-pepper hair from his right eye, then rammed another cartridge into the Henry's chamber. He had his back to the bank, but now, bringing the Henry across his body from right to left, he edged a peek over the lip.

Two men ran toward him, crouching. Thirty feet away and roughly twenty feet apart, one of them was big and fleshy, the other tall and lean and with dark eyes set close against a hawk-like nose. A third man, short and stocky, moved more slowly behind them, crouched over the Winchester in his hands.

Stillman thrust the Henry up over the cutbank, resting the barrel on the grassy lip.

"There he is!" the largest of his stalkers shouted, dropping to a knee and raising the rifle in his hands.

The Henry roared.

The bullet punched through the big man's left shoulder, knocking him back. He grimaced, groaning loudly. His rifle sagged in his hands.

While the other two yelled and dropped to the ground, Stillman ejected the spent round from the Henry's action, drew a hasty bead on the big man again, and drilled the next round through the middle of the man's broad forehead.

Blood spewed out the back of the man's head.

He grunted and sagged backward over his boot heels. He dropped his rifle and threw both arms out to his sides, sort of sagging there against his heels before rolling slowly to one side and dropping to the ground.

Stillman pulled his head down beneath the lip of the cut just before two more whistlers caromed toward him, one spanging off a near stone to his right, the other slapping into the stream behind him. He aimed at the nearest man, hunkered down behind a low hummock extending his own rifle in Stillman's direction.

Sensing another bullet was about twang toward him, Stillman pulled his head down.

The killer's rifle barked. The bullet tore into

the lip of the cut where Stillman's head had just been.

He put his head there again, extending the Henry, and fired at the man behind the hummock as the man raised his own rifle to cock it. The lawman fired two more times, watching his bullets tear up the sod of the hummock. One smashed into the rifle with a clanking thud.

The man threw the rifle into the air, screamed, and huddled low against the ground, wailing.

Stillman pulled his head down again as the stocky gent flung two rounds at him, both sailing wide and plunking into trees on the other side of the creek behind him. Pressing his back to the embankment, the sheriff quickly opened the Henry's loading tube and dropped several shells into it, replacing the ones he'd fired.

Clicking the steel lock into place beneath the barrel, he turned to his left and crawled along the base of the cutbank, heading downstream.

The stocky gent continued firing lead at him. The bullets tore into the sod at the lip of the cut or splashed into the creek. A couple screeched on over the creek bed to crack into pines on the other side.

The man didn't know where Stillman was.

Good.

Intending to work around him, Stillman kept

crawling until he'd gone maybe fifty yards from his starting point. The man he'd just shot was still yowling. He must have rolled onto his back, because Stillman could hear him more clearly bellowing, "Kill him, Scrim! Kill that devil! He kilt Utah an' he done kilt me, the son of a two-cent whore! I'm bleedin' like crazy over here!"

"Shut up, Mort!" the stocky gent returned from farther away.

"Kill him!"

"I said shut up!" Scrim screeched.

Stillman edged a look up over the bank.

The third man, Scrim, had begun backing toward the burning cabin. His horse stood beyond him, near the outhouse and woodshed, reins hanging, staring at the man backing toward him. Scrim pumped cartridges into his carbine's action and fired sporadically as he made his slow, desperate way to his horse.

He was trying to get out of the nasty situation he'd found himself in—on the trail of Fay and the doctor but unexpectedly running afoul of Stillman. He hadn't counted on that. He also hadn't counted on being the last survivor of his five-man pack of blood-thirsty wolves.

He was scared.

He should be.

Stillman stepped up onto the bank, dropped

to a knee, aimed the Henry, and fired. Scrim had just seen him and had started swinging his rifle toward him. Stillman's bullet tore into the man's left knee.

Scrim yelped and leaped back on his still-healthy right leg.

Then he fell.

"No!" he cried.

Stillman rose and started walking to the fallen killer. He held the Henry with his right hand wrapped around the brass breech. He strode purposefully, flames of fury still burning in his chest. Blood boiled in his veins.

Scrim looked over his shoulder at the lawman stomping to him, then rose to his hands and knees and crawled for his horse. He gained his feet and began dragging his bad leg toward the mount that was edging warily back away from him.

Stillman raised the Henry, aimed, and fired.

He watched in satisfaction as his bullet hammered into Scrim's left calf.

Scrim screamed as he dropped to both knees and rolled onto his back.

He sat up and turned his pudgy face to Stillman. The man's brown eyes were wide, round, and glassy with terror. He had a week's worth of red beard stubble on his jaws. "No!" he cried when he saw Stillman striding in his direction again.

He scuttled back on his butt.

He only made it a couple of feet. His horse had run off by now, anyway, so there was nowhere for him to go.

Stillman drew up to within six feet of the man and raised the Henry.

"It's gonna be a real pleasure killin' you, my friend," he said, his face implacable, his blue eyes as cold as death. "You held up the wrong damn stagecoach!"

"No, wait!" The man's eyes opened even wider as he continued inching backwards on his butt, both legs leaving bloody smears on the blond grass beneath him.

Stillman cocked the Henry.

"I got rights!"

"Yes, you do." Stillman drilled the man through his belly. "You got the right to die slow, howling, you son of a bitch!"

That's just what Scrim did. Lying on his back, cupping both hands to his bullet-plundered midsection, he squalled like a gut-shot coyote, loosing his shrill cries into the clear, bright, Montana sky.

Too late, Stillman spied movement off the far corner of the privy, which stood maybe thirty feet to his left and a little ahead of him.

A pistol flashed and roared. The bullet burned across his left side. Stillman swung the Henry toward the outhouse. The man who'd fired the pistol pulled it and as his head behind the privy wall.

"Dude," Stillman said through gritted teeth. He triggered the Henry from his right hip, grimacing against the pain in his side.

The Henry bucked and caterwauled as Stillman fired, levered, fired again, again…again. He watched his .44-caliber rounds fairly honeycomb the rickety wooden structure, letting daylight all the way through it.

Beneath the rifle's roar, a man screamed. The scream rose again as Stillman continued flinging lead at the privy.

As the Henry's hammer clicked, signifying Stillman had emptied the magazine, Dude stumbled out from behind the bullet-riddled structure. He ran, stumbling over his boot toes, to Stillman's left, crying. He was more dead than not, bleeding from a good half-dozen wounds all over his body.

He didn't run far, maybe twenty feet. Then his knees buckled and he dropped, kneeling there, facing away from Stillman.

The lawman brushed his hand across his side.

Just a burn. It hurt, but it wasn't much. He'd allowed his rage to distract him; he'd let his guard down.

He walked over to where Dude still knelt as though in prayer, though the man's bloody arms and hands hung straight down against his sides. Stillman walked around and stopped in front of him, his shadow angling across him.

He saw the scratch marks on the man's face.

"You bastard!" Stillman wound up and drove his right fist against the man's face.

Besides the smack against the man's flesh, Dude didn't make another sound. He fell to one side then, with a ragged sigh, blood oozing over his bottom lip, he rolled onto his back and stared up at Stillman, his chest rising and falling slowly as he breathed his last breaths.

Stillman bent over him, his jaws hard, flames of fury fairly leaping from his eyes. "You're dead, Dude. You messed with my wife and my friend, and you're dead because of it!"

Dude's heavy-lidded eyes stared up at the enraged lawman. His features slackened as the wings of death swooped over him.

"Ah, hell," Dude said. "All that money...fer nothin'..."

The money.

"Where is it?" Stillman asked, glancing around,

expecting to see one of the horses packing the loot from the stage.

Dude stared up at him. "Dutch…has it…the old bastard…"

Stillman frowned. "Dutch?"

Then he realized that while Dude still stared up at him, he was no longer seeing him. The killer's eyes had gone opaque in death.

Scrim still howled where he sat, holding his guts, but his complaints had been growing steadily weaker.

Stillman straightened, stared into the distance for a time, pensive. Then his mouth corners quirked a devious grin. "Dutch," he grunted. "You old devil."

What had Dutch done with the money?

Hoof thuds rose to Stillman's left.

He whipped around, raising the Henry as he momentarily forgot the rifle was empty. He lowered it again, cursed.

Fay trotted to him atop Sweets, heading up from the creek. The doctor rode along behind her, keeping the dun at a walk, following from a meek twenty or thirty feet back. The doctor looked sheepish; Fay stared at Stillman, her brown eyes cast with worry, her lips stubbornly compressed.

She glanced at Dude and at the still wailing

Scrim, then returned her gaze to her husband.

Stillman drew a deep breath. "Just couldn't do it, could you? Not even this one time."

Fay stopped Sweets before him. "Do what?" she asked with a look of mock innocence.

"Obey me even one time?"

She hiked her shoulder. "I didn't want to break my record." Her gaze went to his bloody side, and she leaped down from her saddle. "Ben, you're shot!"

Stillman glowered up at Evans. "Doc, can't you keep track of even one damned, contrary woman?"

Evans grimaced. "Obviously, Ben, not unlike yourself, I have not mastered the art."

Having inspected his wound and apparently deeming it non-life-threatening, Fay peered up at Stillman hopefully. "Are they all dead?"

Stillman laid his hand against her cheek, offered a reassuring smile. "They're all dead."

She smiled. "Can we go home? I want to see little Ben. I want to sleep in our bed again!"

"And here I thought we were having so much fun together," Evans said.

"You bet we can," Stillman told her. "I don't see any reason not to get started right away, in fact."

As he led Fay to the bay, he glanced at the sky. Big Sandy was about a day's ride. If they rode till dark tonight, they should be able to make it by noon tomorrow.

He helped Fay into the saddle, then shoved the Henry into its sheath and mounted in front of his wife.

"What about him?" Fay asked, glancing at Scrim, still sobbing and grunting.

"He'll run into St. Pete soon," Stillman said. "That'll shut him up. Come on, Doc," he called, turning Sweets back toward the creek.

"Don't worry," the doctor said. "I'm right behind you."

Stillman didn't see them, but others were behind him, too.

Phil Triber, Triber's son, Cole, and the three Milliron men had seen the smoke from the cabin and were galloping toward it.

Chapter 24

Asleep in the tall grass, Stillman waved his hand at whatever was tickling his face—a fallen leaf or a fly. The sun felt good, angling down through the trees to bathe his naked body, dry now after the swim he'd taken with his wife.

Again, the tickling sensation.

He waved his hand again, but whatever was nettling him was more persistent this time. He opened his eyes, frowning. Right away, the frown became a smile as he saw his wife, her long, damp hair framing her face, smiling down at him. Fay held a brome grass straw in her right hand.

She flicked it again playfully.

"Sorry to wake you," she said, and leaned forward to gently kiss his lips. "Getting late. Won't be long until the sun's down. Doc's probably wondering what happened to us."

Stillman placed his hand against the back of

her neck, drew her to him, and kissed her passionately, savoring the silky softness of her lips on his. When she pulled away, he said, "I got a feelin' the Doc knows exactly what's been goin' on down here."

He grinned.

They'd stopped and set up camp on a secluded, flat-topped bluff around three in the afternoon. Stillman had been too tired to keep going. Now that he no longer needed to push, he decided to stop early. They were all tired, all badly in need of rest.

Once they'd tended the horses, gathered wood for a fire, and arranged their gear, Evans settled into his bedroll on the butte and fell instantly asleep. Fay, who had investigated the area while gathering wood, had led Stillman down to a pretty little swimming hole on the creek that wrapped itself around three sides of the wooded bluff, roughly a quarter mile from the camp.

They'd undressed, made long, passionate love in the tall, soft grass along the creek bank, birds piping, squirrels chittering, and the creek muttering sweetly around them. Stillman had thought he'd be too exhausted for passion, but he'd been wrong. Seeing his wife's lovely body again, after he'd been terrified for too long that he'd never see her alive again, had made him feel twenty years younger and not so tired, after all.

When they'd finally sated their passion, they'd leaped like children into the swimming hole. They'd frolicked like young lovers playing hooky from school, swimming and splashing, chasing each other from one bank to the other, then coming together to make love again—slower, this time; longer--with Fay backed against a beaver dam, her long legs open to her husband.

Pleasantly sleepy, they'd returned to shore and slept entangled together in a sun-washed patch of grass rippling softly in the hot summer breeze. Judging by the low angle of the sun, they'd slept for a couple of hours.

Now Fay laid her head upon Stillman's broad chest and slid her open hand down his belly. "I love you, Sheriff. Thank you for rescuing us from those madmen."

"Hell, you rescued yourselves—you an' the doc. How did you find that escape hatch, anyway?"

"By accident."

"Lucky accident."

"If you hadn't come along when you did, we'd still be out there, stumbling around."

"Yeah, well, I did come along, honey." Stillman squeezed her, kissed the top of her head. He smiled, thoughtful. "Doc—he's got some sand in him, don't he?"

"Do you know what he did?"

"What?"

"Dutch wanted to kill me to get me out of the way, but Doc told him that if he did, he wouldn't tend his son. He meant it, too. If they'd killed me, he'd have made it so they'd have had to kill him, too. That's why I'm alive."

Fay lifted her head and gazed down at her husband. "I think I've misjudged him, Ben. You know—on account of his nefarious dealings with the women of Clantick. I don't think he's such a bad man, after all. He's not really as self-centered as I thought. He would have died for me."

"Hell, I could've told you that."

"I know." She smiled admiringly. "You've always defended him. I should've listened."

"Well, now you know."

She gazed into his eyes pensively for a time, her mind on Evans. Suddenly, she smiled curiously and said, "What about our son? Who's looking after him?" She arched a schoolmarmish brow. "Mrs. Finnegan, I hope."

That was who usually looked after little Ben for Fay—their rotund, red-headed Irish neighbor lady who'd long since raised her own brood and still loved tending sprouts of all shapes and sizes, and who dearly spoiled little Ben as often as she could.

Unfortunately, she'd taken ill.

"Um…" The question had caught Stillman off-guard. He didn't want to tell Fay he'd left their only son in the hands of Miss Nat Drucker and Tonya French in the Drovers Saloon in Clantick. Not that said women weren't fully capable—every bit as capable as Molly Finnegan, in fact--but Fay, being from a cultivated and well-bred family of the French persuasion, didn't consider sporting girls the right sorts of caretakers for her son.

Not even one who called herself "French."

Stillman didn't blame her for such prejudices. They were common ones amongst women-folk not of the sporting variety. Fay could be forgiven for being extra particular and protective—even overly so--when it came to her child.

However, the fact remained…

"Ben!"

Her sharp tone made him flinch. "What, honey?"

"You didn't leave little Ben with Leon, did you?"

"Oh!" Stillman laughed and pulled her head back down to his chest. "No, no, no…don't you worry about that. I learned my lesson last time!"

He'd once left little Ben with Leon for a few minutes in the sheriff's office, when Fay had gone to a funeral and Mrs. Finnegan had been out of town. Fay had found little Ben in the jailhouse eating rattlesnake stew with Leon out of a bowl she'd deemed hadn't been washed since its manufacture.

Stillman had taken a good tongue-lashing for that one. As had poor Leon, who'd seen nothing wrong with feeding a little boy rattlesnake stew out of a bowl "just as clean as [his] own."

"Whew!" Fay said, pressing her lips to his chest.

They lay there in silence for a minute. Stillman wondered if Fay could hear his heart picking up speed as he thought through his lie options…

Suddenly, she lifted her head and turned her face to his, frowning curiously, maybe a little suspiciously. "Who, then?"

"Oh, don't you worry, honey. little Ben is being about as well cared for as any man…er, I mean… toddler could be. Come here…"

He gently pulled her head up toward his, kissed her, then rolled her onto her back.

"Again?" she laughed. "You're gonna kill yourself, Ben!"

"Oh, but what a way to go!" he said, and shifted her attention from the topic of little Ben in the most pleasant way possible.

***

Evans woke to a loud cacophony. The din rattled his eardrums.

He lifted his head from the saddle he'd been using as a pillow and looked around, scowling his annoyance. After scouring the sun dapples and shadows for nearly a minute, his gaze landed upon the culprit.

A squirrel sat on a pine bough roughly fifteen feet from the ground, to the doctor's left. The beast was bent down over the branch it perched on, its shaggy tail curled over its back. Its little molasses-colored eyes were fixed on the doctor with a sharply wicked cast, and it was giving Evans holy hell, stretching its lips—did squirrels have lips?—back from its sharp little front teeth.

The castigation was a steady, unceasing onslaught, a veritable squirrel tirade.

"Oh, pipe down, you nasty little varmint."

That only seemed to incense the malevolent beast more. The din grew louder, a high-pitched, screeching caterwauling the likes of which the doctor had never heard before.

"I haven't been read out like that since the last time I spoke to—or was spoken at—by that infernal harpy, Katherine Kemmett!" Evans picked up a pine cone and threw it at the beast.

It struck a branch far beneath the squirrel's perch and thudded to the ground. The doctor found another cone, tossed that one with a little more vigor, grunting and wincing against the pain the movement evoked in his wounded calf. That cone got close enough to the squirrel--bouncing off a branch a few feet away from it before dropping to the ground--that the beast finally shut its ugly trap.

It scampered up the trunk and climbed another fifteen feet higher to light on yet another branch.

It hunkered low to resume its tirade but more half-heartedly, with less vigor than before.

Still, the damage was done.

Evans was awake.

"Consarned varmint. A pine forest out here in the great outdoors would be an ideal place without its noisy denizens."

Evans sat up higher against the saddle and looked around. He hadn't realized it, but he'd been talking to himself. Neither Ben nor Fay was here. Evans had woken up a little while ago to build a coffee fire. After he'd brewed and drunk a cup of the mud, sitting here all by himself, he'd fallen asleep again.

In the interim, the fire had burned down to gray ashes beneath the iron tripod he'd placed over it. And still he was alone.

He glanced at the sun. It was angling over the

dark western mountains and would be down in a couple of hours.

The shadows were growing long. Mourning doves were cooing—a much pleasanter sound, if a little elegiacal, than the blasted squirrel. Evans had been here alone on the flat top of the bluff for quite some time. He'd had a good long relaxing nap—two naps, in fact—but now that he was awake again, he felt a building worry over the fate of his two trail partners.

Anxiety evoked by his previous trouble still felt fresh inside him.

"Where in the hell are you two?" he asked aloud, continuing to peer around.

He grabbed the branch he'd used earlier for a crutch, and hoisted himself up from the ground. He limped off to the left, moving through the trees and large rocks peppering the bluff top.

Strange sounds came to him, carried by the breeze. They intermittently clarified and obscured as the breeze rose and abated. A man and a woman. Lovemaking sounds.

He'd heard them splashing around like children earlier, and now...

Evans gave a wry chuff.

Well, at least they were all right, the doctor silently opined, feeling a little sheepish about tipping an ear to the breeze, listening to the sounds again. He closed his eyes and smiled, remembering...

It had been a while for him.

Finally, shame forced him to stop listening. Employing the branch, he shambled to the opposite side of the bluff, the northwest side, from where he could no longer hear the nettling sounds of a man and a woman in love. He stared over the bluff's long, gentle decline toward the tableland below.

To the south lay rolling prairie interrupted here and there by the dark humps of island mountain ranges and bluffs like the one he now occupied. Below to the north was the line of pines and deciduous trees marking the course of the creek in which his friends had been playing like forest sprites.

Randy forest sprites, at that.

The doctor felt a little nettled. How dare they leave him alone so long? Didn't they care that he was wounded? Wounded and alone? Tired and hungry?

Lonely...

But that was his own damned fault, wasn't it? At least, the lonely part. He could have had a woman, a perfectly good woman in Katherine Kemmett as long as he didn't focus too closely on the harpy side of her. But she was a good, kind, attractive woman, overall.

Instead, he'd allowed his own dark desires to lead him astray…and into the hands and arms…and between the legs…of pretty Evelyn Vincent, waitress at Sam Wa's café. A woman young enough to be his daughter.

"Utter blasted fool," he bit out, sitting on a large rock and facing the direction of the camp.

He'd always been envious of Ben and Fay's relationship. He'd never known a more perfect marriage. In fact, he'd known of very few even good marriages. Ben and Fay were truly, deeply in love, even after several years of marriage. They'd never seemed one bit tired of each other.

Sure, they had their arguments—all husbands and wives did—but there was no doubting their love. Anyone could see it in their eyes.

Pure, unadulterated, untrammeled, undying love.

Damn them, anyway!

Ben and Fay had each other, and they had their boy. What did Evans have?

He had a dog. A wild one at that, one who tore up the flower beds around his house looking for old bones he'd previously buried. Buddy was a wild dog, a stray collie-type Evans had started feeding around a year ago. Eventually the pair, not unalike in their reclusive, cantankerous natures, had become friends of sorts.

At least, they'd become companions.

The doctor wasn't even sure Buddy would be at his house when he finally returned to Clantick. The dog might have figured Evans was never coming home and simply moved on to the next meal provider. Buddy had been on his own long enough, however, that he was perfectly capable of securing his own meals in the form of rabbits and gophers and even the rattlesnakes he so deftly caught, somehow avoiding a nasty inoculation of venom, in the buttes along the Milk River.

Evans's only companion had likely moved on, and Evans himself would probably return home to an empty house.

Here he was in his early middle years, alone. And all because of his own damnable weaknesses. Because of those weaknesses, he would most certainly die alone, surrounded only by his books and his whiskey and possibly another shaggy stray or two, a couple of mice-eating cats a-prowl in the attic.

He'd have a heart stroke and he'd die in bed, or he'd fall down his stairs drunk one night, and no one would find him until one of his few friends in town came to investigate and find the grisly scene—a bloated corpse or, worse, a dead man feasted upon by his critters.

Evans croaked out a wry laugh.

"No better than what I deserve," he groused. He dug a half-smoked cigar from a pocket of his torn, dirty coat. "Damn fool!"

He snapped a luficer to life on the rock.

Someone blew it out--the same man who said, "Don't be so hard on yourself, Doc."

There was the click of a gun being cocked. The cold, hard barrel was pressed against the back of the doctor's head. "But don't call out, or I'll put you out of your misery right quick, hear?"

Chapter 25

"Sorry we left you alone so long, Doc," Stillman said, leading Fay back up the bluff. "I reckon time got away from..." He let his voice trail off when, coming out of the trees and entering the camp, he didn't see the doctor where he'd expected to see him—lying back against his saddle.

In fact, the man's saddle was no longer where Stillman had last seen it.

There was no fire, either, and it was getting cool this late in the day.

Stillman and Fay exchanged an anxious glance.

"Doc?" Fay called, moving forward and looking around. "Doc, where are you?"

"His saddle's gone."

"What on earth...?"

Stillman walked back down the bluff to the east, toward the creek, but swerved off the trail to his right. Only Sweets stood at the picket rope he'd tied between two box elder trees. "What the hell...?" he muttered.

Fay walked quickly, growing more and more anxious, behind him. "The dun's gone?" she asked, staring at the rope.

"Yep."

"Oh, lord. Do you suppose he got angry and decided to ride on to Big Sandy without us? Angry because we left him alone so long? The poor man. How thoughtless we were, Ben! He has no one! And he's injured!"

"No. That's not it." Stillman walked around near the picket rope, bent forward to scrutinize the ground.

"What do you mean? What else could it be?"

Stillman dropped to a knee, ran his finger around the outline of a horse's hoof—one print overlaid on another. "There were riders here. Other men here. Several." Seeing something a little way beyond him, he straightened, walked over, crouched again, and picked up a half-smoked quirley that had been stepped on. "Fresh cigarette," he said, and tossed the stub away angrily. "Doc smokes cigars. Someone else was here. They took him."

Stillman kicked a rock.

"Who, Ben?" She could tell he knew.

"Phil Triber."

"The man whose money was on the stage."

"That's right."

Fay shook her head. "I don't understand…"

Stillman didn't respond. He was too busy studying the overlaid tracks surrounding him, walking here and there, kicking fallen leaves and deadfall out of his way. He followed the fresh tracks out of the woods and over the eastern shoulder of the bluff. Fay followed him, looking weary, worried…

Finally, Stillman stopped. He gazed off to the northwest.

"They took him that way," he said. "Toward Big Sandy."

"Why?"

Stillman scowled, chewed his bottom lip. "Not sure…"

He had a pretty good idea. He just didn't want to share it with his wife. Since he hadn't yet retrieved his money and probably knew Dutch's gang had become crow bait, Triber undoubtedly thought Stillman had it. Or knew where it was.

The rancher knew Stillman wouldn't just hand it over to the man who'd tried to kill him and send Triber, his son and his hands on their way.

That little misadventure had put them at odds.

That little misadventure had put Triber in Stillman's sights. Triber was due before a judge to answer for his attempt on Stillman's life. The rancher knew all too well about Stillman's reputation for uncompromising law and order to think the sheriff would let that attempt on his life go.

He was right.

So he'd taken Evans as bait with which to lure Stillman into a trap.

A trap in which Triber likely had no intention of letting Stillman come out alive. It was a most convenient situation for the raptorial rancher. He could just tell anyone who asked that Stillman had been killed by Dutch Wayne's gang when he'd so gallantly hounded the gang to retrieve his wife and Triber's money.

Triber had probably deemed it too risky to make a play on Stillman earlier, when the lawman had been distracted down by the creek. Too many dangerous variables there, with all the sun dapples and shadows. And Stillman, who had had his Henry close to hand, would have fought savagely to protect his wife. If they'd simply ambushed Stillman and Fay, Triber most certainly never would have reclaimed his money. They'd probably seen it was nowhere in or around the camp or with the horses.

Maybe Stillman had squirreled it away somewhere, figuring he'd retrieve it later, after he'd returned his wife and friend to safety.

By taking the doctor as bait, Triber had drawn out the matter, reducing his risk by setting the time and place of his meeting with Stillman himself.

Triber had no idea, of course, that only Dutch Wayne knew where the stolen money was hidden. The old outlaw had taken the secret to his cave-grave. Stillman didn't give a damn about the money. All he cared about was getting Evans back and dragging Triber before a judge.

"You're not telling me everything, are you?" Fay asked, looking up at her husband. She slid a lock of still-damp, windblown hair from her left eye.

"I'll tell you later," the sheriff said, drawing her close, pressing his lips to her temple. "When I know for sure myself." Pulling away from her, he started up the butte. "Time to break camp."

"You're going after them now? It'll be dark soon."

"I know," Stillman said, glancing over his shoulder at her. "But I think I know where they might be headed."

Fay hurried up behind him, lifting the hem of her trail-worn frock above her bare ankles and the shoes Hilda Stryk had given her. "I'm going with you," she insisted.

Stillman took her hand and kissed it as they continued toward the camp. "My darling, I wouldn't have it any other way."

***

After a half-hour's ride, Stillman reined Sweets to a halt.

The sun had gone down behind the tall spine of the Rocky Mountains to the west. While the last green and salmon daylight had bled from the sky, leaving the land in darkness, stars had pricked to life, and a sickle moon was rising, offering enough illumination to reveal the age-silvered sign poking out of the ground, listing badly to the east, on the right side of the trail.

Fay leaned out from the saddle, behind Stillman, to read the sign's badly faded, hand-painted letters: "Paris…?"

She looked at Stillman, one brow lifted skeptically.

Stillman shrugged. "At one time, there were high hopes for this town. Back when gold was discovered in Frenchie's Wash, just east of here." He smiled. "French. Paris. Get it?"

Fay glowered at him.

"Yeah, I know. The joke hasn't gotten any funnier over time."

Stillman stared down Paris's main street. Paris had not lived up to its ambitious name. Little more than a half-dozen widely-spaced shacks, some with false facades, facing each other from each side of the main street, comprised the entire town. Tumbleweeds had blown up against the rickety buildings—thorny, ball-shaped ramparts piled in futility against the wild prairie threatening from all sides. A few more shacks, blurred and silent shadows in the darkness, flanked the main ones, overgrown with brush and weeds.

The town was as dead as a stump.

Not quite.

Staring ahead along the broad main street nestled in the grassy buttes of this remote country twenty miles east of Big Sandy, Stillman thought he saw light filtering out from one of those half-dozen shacks on the main street's right side. He lowered his gaze to the trail before him.

Six sets of fresh hoof prints shown clearly in the dirt of the two wheel ruts divided by knee-high brome and wheat grass as well as spidery tufts of sage.

Crickets chirped in the brush. An owl hooted.

Those were the only sounds.

The air had lost its previous damp heat and acquired a refreshing coolness, welcome after the warm summer day.

"Do you think they're here?" Fay asked behind Stillman, keeping her voice low.

Stillman gazed at what he thought was light stretching out onto the street, from the fourth building ahead of him. It was a two-story log shack with a false façade and what appeared a roofed, street-level boardwalk running along its front wall.

The light seemed to move a little, to shimmer. But that was probably only a shadow passing in the window to the right of it.

Stillman had been through here only a few times. Paris had been a ghost town for as long as he could remember. He hadn't remembered anyone living here, much less anyone running a business here. Paris was home now only to hawks and coyotes.

Turning his head to one side, he answered his wife's question. "Yeah, I think they're here. Light just ahead."

He'd stopped the bay about thirty yards from the first buildings marking the town's edge. Now he reined Sweets to the right, angling him forward so that they pulled up to the side of the first shop on that side of the trail, shielding them from view of anyone who might be lurking.

Stillman had suspected Triber would lead him here. What better place to murder a lawman than in a remote ghost town?

The sheriff swung his right boot over his saddle horn, leaped to the ground with a quiet grunt. He turned to Fay as she slid forward onto the saddle and handed her the reins.

"How many of them are there, Ben?"

"Five."

"Tall odds. Maybe we should ride to Big Sandy and send a telegram to Leon."

"And leave Doc with Triber?"

Fay sighed. "I know. It's just...that..."

"I have to get him out of there." Stillman moved close to Fay's left leg and narrowed a commanding eye at her. "I want you to stay here. It's going to be hard to hear this, honey, but if men other than myself and the doc leave that building ahead of us, you hot foot it out of here. All right? Will you do that?"

Fay shook her head slowly, sniffing back tears. "No."

"Ride back the way we came. After a mile, you'll see the old freight road that will take you west to Big Sandy."

"No!"

Stillman placed his left hand on her left knee, and squeezed. "Yes."

"Ben, I can't—"

"Listen." Stillman squeezed her knee a little

harder. "You have to think of our son."

Fay sniffed again, looked down at him. Tears shone in her eyes. "Those men...Triber...he doesn't just want his money, does he?"

Stillman only stared at her.

"Does he?" Fay asked, hardening her voice with anger.

"No." Stillman shook his head, lowered his gaze.

"He wants you dead."

Stillman looked up at her again. "Wanting and getting are too different things. The doc and I will be the only two men walking out of there, if there's no other way to handle this matter except with lead. But in case I don't walk out, you have to promise me you'll do as I say."

He paused, hardened his eyes and gritted his teeth. "And do it this time. For our son."

Fay stared at him, lines of sorrow cut across her forehead. Tears dribbled down her cheeks. "I just want all of this to be over. I want to go home. I want us to be together with our son!"

"I do, too, honey. I do, too."

Stillman walked to the other side of the horse. He pulled the Henry from the boot, quietly levered a round into the action.

He peered up at his quietly sobbing wife again, and said, "I'll see you soon. Remember your promise."

"You come back to me, dammit, Ben!" she quietly but angrily beseeched him.

He smiled then swung around and tramped off to the rear of the building hunched darkly before him.

Chapter 26

A noise rose from the darkness near Stillman.

It came again, louder this time—a heavy thud. A shadow moved, an object arcing out from the rear of a building on his left. The object caromed toward the sheriff.

He started to swing his rifle up and around, but he knew he wouldn't get it raised before whatever was heading toward him reached its destination.

But then the thing switched course and landed on the ground two feet in front of Stillman's boots. The cat gave a low, groaning, meowing grunt then issued a shrill, indignant cry as it dashed off across the alley and into the darkness.

Stillman lowered the Henry and let out a relieved breath.

Just a cat, undoubtedly in Paris hunting mice in the old trash heaps. The sour smell of a wild animal lingered in Stillman's nostrils. The poor feline had probably been left behind by a long-fled inhabitant to fend for itself.

Holding the Henry in both hands, Stillman continued forward, moving slowly, half-expecting an ambush. But then, if Triber had wanted to ambush him, he could have done so before now.

Still, the lawman moved with caution.

The second and third buildings fell behind him on his left. Now he crossed the broad gap between the third and fourth buildings. The pattering of a piano had grown steadily louder as Stillman had moved toward the fourth building. He could hear its muffled notes better now. It sounded like a not-bad rendition of the tinnily jubilant "Frog Legs Rag."

The joyful chords of the song seemed to be laughing at the lawman out here on a grave and dangerous mission.

He stopped at the rear of the fourth building, inside which the song was being played, and scrutinized the back wall. A rear, first-story door was situated near the building's far corner. A rickety stairs rose to another, second-floor door.

Wood was stacked to the lawman's right, a good distance from the building--a precaution in case of fire. It wasn't old wood. Not wood left from when the town had been abandoned after

Frenchie's vein had pinched out well ahead of its projected time, and those who'd begun to establish Paris had lit out for more promising diggings. This wood had been recently cut and seasoned. Some of it had been split; the split stuff lay in a large, vaguely pyramid-shaped pile fronting the stacked logs.

A splitting maul angled up out of a chopping block.

Stillman strode to the first-floor door, near the log building's far corner. He reached for the handle and wasn't surprised to find it hanging free in its frame, neither latched nor locked.

He swung it open quickly, used his left boot to keep it from swinging back again, and aimed the Henry through the doorway, extending it out from his right hip.

"Stillman! There you are!" The deep male voice echoed around the room. "Come on in and let's have a palaver!"

The piano playing broke off abruptly, reverberations of the last notes still caroming around the smoky, dimly lit, low-ceilinged, wooden-floored room before Stillman.

The lawman walked slowly into the saloon and stopped. The bar lay just ahead and on his right. A man stood behind the bar, aiming a Winchester rifle at him. One of Triber's men.

Triber and his son and the two other hands sat at a table to the left of the bar, maybe fifteen feet beyond where Stillman stood in the open rear doorway. The doc sat there, as well, on a chair between Triber and his rat-faced son with the hook-shaped car on his pudgy left cheek.

The piano abutted the wall to Stillman's left. The man who'd been playing it had swung around on his seat to regard the lawman a little nervously, hands on his thin legs clad in butter-scotch corduroy with patched knees. The rest of him was as thin as his legs.

Bald as an egg, he had large, pale blue eyes. They were big and eerie-looking, as though they'd outgrown his age-shriveled head. A half-smoked quirley dangled from one corner of his mouth.

"Hi, Billy," Stillman growled.

The piano player smiled. Or maybe he flinched. "Ben."

Billy Northcutt had been a cow puncher throughout northern Montana, and Stillman could see the years had caught up to him. He looked frail and a little crooked, and he couldn't have weighed more than a sack of underweight potatoes. Stillman hadn't seen him in years; hadn't thought of him in nearly as long.

"Still kickin', I see," Stillman added absently, as

he scrutinized the men before him, all watching him closely, deviously.

He concentrated his attention on Triber. The rancher sat at the table to the right of the bar, holding a poker hand, a cigar smoldering in an ash tray near his right elbow.

A big, gutta-percha gripped Russian .44 lay near the ash tray. Triber's son, Cole, also held a hand of cards atop the table. His other hand was somewhere under the table, probably on his six-gun.

The two other men at the table, Triber's hands, were also playing poker. Four-handed poker. The two hands were a couple of grinning, snake-eyed devils, peering over their shoulders at Stillman standing behind them.

Make that three snake-eyed devils. The third Triber hand stood behind the bar, aiming that damned Winchester at Stillman's head.

Flanking the two Tibers, fathers and son, Evans sat up straight in his chair, a gag tied over his mouth. His arms had been wrenched behind him and his hands tied behind the chair back. Light from a lantern hanging low over the Tribers's table reflected in the doctor's glasses so Stillman could just barely see the man's gaze directed at him, Stillman.

Evans tried to say something but the gag garbled his words, so he stopped trying and merely shook his head in frustration.

"Billy did me a favor by opening this old watering hole," Triber said conversationally. "We needed a place to wet our whistles somewhere out here in these coyote-infested buttes so far from home. I run cattle through here, and so do Dwight and Dwayne Loggins. A man needs a place to stop and rest a spell, enjoy a little of the snake pizen."

"When I retired from punchin'," Norcutt said from the piano bench, "I didn't have nothin' else to do, so I opened her back up."

"The Rustlers' Saloon," Stillman said, glancing around the storied, crudely appointed room.

"Appropriate name," said Triber. "Back twenty years ago, when the gold played out—if there ever really was any gold in Frenchie's Wash—this place was mostly only patronized by cattle rustlers. I hung six of them at one time from that balcony back there." The rancher raised his gray eyes. "Up behind you there, Sheriff."

Stillman glanced over his left shoulder to see the balcony running along the saloon's rear wall. The second story used to house the whores' cribs n. A length of frayed rope still hung from the bottom rail of the rickety pine railing. A necktie left over from a long-ago party.

Stillman turned back to Triber, who regarded him with a thin, gloating smile.

"I had Melvyn Fryburg killed in here," he continued bragging, delighting in confessing his sundry sins to Stillman now that he had the upper hand and figured Stillman would be dead soon, anyway. "He was standing right there at the bar, near where Val is standing now."

Val was the hand aiming the Winchester at Stillman's head.

"I paid Burt Walsch two butchered beeves, two bottles of bourbon whiskey, and fifty dollars in silver to shoot the son of a bitch in the back," Triber crowed, then slowly lifted his cigar to his mustached mouth and took a couple of puffs.

Melvin Fryburg had been a deputy U.S. marshal of some renown, one of the men Stillman had looked up to when Stillman had first been awarded his own commission, back when he was still in his twenties and relatively new to the territory. Fryburg had nearly been Stillman's age now when he'd died here in the Rustlers, though all Stillman had known up to now about his death was that he'd been found with a bullet in his back in Frenchie's Wash.

The carrion eaters had been working on him so long that only the badge still pinned to his shirt had identified him.

It had been widely suspected that either Triber or the Loggins had murdered him, or had had him murdered.

Stillman stared stonily at the rancher.

The man kept his eyes on the lawman, silently jeering, taunting.

Cole Triber gazed at Stillman, too, his head with his broken, swollen nose canted down, like that of a perpetually guilty dog. But a smile curled one side of his upper lip, and his brown eyes shown glassy with glee and drink as he, too, gazed through the smoky shadows at the lawman.

The two hands at Triber's table continued leering over their shoulders at Stillman.

The lawman walked slowly forward, not making any sudden moves that might make Val nervous, and kicked out a chair at a near table, two tables away from Triber's table. He laid the Henry on the table and sagged heavily into the chair. He removed his hat, flung that onto the table, as well, then scrubbed his hand through his hair with a sigh.

He sat back in the chair, glaring at Triber and pointing his chin at Evans. "Let him go."

"Where's the money?"

"I don't know."

"That's the way you're gonna play it, Sheriff?"

Triber plucked the cigar from the ash tray again, took another drag. "Better think it over."

"What's it for?" Stillman asked.

Triber's smile faded. He slid his eyes, which now owned a wicked cast, to his son sitting to his right. Cole Triber hunkered ever-so-slightly lower in his chair, as though cowering from another possible assault from his father.

Triber returned his gaze to Stillman, drew a deep breath, and let it out slowly. "My son, you understand, is a bad apple. But, then, you already knew that. As did I and most of the Highline."

Again, he cut his hard, angry gaze to his son, who winced a little, probably thinking about his tender nose, not wanting any more damage done to it. Stillman had to admit it looked sore as hell.

Triber's cunning, victorious smile returned his lips as he explained to the sheriff, "You see, my son killed a girl. A young gypsy girl who'd been camping on the outskirts of Big Sandy. Cole had gone into town to get drunk, as he always does on Friday night, at the Pioneer Saloon. On the way back home the next morning, he came upon the girl hanging wash to dry in the woods there by Big Sandy Creek. He grabbed the girl and dragged her off into the--"

"Pa!"

Triber swung around to face the exasperated

young man. The rancher leaned toward him, bunching his fists, and thundering, "Keep your damn mouth shut!" He sealed the command with a hard glare.

Cole sagged back in his chair, regarding his father with real fear in his liquid brown eyes.

Turning back to Stillman, Triber poked the cigar into his mouth again, took a puff, blew the smoke over the table. The smoke encircled the low-hanging lamp like a giant spider's web. "Of course, she fought him. She wouldn't submit to my son's goatish wishes. He'd spilled plenty of seed the night before, on the second floor of the Pioneer. But that hadn't been enough for Cole. No, sir. He saw this girl and just had to have her. I hear she was even rather plain-faced."

Tiber glanced again at the young man sitting in shock beside him, and flared a nostril distastefully.

To Stillman, the rancher said, "Like I said, she fought him. Cole says the girl tripped and fell and hit her head on some rocks. The girl's brother, who'd been running for Cole and his sister, that Cole had struck her, and she'd fallen onto the rocks accidentally." The older man shrugged. "It doesn't really matter, though. However you want to shape it, it sizes up to murder. There were witnesses besides the girl's brother. And Dayton

Peale had to stick his nose in it, too."

Dayton Peale was the ex-tracklayer who now served as Big Sandy's town marshal.

"That fifty-thousand dollars was to pay off the girl's family, the witnesses to the murder"—again, Triber glanced at his son—"and Peale...so they wouldn't take their story to you, Sheriff of Hill County."

"I see," Stillman said with a knowing smile. "Now you don't have to worry about me. At least, in a few minutes you won't. You'll supposedly have your money back, and there won't be any lawman to turn to in Clantick. At least, there won't be an officially seated sheriff until the county commissioners can get around to a special election."

Triber wasn't awarding much credit to Stillman's deputy, McMannigle. He should have.

"And by that time, the murder will fade from people's memories," the rancher said. "They'll decide it's not worth butting heads with me over a simple gypsy girl. A rather plain-faced one, at that."

"Her family probably won't see it that way. But they're just gypsies. What are they going to do on their own?"

Triber grinned and slapped the table. "Exactly! Couldn't have put it better myself."

"What about Peale? He's the stubborn sort, not a half-bad town tamer."

"If he won't listen to reason, I'll put a bullet in him. I should have in the first place. Just like I did with Melvin Fryburg. The witnesses, too, if they won't listen to reason. Hell, I should've even killed the gypsies. Every last one. Why, they're little better than chicken-thieving dogs, after all."

"Why didn't you just kill me in the first place? Put a bullet through the courthouse window. I'm sure you know where my office is now, in the new building."

Triber chuckled deviously. "Live and learn, Sheriff. Live and learn."

Stillman leaned forward, resting an elbow on the table, and pointed at Cole. "All that killing... all that expense...for that worthless little privy rat?"

"I know, I know," Triber said, sadly wagging his head while his son glared incredulously at both him and Stillman, "but he's all I got. What does a man have if he doesn't have a legacy?"

The rancher sucked on the cigar again. "At least, I hope your wife is all right." He blinked, smiled seedily. "She sounded fine earlier—at least she did from up on the butte where we ran into the doctor here. She sounded downright happy to see you alive, in fact!"

The other men, including Cole and Val, snickered. Billy Northcutt must have slipped away during the conversation, because he no longer sat on the piano bench. He'd likely done the wise thing and headed for safer ground.

A fresh wave of rage burned through Stillman. He glared at the rancher, wanting to snap up the Henry and blow a bullet through the man's smug face. But he saw Val and the Winchester in the periphery of his vision, and suppressed the urge. "You think you're pretty smart—don't you, Triber?"

"Yes, I do." Triber hardened his jaws. "Now, I'll only ask you once more--where's the money?"

"I don't know.

Triber plucked the big Russian revolver off the table, cocked it and aimed it slightly behind him and to his right, at Doc Evans's forehead.

Evans winced and squeezed his eyes closed.

Triber hardened his jaws, and said, "Is that the way you're gonna play it, Sheriff? If so, this man will die."

Chapter 27

Stillman's gut tightened with dread as he stared at the cocked revolver Triber held to Evan's head. He licked his lips and said, "Don't you wonder how Dutch Wayne knew about that money?"

Triber frowned. "Huh?"

"How do you suppose Wayne knew that stage wash hauling your loot? That coach rarely hauls anything more valuable than the U.S. Mail. Money of any amount is usually sent north via the train these days. Stagecoaches are too slow and unreliable now that we have the iron horse.

"No man is stupid enough to risk his life holding up a stage just to see if it's carrying anything valuable. There's not even enough passenger travel out here to make it worthwhile to rob reticules and wallets."

Triber stared at him. The rancher's right eye twitched.

"Yes…" Triber said. "That…is…strange…"

Stillman slid his gaze to Cole. "Ask your son."

Cole's cheeks turned cherry red. Rage sparked in his eyes. "Shut up, you old coot!"

To Triber, Stillman said, "He sicced Dutch on that stage for a cut of the take down. Dutch told me himself. His dying words."

Incensed, Cole turned to his father. "No, I didn't!"

The other men looked uneasy. Val shifted his weight, moving the Winchester slightly, rolling his eyes to the Tribers.

"He was going to take his inheritance a little early and get out from under your thumb," Stillman said, his shrewd, mocking smile still quirking his lips.

"Don't listen to him, Pa!"

Triber had kept his gaze on Stillman, but now he turned his smoldering gaze on his son. As he did, he pulled the Russian down away from the doctor's head.

Stillman looked at the Henry. Now. His time was now.

But, dammit, Val was aiming the Winchester at him again, staring along the barrel at Stillman's head. The lawman would never get the rifle raised before the rifleman jacked a round through his brain plate.

"Pa, don't listen to him!"

Stillman readied himself to make his move despite Val and the Winchester.

Quietly, Triber said, "It's true, isn't it?"

"No, it ain't, Pa. No, it ain't!" Cole turned his flashing brown eyes on the sheriff. He had his hand on the grips of his holstered revolver. "He's lyin'! He's lyin'! He's tryin' to turn you again' me—don't ya see?"

Again with quiet menace, Triber said, "Pipe down, boy. I'll see to you later."

He turned to Stillman again. "Where is my damn money?" he shrieked, stretching his lips back from his square, ivory-colored teeth. He started to lift the Russian again toward Evans's bespectacled head. "Tell me now, or so help me, this man's brains will be—"

He stopped as the front door scraped open, groaning on its ancient hinges.

All eyes, including Stillman's, turned to see a young blond woman poke her head through the door, her wide blue eyes searching the room anxiously. "Doc...?"

As her gaze found Evans, she clamped a hand over her mouth in shock. Stillman saw that Val had turned his head full away from Stillman to stare at the girl. The Winchester sagged in Val's hands.

Stillman whipped up the Henry. He clicked the hammer back and, straightening, pressing the butt plate against his right shoulder, swung toward Val. Val was turning back to Stillman, eyes widening, raising the Winchester once more.

Stillman had him dead to rights, and Val knew it.

"No!" Val shouted.

The man's shout was drowned by the Henry's boom.

Val dropped the Winchester and flew against the back bar, clutching the wound in his neck. Stillman racked another round into the Henry's action and turned to where Cole, cursing shrilly, bounded up out of his chair and raised his Colt. He didn't quite get the hammer cocked before Stillman triggered the Henry again.

That slug slammed into Cole's upper center chest, punching him back into his chair. He and the chair went over backward to hit the floor with a resounding thud.

The other two men and Triber moved on Stillman now. The lawman saw them through his own wafting powder smoke and in the periphery of his vision.

He didn't have time to lever another round. Instead, he dropped the Henry and flung himself to the floor, left of his table but only after smashing his right arm down against the table's edge. The table fell toward him, partly in front of him, acting as a shield as two bullets meant for Stillman hammered into it.

Stillman rolled wide of the table, avoiding two more bullets as the crashing of the guns roared in his ears. As he rolled up onto his left shoulder and clawed his Colt Frontier .44 from the holster on his left hip, he saw the two remaining Milliron men extending smoking pistols at him, tracking him as he moved.

Stillman aimed swiftly, shot the man on the left.

He rolled again, kicking away a chair and pulling another table down in front of him.

Good thing he did, or the bullet fired by the last-standing Milliron hand would have cored him a third eye. He winced as the wood slivers from the table bit into his right cheek. He snaked the Colt over the top of the table, aimed at the Milliron man as the man clicked back his Remington's hammer and started to aim at Stillman once more.

Stillman's Colt bucked.

The Milliron man grunted, stretching his lips back from his teeth and flinging his own shot into a faded oil painting hanging on the wall behind Stillman. Stillman fired two more rounds over the edge of his covering table, and the last-standing Milliron man went rolling over the table at which he and the three others, including Phil Triber, had been playing poker.

A whiskey bottle and four glasses crashed to the floor.

The last Milliron rider landed with a thud and a heavy, final grunt to the left of Doc Evans, who remained tied to his chair, staring wide-eyed through the wafting powder smoke at Stillman.

Stillman gazed over the edge of his table.

Phil Triber was on one knee, just beyond a ceiling support post and the overturned table. Stillman could see only the man's head and shoulders. He knelt beside his dead son. Stillman saw Cole Triber's boots extending out to the left of the overturned gambling table.

Toe down.

Stillman was about to rise, but then Triber lurched to his feet. He still had the Russian in his right hand.

"You killed my son, you son of a bitch!" Triber raised the Russian toward Stillman.

He tried to raise it, rather.

Evans threw himself and his chair against the man, knocking Triber's gun hand down.

"Damn you!" Triber bellowed as the doctor slammed to the floor.

Triber pulled his revolver back up, but before he could get off a shot, Stillman drilled him through his left shoulder. The man yelped and flew backward, dropping the Russian.

Stillman heaved himself to his feet, stepped over the fallen table before him, and hurried over to where Triber, lying belly down on the floor, was stretching his right hand out toward the Russian.

Stillman stomped down on the man's right hand.

Triber cursed.

Stillman tattooed the back of the man's head with the barrel of his .44, laying him out cold.

"Doc!" the girl yelled again.

Stillman looked up to see the girl—a pretty blonde in blue denim trousers and a blue-and-white plaid shirt and with what appeared a .41-caliber pocket pistol wedged behind her wide, black belt--run to where Evans lay on his side, still bound to the chair, and gagged.

"Oh, Doc—please don't be dead, Doc!" the girl cried.

Evans looked up at the girl, frowning curiously. He rolled his eyes to one side, regarding Stillman dubiously.

"Here, here," the sheriff said, dropping to a knee beside Evans and the girl draped over him.

"Let me cut him loose, Miss. Give me some room."

Stillman used his folding Barlow knife to cut through the ropes, freeing the doctor's hands. He jerked the bandanna from the sawbones's mouth.

"Dixie!" Evans said in astonishment, rolling onto his back and kicking away the chair. "What in blue blazes are you doing way out here?"

"Ben!" Stillman turned to see Fay standing just inside the saloon's open doorway, flushed and out of breath. A lock of hair hung over her right, worried eye. She swept the stray lock away, moving slowly forward, looking around at the carnage littering the floor of the old Rustlers' Inn.

Stillman held up a hand to her and glanced at Evans and the girl again.

"Oh, doc!" the girl cried, wrapping her arms around Evans's neck, hugging him close and sobbing. "I thought for sure you were dead! I thought for sure they'd killed you like they killed my pa!"

"Your pa?" Stillman and Evans said at the same time.

She nodded, sobbing. "Burt Conway, Marshal of Rocky Ford. Pa went after the killers, but they shot him and sent him home tied over his saddle! I saddled up and went after those devils myself. Pa taught me how to track an' shoot just fine!"

She sleeved tears from her cheeks. "I'm so glad they didn't do the same to you, Doc!"

"There, there, Miss Dixie," Evans said. "I'm fine. Just fine. A little worse for the wear, is all."

"Conway's dead," Stillman muttered. "I'll be damned."

Stillman glanced at Fay, then went over and picked up Triber's Russian. He wedged the pistol behind the waist band of his pants, then pulled a set of handcuffs from the back of his cartridge belt. He cuffed the still-unconscious rancher's hands behind his back.

He glanced once more at Evans and the pretty blonde now making goo-goo eyes at each other down there on the floor, then walked to where Fay stood beside the bar.

He took his wife in his arms, hugged her close.

"Are you all right?" she asked.

"Not a scratch. At least, no more than when I entered the place."

"How 'bout the doc?" Fay asked.

"Well…look for yourself."

Evans and the girl were holding hands as they both climbed to their feet, smiling at each other, speaking softly, intimately together.

"How do they know each other?" Stillman asked. "She's young enough to be—"

"His daughter, I know. It's a long story. She rode into town a little after you left me. I tried to keep her with me, but she was so worried about the doc, she ran away from me. I wasn't sure if I should go after her or not. I thought I might only make things worse for you."

"Come on." Stillman took Fay's hand and led her into the clean night air, away from the carnage and the cooing lovebirds.

"That's Conway's daughter, eh?" Stillman asked, still holding his wife's hand.

"Yes. Dixie. A big admirer of the good doctor. Apparently, her admiration knows no bounds. Too bad about her father. I remember Dutch and his men spying a man following us—one wearing a badge. After Dutch looked the man over through his spyglass, he identified him as Conway. He sent a couple of men back to 'discourage' the marshal, as Dutch put it. Apparently, that's exactly what they did, and more."

Stillman had vaguely wondered why he'd never run into the Rocky Ford town marshal somewhere along the killers' trail. Now he knew why.

"Dixie's lucky she didn't get herself killed. That's damned near what she did." Though Stillman had to admit she had saved his and the doctor's life, albeit inadvertently.

"A rather headstrong girl, I would say. And one who seems to be very taken with Doctor Evans."

"Well, don't that beat all!" Stillman exclaimed, staring through the window at where Evans now sat at a table and the girl poured him a drink from a labeled bottle she must have found behind the bar. She was chattering away, telling Evans how frantic she'd been.

"He certainly does beat all," Fay quipped. "He certainly does do that."

Apparently sensing Stillman and Fay staring in at him, Evans turned to the window. The doctor grinned, raised his filled shot glass in salute, and threw back the liquor.

"Now, if that's not a healing elixir, I don't know what is!" Stillman heard him exclaim through the open door. "Heal me some more, Miss Dixie. Heal me some more, sweet child!"

Epilogue

Stillman turned the double-seated buggy off the main trail winding along the Milk River west of Clantick and pulled it onto the rocky two-track trail that climbed a crease between two haystack buttes.

The iron-shod buggy wheels clattered over ruts, chuck holes, and half-buried stones. Meadow larks cooed from breeze-brushed, sunlit weed tips along the trail. There wasn't a cloud in the deep-blue Montana sky, and the Milk River slid slowly between its chalky banks, gurgling softly.

Doc Evans lounged on the rear leather seat behind Stillman and Fay, who rode beside the lawman, lifting her face to the warm afternoon sunshine, smiling dreamily, no doubt anticipating her imminent reunion with their son.

Evans, too, looked cheerfully contemplative.

"How you doing, Doc?"

The doctor glanced at Stillman through his round spectacles, the left lens of which had cracked sometime during the sawbones' ordeal in the shadow of the Highwoods.

"Me?" Evans smiled. "I'm fine. Just fine, Ben!"

The smile blossomed into a devilish grin.

The sawbones had spent the previous night with Dixie Conway, in the Hotel Baldwin in Big Sandy. It had been a fairly chaste tryst, as the two had slept in separate rooms, the doctor insisting to Stillman and, more importantly to the critical Fay, that their relationship was purely platonic, albeit laced with a little innocent flirtation.

But the two had dined together in Miss Claudia Prince's Bluebird café, and they'd sat together for a couple of hours on the hotel veranda while the day had turned to dusk and then evening, playing euchre, chatting, whispering, chuckling, laughing, and sitting quietly together in the hotel's wicker swing.

It had turned out that Dixie had learned from Dr. Barney that Fay was not, in fact, Evans's wife, as Fay had fibbed to the girl upon their first meeting...

In Big Sandy, Dixie had doted protectively on the doctor, helping him medicate and rewrap his wounded leg after securing him a hot tub with fresh, clean towels at Big Sandy's tonsorial parlor owned by a Chinaman named Chow Ling. She'd overseen his haircut and then, having also found him a bona fide wooden crutch, helped him back to the hotel for an afternoon nap.

They'd parted only a few hours ago, when Dixie had seen Evans, Stillman, and Fay off on the train heading north to Clantick. She'd given the doctor a big hug and a peck on the cheek, which had caused his sunburned face to blossom rose, then leaped in a lively manner onto her horse and set off for home.

She had to plan her father's funeral, and do her grieving. Now that she'd made sure the doctor was safe, she could do both of those things in peace.

"You old devil, Doc," Stillman said, chuckling.

Fay gave him her best schoolmarmish look. "Don't encourage him."

"Ah, the doc's just having fun."

"I'll say I am," Evans said, half under his breath, chuckling as he looked away, grinning.

Fay turned around in her seat to regard the man severely. "Doc, you haven't encouraged her, have you? I mean, you do realize that she is half your age."

"I beg your pardon," Evans said haughtily. "Dixie is eighteen years old. In this country and in these times, that is a full-grown woman. Why, my mother married my father when she was only fifteen, and he was...well, he was at least ten years older than she!"

"My god!" Fay said.

"What, pray tell? Ben, bring this woman to heel!"

Keeping his head aimed forward as the stocky roan in the traces pulled the buggy to the top of the hill, Stillman only laughed.

"You've encouraged her, haven't you?" Fay pressed, extending her left arm along the top of the seat back and pointing at the doctor.

"Um...well..." Stillman heard the sheepish wince in the doctor's voice.

"Don't tell me she is planning to move up here, to Clantick?" Fay said, no little rebuke in her tone.

"Um...well..."

"Doc!"

"The poor girl has little now that her father is gone. She has no other family, only a few friends in Rocky Ford, so I...I...well, I offered her...a...a job."

"A job?" Fay paused. "As your assistant, I bet. Hah!"

"Sure," Evans said innocently. "Why not? She's a very good assistant. She's been assisting Dr. Barney for the past two years, but Barney will be retiring soon, so... She might even tend my house for me. Lord knows, it could use it!"

He chuckled.

"A single young woman is going to be assisting a bachelor doctor—a known scoundrel of a bachelor doctor, I might add--without benefit of a chaperone?" Fay intoned.

"What does she need a chaperone for? She's a full-grown woman! Oh, Ben, won't you please rein in your wife. I'm begging you!"

Stillman was glad to see Evans's old, three-story house rise before him atop the butte, eyesore though it was. The house had been built by a prominent member of the Clantick community many years ago, and then abandoned when the man had died and his family had left.

The old Victorian castle-like rambling structure had been in ill-repair before the doctor had bought it and moved in. It had fallen into even severer disrepair since. Several years ago, it had needed several coats of fresh paint.

It hadn't received them.

Now the place looked gray and bleak and abandoned, with wild shrubs and weeds growing up along its stone foundation. The broad front porch was missing boards. The roof was missing shakes. Several windows were boarded over.

In fact, the whole listing affair, with its first-floor bay windows filled with cracked colored glass, its two turrets and gingerbread trim, looked like an ancient, derelict ship that had run aground long, long ago and was waiting for one more last tide to drag it out to sea for its long-awaited, final burial.

If Dixie Conway moved up here from Rocky Ford to tend the doctor's house, she had her work cut out for her, Stillman silently opined, unable to squelch a chuckle.

"What are you laughing at?" Fay said to him. "He's incorrigible!"

Stillman shrugged as he reined the roan to a halt in front of the doctor's dilapidated front porch. "Well," the lawman weakly responded. "He's the doc..."

That pretty much said it all as far as Stillman was concerned.

As the sheriff helped the wounded sawbones out of the buggy, barks rose from the far side of the house. The drumming of four padded feet rose, as well, growing in volume until a shaggy, black and white collie dog ran out from around the house's north side, barking gleefully, ears pricked.

"Buddy!" Evans said. "Buddy, it's you! I'd thought for sure you'd have abandoned me for some charlatan with a freshly filled game shed!"

Evans crouched to pet the barking dog.

Stillman set the man's luggage on the porch. "You need help getting inside, Doc?"

"No, I'm fine, Ben." Evans sat on the porch steps, the tail-wagging dog sticking close to him, whining and barking.

The doctor pulled a half-smoked cheroot from his coat pocket. He produced a lucifer from the same pocket. He plucked his freshly filled traveling flask from another pocket, and grinned up at his old friend. "I'm gonna sit here and have a smoke and a belt or two. And pet my dog awhile. Ruminate on my close brush with death."

He glowered at Fay, who'd climbed down from the buggy to stand beside her husband, one arm wrapped around Stillman's waist. "Remind me never to ride another stagecoach with your wife, Ben. She's not only a harpy—why, she's a jinx, to boot!"

He struck the match to life on the stone step.

Fay laughed, crouched over the doctor, and pecked his cheek while he lit his cigar, pretending to ignore her. "Despite my disapproval of your, um, dealings with Miss Dixie Conway, not to mention most everything else in your personal life, I deeply, sincerely thank you, Doc."

"Thank me?" Evans frowned, befuddled, as he puffed the cigar. "Whatever for?"

"For saving my life, you fool."

"Oh, hell."

"I want to thank you, too, Doc," Stillman said, drawing Fay close against him. "For getting her out alive."

Evans looked at Fay. He pulled the cheroot out from between his lips, and said, "We got each other out alive."

He winked.

Fay leaned down to peck his cheek again, and squeezed his shoulder with genuine affection.

"Ah, hell," Evans said, flushing.

His gaze turned thoughtful. He lifted his eyes to Stillman again, beetling his freshly trimmed brows curiously. "What do you suppose Dutch did with it, Ben? Triber's loot."

Stillman shrugged. "Your guess is as good as mine, Doc."

He turned to stare back toward the Highwood Mountains, out of sight beyond the first front of the Two Bears rising in the south. He'd left Phil Triber with Big Sandy Town Marshal Dayton Peale. The outlaw rancher was safely locked away in one of Peale's iron cages.

When the man had recovered from his shoulder wound enough for travel, Stillman would ride down and fetch him. The rancher would be tried for attempted murder and sundry other crimes the county prosecutor would be charging him with soon, right here in Clantick's new courthouse.

As for Triber's stolen money, however...Dutch Wayne had taken its whereabouts to his grave.

Turning back to the doctor, Stillman said, "I reckon no one will ever know. Pretty remote country down there. Few travel through it. Cows and cow punchers now and then, but..."

"Yeah," Evans said, also staring south. "A lot of money waiting to be found by some lucky pilgrim."

"You got that right."

Fay said, "See you later, Doc. You behave yourself, hear?"

Evans grumbled as Fay turned to her husband and squeezed his hand. "Now then, let's get on over to Mrs. Finnegan's place. I can't wait to see my boy again!"

Stillman helped her back into the carriage, smiling stiffly. Nervously. As he climbed in beside her and turned the roan away from the doctor's house, Evans heard him say, "Now, uh... about that."

"About what?"

"Mrs. Finnegan."

"What about her?"

"Well, now, see...?"

"No, I don't see," Fay said, her voice growing

shrill. "See what…? What have you done with little Ben?"

Evans sat on his porch steps, patting Buddy's head and watching the buggy dwindle into the distance. He puffed the cheroot and watched the wheeled contraption drop down the side of the bluff and disappear.

His friend's voices and the clomping of the roan fell silent.

"Now, you see that right there, Bud?" Evans said to the dog, pointing his cigar at where the buggy had disappeared and lifting his flask to his lips. "That right there, what that poor man is going through right now, is why I got you instead of some harpy stomping around the place!"

He chuckled and took a long drink.

Buddy leaped up, planted his paws on the saw-bones's shoulder, and licked his cheek.

FROM BEST-SELLING AUTHOR PETER BRANDVOLD COMES A BRAND-NEW WESTERN ADVENTURE SERIES...

Mike Sartain, The Revenger, grew up in the French Quarter of New Orleans where he was taught how to fight by some of the toughest, meanest SOBs in any port. He was taught how to love by some of the most beautiful women in the world.

After the War Between the States, the former Confederate came west and joined the frontier cavalry. Wounded by Apaches in Arizona, he was nursed back to health by an old desert rat and his beautiful granddaughter, Jewel.

When the prospector and Jewel were viciously murdered by marauding Yankee bluecoats, Sartain hunted the soldiers down and killed them one by one in his own fierce Cajun style, for Jewel had been carrying Sartain's unborn child. That's how Mike Sartain's lust for revenge got started. That's how he became a wanted man, with a dead-or-alive price on his head.

Now, with no choice but to keep on riding, The Revenger rides for anyone who has an ax to grind...

AVAILABLE NOW ON AMAZON

ABOUT THE AUTHOR

Peter Brandvold grew up in the great state of North Dakota in the 1960's and '70s, when television westerns were as popular as shows about hoarders and shark tanks are now, and western paperbacks were as popular as Game of Thrones.

Brandvold watched every western series on television at the time. He grew up riding horses and herding cows on the farms of his grandfather and many friends who owned livestock.

Brandvold's imagination has always lived and will always live in the West. He is the author of over a hundred lightning-fast action westerns under his own name and his pen name, Frank Leslie.

www.ingramcontent.com/pod-product-compliance
Lightning Source LLC
Chambersburg PA
CBHW020529020726
47494CB00006B/1689